Edgar Wallace was born illegitimately
adopted by George Freeman, a porter ;
eleven, Wallace sold newspapers at Ludgate Circus and on leaving
school took a job with a printer. He enlisted in the Royal West Kent
Regiment, later transferring to the Medical Staff Corps and was sent
to South Africa. In 1898 he published a collection of poems called
The Mission that Failed, left the army and became a correspondent
for Reuters.

Wallace became the South African war correspondent for *The
Daily Mail*. His articles were later published as *Unofficial Dispatches* and
his outspokenness infuriated Kitchener, who banned him as a war
correspondent until the First World War. He edited the *Rand Daily
Mail*, but gambled disastrously on the South African Stock Market,
returning to England to report on crimes and hanging trials. He
became editor of *The Evening News*, then in 1905 founded the Tallis
Press, publishing *Smith*, a collection of soldier stories, and *Four Just
Men*. At various times he worked on *The Standard*, *The Star*, *The Week-
End Racing Supplement* and *The Story Journal*.

In 1917 he became a Special Constable at Lincoln's Inn and also
a special interrogator for the War Office. His first marriage to Ivy
Caldecott, daughter of a missionary, had ended in divorce and he
married his much younger secretary, Violet King.

The Daily Mail sent Wallace to investigate atrocities in the Belgian
Congo, a trip that provided material for his *Sanders of the River* books.
In 1923 he became Chairman of the Press Club and in 1931 stood as
a Liberal candidate at Blackpool. On being offered a scriptwriting
contract at RKO, Wallace went to Hollywood. He died in 1932, on
his way to work on the screenplay for *King Kong*.

The
Frightened Lady

HOUSE OF
STRATUS

This edition published in 2001 by House of Stratus, an imprint of Stratus Holdings plc, 24c Old Burlington Street, London, W1X 1RL, UK.

www.houseofstratus.com

Typeset, printed and bound by House of Stratus.

A catalogue record for this book is available from the British Library.

ISBN 1-84232-686-4

1

American footmen aren't natural: even Brooks admitted as much to Kelver, the butler, thereby cutting the ground from under his own feet.

He was a stout man, tightly liveried, and wore spectacles. His hair was grey and thin, his voice inclined to be squeaky. Sticking out of the pocket of a red-striped waistcoat, which was part of his uniform, there was visible a broken packet of gum. He chewed most of the time, his jaws moving almost with the regularity of a pendulum. Gilder, of an exact and mathematical turn of mind, had clocked him as fast as fifty-six to the minute, and as slow as fifty-one. In the privacy of his room Mr Brooks smoked a large pipe charged with a peculiar sugary blend of tobacco that he imported expensively from California.

Neither Mr Brooks, the footman, nor Mr Gilder, the footman, fitted the household of Marks Priory, nor did they fit the village of Marks Thornton.

They were poor footmen, and never seemed to improve by practice and benefit from experience.

Yet they were nice men, if you can imagine such abnormalities as American footmen being nice. They interfered with none, were almost extravagantly polite to their fellow-servants, and never once (this stood as a monumental credit) did they report any other servants for a neglect of duty, even when neglect worked adversely against their own comfort.

They were liked, and Gilder a little feared. He was a gaunt man with a hollowed, lined face and a deep, gloomy voice that came

1

rumbling up from some hollow cavern inside him. His hair was sparse and black and long; there were large patches on his head which were entirely bald, and he was immensely strong.

There was a gamekeeper who discovered this – John Tilling. He was a big man, red-haired, red-faced, obsessed by suspicion.

His wife was certainly pretty, as certainly restless and given to dreams which she never quite realised, though imagination helped her nearly the whole of the journey. For example, she found no olive-skinned Romeo in a certain groom from the village. He was ruddy, rather coarse, smelt of stables and beer, and last Sunday's clean shirt. He offered her the mechanics of love, and her imagination supplied the missing glamour. But that was an old scandal. If it had reached the ears of Lady Lebanon there would have been a new tenant to Box Hedge Cottage.

Later Mrs Tilling looked higher than ostlers, but her husband did not know this.

He stopped Gilder one afternoon as he was crossing Priory Field.

"Excuse me."

His politeness was menacing.

"You bin down to my cottage once or twice lately – when I was over at Horsham?"

An assertion rather than an inquiry.

"Why, yes." The American spoke slowly, which was his way. "Her ladyship asked me to call about the clutch of eggs that she's been charged for. You mweren't at home. So I called next day."

"And I wasn't at home neither," sneered Tilling, his face redder.

Gilder looked at him amused. For himself he knew nothing of the unfortunate affair of the groom, for small gossip did not interest him.

"That's so. You were in the woods somewhere."

"My wife was at home… You stopped an' had a cup of tea, hey?"

Gilder was outraged. The smile went out of his grey eyes and they were hard.

"What's the idea?" he asked.

His jacket was suddenly gripped.

"You stay away – "

So far Tilling got, and then the American footman took him gently by the wrist and slowly twisted his hand free.

If Tilling had been a child he could have offered no more effective resistance.

"Say, don't do that. Yeah! I saw your wife and I had tea. She may be a beautiful baby to you, but to me she's two eyes and a nose. Get that in your mind."

He jerked his forearm very slightly, but very violently. It was a trick of training; the gamekeeper stumbled back and had a difficulty in maintaining his balance.

He was a slow-witted man, incapable of sustaining two emotions at one and the same time. For the moment he was too astounded to be anything but astounded.

"You know your wife better than I do," said Gilder, flexing his back. "Maybe you're right about her, but you're all wrong about me."

When he came back from the village – he had been to the chemist's – he found Tilling waiting for him almost on the spot where they had parted.

There was no hint of truculence; in a way he was apologetic. Gilder, by repute, had her ladyship's ear, and exercised a supreme intelligence which had its explanation according to the fancies fair, fantastic or foul, of those who offered a solution to the mystery.

"I'll be glad if you overlook what I said, Mr Gilder. Anna an' me have our little disagreements, an' I'm a high-handed chap. There's been too many visits down at Box Hedge, but you, bein' a family man – "

"I'm not married, but I've got a domestic mind," said Gilder. "Let's say no more about it."

Later he told Brooks, and the stout man listened stolidly, his jaws working. When he spoke, he offered an historical parallel.

"Say, have you heard of Messalina? She was an Eyetalian woman, the wife of Julius Caesar or somep'n."

Brooks read a great deal and had a skimming memory for facts.

Still, a footman who was an American citizen and who even knew that Messalina had lived, and could produce her in any recognisable form to illustrate a situation, was phenomenal.

Place him and his companion against the background of Marks Priory and they became incongruous.

For Marks Priory had its footing set by Saxon masons, and the West Keep had gone up when William Rufus was hunting in the New Forest. Tudor Henry had found it a ruin, and restored it for his protégé John, Baron Lebanon. It had withstood a siege against the soldiers of Warwick.

It was Plantagenet and Tudor and Modern. No eighteenth-century builder had desecrated its form; it had survived the rise and fall of the Victorian renaissance which produced so many queerly shaped angels and cherubs and draughty back rooms.

There was an age and a mellowness to it that only time and the English climate could bring.

Willie Lebanon found it an irritation and an anodyne; to Dr Amersham it was a prison and a disagreeable duty; to Lady Lebanon alone it was Reality.

2

Lady Lebanon was slight, petite by strict standards, though never giving you the impression of smallness. Yet people who spoke to her for the first time carried away a sense of the majestic. She was firm, cold, very definite. Her black hair was parted in the middle and brought down over her ears. She had small, delicate features; the moulding of her cheeks was aesthetic. In her dark eyes burnt the unquenchable fires of the true fanatic. Always she seemed conscious of a duty to aristocracy. The modern world had not touched her; her speech was precise, unextravagant – almost you saw the commas and colons which spaced her sentences. She abominated slang, smoking in women, the vulgarity of ostentation.

Always she was conscious of her descent from the fourth baron – she had married her cousin – and the tremendous significance of family.

Willie Lebanon confessed himself bored with the state in which he lived. Though he was small of stature, be had passed through Sandhurst with distinction, and if his two years' service in the 30th Hussars had failed to stamp him soldier, the experience had enhanced his physique. The bad attack of fever which brought him home (explained Lady Lebanon, when she condescended to explain anything) was largely responsible for Willie's restlessness. The unbiased observer might have found a better reason for his exasperation.

He came slowly down the winding tower stairs of Marks Priory into the great hall, determined to "have it out" with his mother. He

5

had made such resolutions before, and half-way through the argument had wearied of it.

She was sitting at her desk, reading her letters. She glanced up as he came into view and fixed him with that long and searching scrutiny which always embarrassed him.

"Good morning, Willie."

Her voice was soft, rich, and yet had in it a certain quality of hardness which made him wriggle inside. It was rather like going before the commanding officer in his least compromising mood.

"I say, can I have a talk with you?" he managed to jerk out. He tried to recall to himself the formula which was to support him. He was the head of the house, the lord of Marks Priory in the County of Sussex, and of Temple Abbey in the County of Yorkshire...the master! He had only a vague and dismal satisfaction at the knowledge, and certainly was no nearer to the dominating mood which he was trying to stimulate into being.

"Yes, Willie?"

She laid down her pen, settled herself back in the padded chair, her delicate hands lightly clasped on her lap.

"I've sacked Gilder," he said jerkily. "He's an absolute boor, mother; he really is. And he was rather impertinent... I think it is rather ridiculous, don't you, having American footmen who really don't know their jobs? There must be hundreds of footmen you could engage. Brooks is just as bad..."

He came to the end of his breath here, but she waited. If she had only said something, or had grown angry! After all, he was the master of the house. It was too absurd that he could not discharge any servant he wished. He had been in command of a squadron – it was true, only while the senior officers were on leave – but the commanding officer had commended him on the way he had handled the men. He cleared his throat and went on.

"It's making me rather ridiculous, isn't it? I mean, the position I am in. People are talking about me. Even these pot-house louts who go into the 'White Hart.' I'm told it is the talk of the village – "

"Who told you?"

Willie hated that metallic quality in her voice, and shuddered.

"Well, I mean, people talk about me being tied to your apron strings, and all that sort of thing."

"Who told you?" she asked again. "Studd?"

He went red. It was devilish shrewd of her to guess right the first time; but he owed loyalty to his chauffeur, and lied.

"Studd? Good heavens, no! I mean, I wouldn't discuss things like that with a servant. But I've heard in a sort of roundabout way. And anyway, I've sacked Gilder."

"I'm afraid I can't do without Gilder. It is rather inconsiderate of you to discharge a servant without consulting me."

"But I'm consulting you now."

He pulled out the settle on the other side of the desk and sat down; made an heroic effort to meet her eyes, and compromised by staring hard at the silver candlestick on the cabinet behind her.

"Everybody's noticed how these two fellows behave," he went on doggedly. "Why, only once in a blue moon do they say 'my lord' to me. Not that I mind that. I think all this 'my lording' and 'my ladying' is stupid and undemocratic. They do nothing but loaf around the house. Really, mother, I think I'm right."

She leaned forward over the writing-table, her thin, clasped hands resting on the blotter.

"You are quite wrong, Willie. I must have these men here. It is absurd of you to be prejudiced because they are American."

"But I'm not — " he began.

"Please don't interrupt me when I am talking, Willie dear. You must not listen to what Studd says. He's a very nice man, but I'm not quite sure he's the kind of servant I want at Marks Priory."

"You're not going to get rid of him, are you?" he protested. "Hang it all, mother, I've had three good valets, and each one of them you thought wasn't the right kind of servant, though they suited me." He screwed up his courage. "I suppose the truth is that they don't suit Amersham?"

She stiffened a little.

"I never consider Dr Amersham's views. I neither ask his advice nor am I guided by him," she said sharply.

With an effort he met her eyes.

"What is he doing here, anyway?" he demanded. "That fellow practically lives at Marks Priory. He's a perfectly loathsome fellow. If I told you all I'd heard about him – "

He stopped suddenly. The two little pink spots that came to her cheeks were signals not to be ignored.

Then, to his relief, Isla Crane came into the hall, some letters in her hand. She saw them, hesitated, and would have made a quick retreat, but Lady Lebanon called her.

Isla was twenty-four, dark, slim, rather lovely in an unobtrusive way. There are two varieties of beauty: one that demands instant and breathless discovery and one that is to be found on acquaintance, and to the surprise of the finder. The first time you met her she was a hardly rememberable figure in the background. By the third time she monopolised attention to the exclusion of all others. She had good eyes, very grave and a little sad.

Willie Lebanon greeted her with a smile. He liked Isla; he had dared to say as much to his mother, and, to his amazement, had not been reproved. She was a sort of cousin, definitely private secretary to Lady Lebanon. Willie was not conscious of her beauty; on the other hand, Dr Amersham was all too conscious, but Lady Lebanon did not know this.

She put the letters down on the desk and was relieved when her ladyship made no effort to detain her.

When she had gone: "Don't you think Isla's growing very beautiful?" asked Lady Lebanon.

It was an odd sort of question. Praise from his mother was a rare thing. He thought she was trying to turn the conversation, and rather welcomed the diversion, for he had reached the bottom of his reserves of determination to "have it out."

"Yes, stunning!" he said, without particular enthusiasm, and wondered what was coming next.

"I want you to marry her," she said calmly.

He stared at her.

"Marry Isla?" aghast. "Good Lord, why?"

"She's a member of the family. Her grandfather was a younger brother of your grandfather, the seventeenth Viscount."

"But I don't want to marry – " he began.

"Don't be absurd, Willie. You will have to marry somebody, and Isla is in every way a good match. She has no money, of course, but that really doesn't matter. She has the blood, and that is all that counts."

He was still staring at her.

"Marry? Good Lord, I've never thought of being married. I hate the idea, really. She's terribly nice, but – "

"No 'buts' Willie. I wish you to have a home of your own."

He might have insisted, and the thought did occur to him, that he already had a home of his own, if he were allowed to manage it.

"If people are talking about you being in apron strings I should think you would welcome the idea. I have no particular desire to stay at Marks Priory and devote my life to you."

Here was a more alluring prospect. Willie Lebanon drew a long breath, swung his legs to the other side of the settle, and stood up.

"I suppose I've got to marry some time," he said. "But she's awfully difficult, you know."

He hesitated, not knowing exactly how his confession would be accepted.

"As a matter of fact, I did try to get a little friendly with her – in fact, I tried to kiss her about a month ago, but she was rather – stand-offish."

"What an awful word!" She shivered slightly. "Naturally she would object. It was rather vulgar of you."

Gilder slouched into view and rescued a bewildered and rather indignant young man from explanation.

Gilder's livery had been most carefully fitted by a good London tailor. He was, however, the type of man on whom clothes were wasted. That mulberry uniform of his might have been bought from a slop shop. The coat hung on him, the shapeless trousers sagged at the knees. He was tall, cadaverous, hard-faced, and his normal expression was one of strong disapproval.

Lord Lebanon waited for the reproof which, by his standard, was inevitable. His mother made no attempt to reprimand the man or ask him to explain the impertinences alleged against him.

"Do you want me, m'lady?" It was a mechanical question. When she shook her head he went slowly out of the hall.

"I do wish you had asked him what the dickens he meant by – " he began.

"Remember what I say about Isla," she said, ignoring his unfinished protest. "She is charming – she has the blood. I will tell her how I feel about it."

He stared at her in amazement.

"Doesn't she know?"

"As for Studd" – her level brows met in a frown.

"I say, you're not going to rag Studd, are you? He's a devilish good fellow, and anyway, he didn't tell me anything."

Later he found Studd working at the car under the wash in the garage.

"I'm afraid I've done you an awful shot in the eye, Studd," he said ruefully. "I told her ladyship that people were saying – you know – "

Studd looked up, straightened his back with a grimace, and grinned.

"I don't mind, m'lord."

He was a fresh-faced man of thirty-five, had been a soldier, and had served in India.

"I shouldn't like to leave this job, but I don't think I'll stick it much longer, m'lord. I don't mind her ladyship; she's always very polite and decent to me, though she does treat you as though you're one of the slave class. But I can't stand that feller." He shook his head.

Lord Lebanon sighed. There was no need to ask who "that feller" was.

"If her ladyship knew as much about him as I do," said Studd, heavily mysterious, "she wouldn't let him into the house."

"What do you know?" demanded Lebanon curiously.

He had asked the question before and had received little more satisfaction than he had now.

"At the right time I've got a few words to say," said Studd. "He was in India, wasn't he?"

"Of course he was in India. He came back to bring me home, and he was in the Indian Medical Service for years, I believe. Do you know anything about him – I mean, about what he did in India?"

"At the right time," said Studd darkly, "I'll up and speak my mind."

He pointed to a recess in the garage. Willie Lebanon saw a shining new car which he had never seen before.

"That's his. Where does he get the money from? That cost a couple of thousand if it cost a penny. And when I knew him he was broke to the wide. Where does he get his money from?"

Willie Lebanon said nothing. He had asked his mother the same question without receiving any satisfactory answer.

He loathed Dr Amersham; everybody loathed him except the two footmen and Lady Lebanon. A dapper little man, overdressed and over-scented; domineering, something of a Lothario if village gossip had any foundation. He had become suddenly rich from some unknown source; had a beautiful flat in Devonshire Street, two or three horses in training, and was accounted a good fellow by the sort of people who have their own peculiar ideas as to what constitutes good fellowship.

The fact that he was at Marks Priory did not surprise Willie. He was always there. He came late and early, driving down from London, spending an hour or two before taking his departure; and when he arrived there came a new master to Marks Priory.

He came downstairs, where he had been standing, and, if the truth be told, listening, a second after Willie had made his escape from the hall, pulled up a chair to the side of the desk where Lady Lebanon was sitting, and, taking a cigarette from a gold case, he lit it without so much as "by your leave." Lady Lebanon watched him with her inscrutable eyes, resenting his familiarity.

Dr Amersham blew a ring of smoke from his bearded lips, and looked at her quickly.

11

"What's this idea about Willie marrying Isla? That's a new scheme, isn't it?"

"Of course I was listening on the stairs," he said. "You're so damned careful about telling me things that I've got to find them out for myself. Isla, eh?"

"Why not?" she asked sharply.

His eyes were red and inflamed; his complexion, never his best point, blotchy; the hand that took the cigarette from his lips trembled a little. Dr Amersham had had a party at his flat, and had had little or no sleep.

"Is that why you asked me to come down? You wanted to tell me this? As a matter of fact, I nearly didn't come. I had rather a heavy night with a patient – "

"You have no patients," she said. "I doubt if there is anybody in London quite so foolish as to employ you!"

He smiled at this.

"You employ me; that is enough. The best patient in the world, huh?"

This was a good joke, but he enjoyed it alone. Lady Lebanon's face was entirely without expression.

"That chauffeur of yours is not too good – Studd. He had the damned impertinence to ask me why I didn't bring my own chauffeur; and he's a little bit too friendly with Willie."

"Who told you?" she asked quickly.

"I've heard all about it. There are quite a number of people in this neighbourhood who keep me posted as to what is happening."

He smiled complacently. He had indeed two very good friends at Marks Thornton. There was, for example, pretty Mrs Tilling, but Lady Lebanon did not know about this. The gamekeeper's wife was an admirer of Studd: the doctor had recently made this discovery and felt smirched.

"What has Isla to say about a marriage?"

"I haven't told her."

He took the cigarette from his lips and regarded it with interest.

"Yes, it's not a bad idea. Strangely enough, it never occurred to me." He pulled at his little Vandyke beard. "Isla...yes, an extraordinarily good idea."

If she were surprised at his approval she did not show it.

"She's a blood relation of the Lebanons, too." He nodded. "Wasn't there another one of the family who married in similar circumstances – his cousin, I mean?"

He looked up at the dark family portraits that were hung on the stone wall.

"One of those ladies, wasn't it? I've a good memory, eh? I remember the history of the Lebanons almost as well as you."

He took out his watch with some ostentation.

"I'll be getting back – " he began.

"I want you to stay," she said.

"I have rather an important appointment this afternoon – "

"I want you to stay," she repeated. "I have had a room got ready for you. Studd, of course, must go. He has been telling Willie the village gossip."

The doctor sat upright. Was Mrs Tilling the kind of woman who talked...?

"About me?" he asked quickly.

"About you? What should they know about you?"

He was a little confused, and laughed.

If she had her views about the quality of his radiance, she did not express them.

He accepted her wish as a command, grumbled a little, but as he had not the excuse that he was unprepared for a stay, he had no excuse at all.

There was no intention on his part of returning to town. Nearby he had a cottage that had been decorated and furnished by the daintiest of London's artistic young men. And he had planned to stay the night there, for he was a man with local responsibilities. Of this fact Lady Lebanon knew nothing.

"By the way," she called him back from the stairs. "Did you ever meet Studd in India? He was stationed in Poona."

Dr Amersham's face changed.

"In Poona?" he said sharply. "When?"

She shook her head.

"I don't know, but from what I've heard he has told people he knew you there; which is another reason why he should leave Marks Priory."

Dr Amersham knew another, but he kept this to himself.

3

Mr Kelver, the butler at Marks Priory, used to stand by the sanctuary door for an hour on a fine evening, looking across the lovely weald of Sussex, wondering, and never exactly reaching any decision on the matter, whether it was consonant with his dignity and his grandeur to be segregated from his employer at nine o'clock every evening. For at that hour her ladyship with her own hands turned the key in the lock of that big oaken door which thereafter shut off the north-east wing of Marks Priory from the rest of the house.

The servants' quarters were comfortable. Within reason, and with Mr Kelver's permission, servants might go in and out of the Priory as they wished, following the path that skirted the woods to the village. But was it not something of an affront to one who had been in the service of a Serene Highness that he, too, must be classified with the excluded?

The sanctuary door was in the north-east wing, and was in a sense Mr Kelver's private entrance and exit, the staff using the little hall entrance which also was the tradesmen's.

A queer household, he thought. He half confided his view to Studd, though he never gave that polite and experienced man his fullest confidence. For Mr Kelver belonged to an age which knew nothing of chauffeurs, and he had never placed these alert and skilful mechanics in the order of domestic precedence. They had been a puzzle to him since they first "came in." A butler of Mr Kelver's experience knew to a nicety the subtle distinctions in importance

15

between a first footman and a lady's maid; unerringly he could balance the weight of cook against valet; but chauffeurs were not so easy.

Studd had been accepted, became "Mister Studd," and was as near to being in the butler's confidence as any servant could possibly hope. And lately Mr Kelver had felt the need of a confidant.

He was thinking about Studd when that man appeared round one of the towers of the Priory. Mr Kelver greeted him with a gracious nod, and Studd, on his way to the garage, stopped. He was a little flushed. At first Mr Kelver, who thought the worst of servants, had the impression that he had been drinking.

"I've just had a few words with Amersham." Studd jerked his thumb over his shoulder. "What a gentleman, eh! And what a doctor! if her ladyship knew what I know he wouldn't last five minutes in this place. Indian Army, eh? I could tell you something about the Indian Army!"

"Really?" said Mr Kelver politely.

He never encouraged gossip, but was generally anxious to hear it.

"It's a funny thing," Studd went on. "I met a fellow down in the village, a queer-looking customer, who said he had been to India. I had a drink with him in the private bar of the 'White Hart.' I didn't say much; I just listened to him. But he's been there all right."

Kelver, thin, aristocratic, lifted his silvered head and looked down his aquiline nose at the little chauffeur.

"Has Dr Amersham been – er – complaining?" he asked. Studd came back to his grievance savagely.

"Something gone wrong with his bus," he said. "He wanted me to put it right in five minutes, and it's a two days' job. You'd think he was the boss here, wouldn't you – honestly, wouldn't you, Mr Kelver?"

Kelver smiled mysteriously and made his conventional reply to such embarrassing questions.

"It takes all sorts of people to make a world, Mr Studd," he said. Studd shook his head.

"I don't know," he said vaguely. "What's this place – Marks Priory, isn't it? Who's the owner – Lord Lebanon, isn't it?"

He extended the fingers of his hand, and ticked off the household.

"Here they are – as they count. Number one, Dr Blooming Amersham, Lord High Controller. Number two, her ladyship. Number three" – he was at a loss for number three – "I suppose you'd say Miss Crane, though I've got nothing against her. Also ran, Lord Lebanon!"

"His lordship is young," said Mr Kelver gently.

It was no answer, and he knew it was no answer. He completely agreed with Studd, but he knew his place. The man who had served the Duke of Mecklstein und Zwieberg, who had been in the household of the Duke of Colbrooke, whose family for generations had served great people greatly, could not with dignity and propriety criticise his employers.

There was a quick step on the gravelled path and Dr Amersham came into view.

"Well, Studd, have you finished the work on my car?"

He had a sharp, rather ugly voice. His manner was normally provocative.

"No, I haven't finished the work on your car," said Studd aggressively; "and what's more, I'm not going to finish the work on your car tonight. I'm going down to the ball."

The doctor's face went white with rage.

"Who gave you permission?"

"The only person in this house who can give me permission," said Studd loudly. "His lordship."

The little beard of the doctor was quivering with anger.

"You can find another job."

"Find another job, can I?" snarled Studd. "What sort of a job, doctor – signing other people's names on cheques?"

The doctor's face went from white to crimson, and then the colour faded till it was grey.

"If I get another job it will be an honest job. It won't be robbing a brother officer – take that from me! And whatever job I take I shan't be pinched for it, or go up for trial for it, or be kicked out of the Army for it!"

17

His tone was significant, accusatory. Amersham wilted under the glare of his eyes, opened his mouth to speak, but could only find a few tremulous words.

"You know too much for your good, my friend," he said, and, turning on his heels, walked away.

Mr Kelver had listened uncomprehendingly, a little aghast at the impropriety of Studd's words, uneasy as to whether he should have intervened, or whether, even without intervention, he was tacitly compromised. If he had been sure of Studd's position in the hierarchy of service...

He had the impression – and here he was right – that Dr Amersham had been unaware of his presence.

"That's got him!" said Studd triumphantly. "Did you see him change colour? He's going to fire me, is he?"

"I don't think you should have spoken to the doctor in that tone, Studd," Kelver was mildly reproachful.

The chauffeur was in the exalted state of one who had spoken his mind, and was superior to disapproval.

"Now he knows his place, and there are one or two other things I could say," he said.

There was a fancy dress ball at the village hall that night, in aid of the bowling club. In the dusk of the evening came a fly from the hall, carrying a pierrot, a pierrette, a gipsy woman and an Indian to the festivities.

Mr Kelver did not approve of servants wearing theatrical costumes – even though they were home-made. It removed them from his jurisdiction. He had a word or two to say about the hour they should return. He was concerned about the impropriety of the pierrette's legs. It was the first time he was aware that the under-housemaid had legs. But mostly he had a word of fatherly advice for the gorgeous Indian, who was Studd.

"If I were you, Mr Studd, I think I should see the doctor in the morning, and apologise. After all, if you're in the right you can afford to apologise, and if you're in the wrong you can't afford not to."

Consciously or unconsciously, he was paraphrasing Mr Horace Lorimer's sagest advice.

After the fly had gone he strolled into the hall, making his final tour before he retired to the servants' wing, putting a cushion in place, removing an empty glass – obviously the doctor's – that had been left on her ladyship's desk.

Later he saw the doctor. He was standing in one of the window recesses in the main corridor, with the two footmen: Brooks, stout and spectacled, and the gaunt Gilder. They were talking together in low tones, head to head. Somebody else saw them. Lord Lebanon, in the doorway of his room, watched the conference, a little amused. He said good night to Kelver as he passed, then called him back.

"Isn't that the doctor?" He was a little short-sighted.

"Yes, my lord; it's the doctor and Gilder, and, I think, Brooks."

"What the devil are they talking about? Kelver, don't you think this is a queer house?"

Kelver was too polite a man, too perfect a servant, to agree. He thought the house was very queer, and the two footmen the most outrageous phenomena that Marks Priory offered. But they were not under his jurisdiction: that fact had been made very plain to him by her ladyship on the day he had arrived. Moreover, they were not excluded from the living-rooms after nine o'clock, but had the free run of the house.

"I have always felt, my lord," he said, "that it takes all sorts of people to make a world."

Willie Lebanon smiled.

"I think you've said that before, Mr Kelver," he said gently, and, surprisingly and a little embarrassingly, patted the aged man on the shoulder.

4

There was a man named Zibriski, who, being of a poetical turn of mind, called himself Montmorency. He was called other names, which were not so polite, by people who found themselves in possession of currency notes which had been printed by the offset process on one of Mr Zibriski's private presses. As curios they were admirable; as instruments of exchange they were entirely a failure. He made a very respectable living; went to Monte Carlo in the winter and to Baden-Baden in the summer; kept an expensive flat in London – two, if his peroxided wife only knew – and drove about in a highly chromiumed American car.

He was no common retailer of spurious notes, but a master man in a very big way. He had a press in Hanover and another in the back part of a small hotel in one of the little streets near the quay at Ostend. His five-pound notes were beautifully printed and most impressively numbered. Cashiers of banks had accepted them; they had passed without detection under the eagle-beaked croupiers of Deauville.

A man, one Briggs, of many convictions, who passed through life with the delusion that dishonesty paid, had for a week past been living in the village of Marks Thornton, being a guest at the "White Hart." He was the sub-agent, and presently Mr Montmorency would call in his glittering car and deliver to Briggs four imposing packages receiving half the market value on account. Briggs in turn would distribute these packages in likely quarters, make a hundred per cent profit, and perhaps a little more if he had the courage to become an active negotiator.

He came to Marks Thornton to await the arrival of the wholesaler, and there arrived at the same time in a neighbouring village two inoffensive-looking strangers who were less interested in Briggs than in Zibriski.

"I followed him to Marks Thornton," said Detective Sergeant Totty. "It's my opinion, nothing will happen there – "

"Your opinion," said Chief Inspector Tanner, of the Criminal Investigation Department, "is so unimportant that I scarcely hear it, and, anyway, it's second-hand; it's a view that I have already expressed."

"Why not take Briggs now?" asked Totty.

He was a man under the usual height, rather pompous of manner, a courageous man but somewhat short of vision. Tanner, seventy-three inches in his stockinged feet, looked down on his subordinate and sighed.

"And charge him with what?" he asked. "You couldn't even get him under the Prevention of Crimes Act. Besides, I don't want Briggs. I want Zibriski. Every time I see a photograph of that man throwing roses at beautiful females in Nice I get a pain. There isn't a police force in Europe that doesn't know that he's the biggest slush merchant in the world, and yet he has never had a conviction. We'll do a little mobile police work tonight, Totty."

"Rather a nice village, Marks Thornton," said Totty. "In fact, I nearly took a room at the 'White Hart.' It's silly, trying to keep observation six miles away. Grand old castle there, too."

Tanner nodded.

"That is the seat of Viscount Lebanon – Marks Priory."

"Very old-fashioned," suggested Sergeant Totty.

"Naturally it would be," said Tanner dryly. "They started building it somewhere around 1160."

In the dusk of the evening they drove over to the village, passed the "White Hart," and went slowly up the hill road which skirts the Priory. From the crest of the hill you had an uninterrupted view of the grim house with the four towers which stood one at each corner of the building. In Tudor days the curtain wall had been pulled down and a monstrous piece of Tudorism had been built into it.

21

Tanner stopped the car and examined the building curiously. "Looks like a prison," said Totty. "Rather like Holloway Castle."

Mr Tanner did not deign to reply.

There was no sign of Zibriski in any of the villages they visited. At eleven o'clock they returned to their lodging. Nor did Zibriski come the next day, nor the next. At the end of the week Tanner went back to London. He had excellent information about the movements of the underworld, so accurate indeed that he was satisfied that Zibriski had been warned of his presence, and had changed his plan. Here, however, he was wrong.

On the night of the fancy dress ball Zibriski arrived, met his agent in his room, and there was a swift exchange of good money and bad. Briggs packed the spurious notes in his bag, and, this done, having that contentment of mind which is the peculiar possession of criminals, he went out for a stroll.

There was some sort of a ball on. He stood outside the village hall, heard the strange sounds which were emitted by a hired jazz band, and, climbing the hill, came to a stile where he sat, filled his pipe, and speculated pleasantly upon his good fortune. For Zibriski notes were good trading, and he was certain of his hundred per cent profit.

He saw somebody coming up the road, a strange apparition, wearing a robe and a turban. There was a half moon that night. Briggs got down from the stile and peeped curiously. An Indian? Then he remembered the fancy dress ball.

The man passed him with a cheery good night. From his voice Briggs gathered that he had been drinking a little. He crossed the stile into the field, on his way to the big house. Briggs resumed his seat on the stile and relit his pipe, which had gone out.

Then suddenly from behind him came the beginning of a scream of mortal agony. It lasted only for a fraction of a second. The man on the stile felt the hair on his head rise. He turned round, trying to pierce the darkness, but could see nothing. The ex-convict took out his handkerchief and wiped his damp forehead.

Then he heard the sound of somebody running towards him and presently he saw a man.

"Who's that?" asked a voice sharply.

In the faint moonlight he saw a peaked face with a little brown beard, and gaped at the sight.

"Who are you?" He was surprised to find how husky his voice was.

"All right! I'm Dr Amersham," snapped the man with the beard.

"Who was that screamed?" asked Briggs.

"Nobody screamed – an owl, I expect."

Amersham turned and faded into the darkness.

Briggs sat for a long time. He was a little terrified, but he had the intense curiosity which is the Cockney's virtue; and presently he swung over to the other side of the stile and moved gingerly along the beaten path. He remembered he carried a little hand torch in his hip pocket, and took it out, throwing a beam of light a little ahead of him, and continued.

He was on the point of turning back when he saw something glitter in the light of his lamp. It came from a heap that lay by the side of the path. He moved forward a pace, and his heart began to beat violently. Briggs hesitated again, set his teeth, and continued his investigation.

It was a man – the man who had passed him in Indian costume. He lay still, motionless. About his neck was a red scarf tightly tied...and he was dead...strangled.

In spite of the horrible distortion he recognised him. It was the chauffeur at the Hall, the man who had drunk with him in the bar...Studd.

Gingerly he felt his pulse, slipped his hand under the embroidered shirt, and felt his heart. Briggs rose, went swiftly down the path, jumped across the stile, his heart beating like a mechanical riveter. He walked slowly back to the "White Hart." Let the police find their own dead. He didn't want to be mixed up in it, and had good reasons.

He left the village early in the morning, an hour before they found the strangled body of Studd the chauffeur.

23

5

Mr Arty Briggs reached Victoria Station, desirous of obliterating himself in the crowded city, but having no very great anxiety. The four plain-clothes men who closed round him as he came through the barrier left him in no doubt as to the seriousness of his crisis.

He was taken to Bow Street, and his bag searched. Nobody took a great deal of notice of his statement that the bag was not his, and that he was merely doing a friendly act for an unknown man named Smith by carrying it. The receptacle contained a great deal that Mr Briggs would very gladly have seen evaporate into air.

"I've never seen the stuff before in my life," he said with oaths, and asked for Divine punishment, instant and drastic, if he were lying.

Later he was interviewed by Chief Inspector Tanner.

"Being in possession of counterfeit notes is a mere trifle compared with what's coming to you, Briggs," said Tanner. "You were in the village of Marks Thornton last night. There was a murder committed. What do you know about it?"

Mr Briggs knew nothing. It was, he said, a great surprise to him that anybody could be murdered in that beautiful place. He asked pointedly if any arms had been found on him, and volunteered to have a stricter and more intimate examination.

"It almost sounds as if you knew this man was strangled," said Tanner.

For his own part he had not the least belief that the man had anything to do with the crime. Briggs was not a killer; he was a regular seller of a commodity which was in demand. Moreover, he was an old lag, and not only his history but his temperament were known to the police.

Tanner could not suspect that this man had seen with his own eyes the strangled chauffeur, and inquiry was not pushed very far. But under the threat of being suspect of the murder, Briggs made a clean breast of the lesser offence, and since there is no honour amongst thieves it was due to his instrumentality that Mr Zibriski was taken off the Havre boat that night and lodged in a Southampton cell.

Tanner went up to see the Chief Constable on his return to Scotland Yard. In answer to his inquiry, the Chief shook his head.

"No, the local police haven't asked for us, and it is unlikely that they will until the scent is so cold that you could freeze mutton on it. It seems to be a pretty commonplace crime, and the locals think it is an act of revenge. This man Studd seems to have made one or two bad friendships, though apparently he had no real enemies."

He had been talking on the telephone to Horsham, and this was the source of his information.

Bill Tanner secured one or two other scraps of information in the course of the evening, but nothing that excited his interest. Studd had had a quarrel with a gamekeeper who had suspected his pretty wife of philandering – unjustly, as it proved. Nobody mentioned the name of Dr Amersham. In the reports which came to Scotland Yard his name did not appear, and it was not until a week later, when the "locals" decided to invoke the aid of the Yard, and Tanner and his shadow went down to Marks Thornton, that he heard of the doctor.

He paid a brief visit to Marks Priory, but was coldly received. Casually he mentioned the name of Dr Amersham to her ladyship.

"He comes here occasionally," she said, "but he was not here on the night of this unfortunate happening. I think he left about ten."

That one glimpse he had of the internal life of Marks Priory told him nothing. It was the typical home of a great aristocrat, and on the occasion of his visit the big hall was in a state of repair. There were scaffold poles against the wall, and Kelver, who was his cicerone, showed him the stone tablets, each holding the coat armour of some ancient member of the family, that were being inset in the walls.

"Her ladyship," said Kelver, with proper reverence, "is an authority on heraldry. She can read a coat of arms, sir, as you and I might read a book. She has an astonishing knowledge of the subject. As you probably know, sir, the family comes from most ancient times. The first Lebanon was knighted by King Richard the First."

"Interesting," said Big Bill, who was no archaeologist. "What can you tell me about Studd?"

Kelver shook his head.

"The tragedy of that happening, sir, has kept me awake at night. He was an extraordinarily pleasant man, quite the gentleman, and I have never known him to quarrel with anybody."

He paused, and Tanner misunderstood his hesitation.

The butler had seen nothing, heard nothing. The first news he had had of the chauffeur's death was that conveyed by the policeman who had found him. He had nothing but praise for the dead man, dismissed as impossible any suggestion that he might have had an enemy.

Sergeant Totty, busy in the servants' hall, brought the same story.

"I cherchezed the femme, but she wasn't there," said Totty. "No woman in it at all."

The trail was six days old. It was impossible to pick up anything that was new. There had been a stranger staying at the village inn – too well Tanner knew who that stranger was. There was the usual story of tramps and gipsies, but the nearest gipsy caravan had been twenty miles away. Poachers did not work the Priory fields, but preferred the coverts of Marks Priory Park, and every local poacher had been accounted for.

Tanner saw the photograph of the dead man, examined and took possession of the scarf that had strangled him: a piece of dull red cloth, in one corner of which was a little tin label sewn by the edges, bearing some words in Hindustani, which proved on translation to be the name of the manufacturer.

He saw Lord Lebanon and questioned him. That young man could offer him no solution. He was really fond of Studd – that much Bill had discovered through the butler – and was greatly upset by his death.

The third important member of the household he met as he walked across the Priory fields towards the village. Isla Crane was walking towards him with quick steps and would have passed him, but he stopped her.

"Excuse me – you're Miss Crane, aren't you? I am Detective Inspector Tanner from the Yard."

To his amazement the colour faded from her cheeks; the hand that went to her lips was shaking. She looked at him in wide-eyed apprehension. He had seen such looks before. People suddenly confronted by the police behave oddly, whether they are innocent or guilty, but he had never expected that a girl of her class would betray such emotion. She was frightened, terrified. He thought that she was on the point of collapsing, and his amazement deepened.

"Are you?" she said jerkily. "Yes – I – somebody told me you were... About Studd's death, isn't it? Poor man!"

"I suppose you saw nothing? You can't throw any light whatever on this matter?" he asked.

She shook her head almost before the words were out of his mouth.

"No...how could I?"

Then abruptly she walked past him. Looking back after her, he had the impression that she was running.

Sergeant Totty, watching her until she was out of sight turned to his superior.

"That's funny," he said.

"It's not funny at all," snapped Bill Tanner. "I've seen scores of people behave like that. It must be pretty rotten for people of that class to be suddenly brought face to face with a murder."

Yet he went on his way a very thoughtful man.

Isla came to the big porch before the main door of Marks Priory. Gilder, the footman, was sitting there in a chair, reading a newspaper. He got up as she approached, his forbidding eyes upon her, and she had passed him when he spoke.

"Seen that cop?"

She turned.

"The detective?"

He nodded.

"Did he ask you any questions, miss?"

She looked at him for a moment uncomprehendingly.

"Did he ask you any questions, miss?" rumbled Gilder. His deep bass voice was a little unnerving.

"He asked me if I had heard anything, that's all," she said, turned swiftly and went into the house.

Lady Lebanon was sitting in the great hall at her desk. For twelve hours out of the sixteen you might find her there. She would spend whole days examining old heraldic inscriptions and reading over the parchment book of the Lebanons. She was an excellent Latin scholar, and had few equals in her knowledge of ancient English. She was examining the book now, making notes on a writing-pad. At sight of Isla she closed the book, put the pad away in a drawer and deliberately locked it.

"What's the matter?" she asked.

The girl was trembling from head to foot. For some time she could not find her voice.

"He's been asking questions," she said at last. "Mr Tanner."

"The police officer? What questions did he ask?" And then quickly: "Did he say anything about Amersham?"

The girl shook her head.

"He never mentioned his name. What is going to happen?"

Lady Lebanon leaned back in her chair, rested her elbows on its padded arms, and folded her hands.

"There are times when I can't quite understand you, Isla," she said with some acerbity. "What is likely to happen?"

"Suppose they find out?"

The calm woman at the desk raised her dark eyes to the girl.

"I really don't know what you're talking about, Isla. Suppose who find out? I wish you wouldn't talk about things that don't concern you."

Isla Crane went to her room early that night. She slept in what was known as "the old lord's room," a great, lofty and gloomy chamber, with a huge four-poster bed that still bore on its headboard the faded arms of some forgotten Lebanon – forgotten except by Lady Lebanon, who forgot nothing. It was a long time before she went to sleep.

"Why the devil did she go to bed so early?"

"Don't be difficult, Willie dear," said his mother. "There's nothing in the world for Isla to sit up for."

She looked at the jewelled watch on her wrist.

"It's nearly your bedtime, darling. Don't stay up late. Have you talked to Isla?"

He shook his head.

"No, I haven't had a chance since this awful thing happened." He bent his head, listening. "That's a car," he said. "Amersham?"

"He's coming down tonight."

"He was here the night of the murder, wasn't he?"

She looked up quickly.

"No, he left very early – about ten, I think."

The boy smiled.

"Mother darling, I saw his car go away at seven in the morning. I was looking out of my window. Somebody else told me that he went away the same night."

"Did you correct them?" she asked sharply.

He shook his head.

"No; why should I?"

He looked up at the vaulted roof and sighed.

"This is a devilishly dismal place," he said. "It gives me the creeps. I don't want to see Amersham; I'm going to my room."

The door opened, but it was not the objectionable doctor. Gilder carried a tray, a siphon and a glass. He poured out a modicum of whisky and splashed soda into it. All the time the unfriendly eye of Lord Lebanon watched his every movement.

He took the glass from the man's hand and sipped it. Not until the glass was empty did he detect the bitter after-taste.

"Funny whisky that," he said...

It was the last remark he remembered making. Four hours later he awoke with a splitting headache, and, switching on the light, found himself in his own room. He was in bed, in his pyjamas. With a groan he sat up, his head swimming. Mr Gilder was a little careless with the drug he had administered.

6

Lebanon rose, walked unsteadily to the door and tried to open it. It was locked. He fumbled for the key, but it was not there. He was confused; his head seemed to be out of control; it lolled from side to side. With an effort he forced himself awake, found the switch and turned it.

He knew intimately only two rooms in the house. At first he thought he was in a third, but gradually, as his perceptions awakened, he recognised familiar objects. There was a bell-push near his bed; he pressed it, sat on the bed and waited. It was a long time before there was any answer, and he was in the act of pressing the push again when he heard a key rattle into the lock, and snap as it turned.

It was Gilder. Something had happened to the debonair Gilder; his eye was discoloured; his collar showed signs of rough usage; the striped waistcoat he wore was a little torn, and two of the buttons were missing. For a long time he glowered sulkily at the boy.

"Do you want anything, my lord?" he said at last, and Lebanon knew that he had forced himself to this polite address.

"Who locked my door?"

"I did," said the other coolly. "A fellow who called this evening started a rough house, and I didn't want you to be in it."

The young man stared at him.

"Who was it?" he asked.

"Nobody you know, my lord," said the other shortly. "Is there anything I can do for you?"

"Get me a drink – something cold and long. That whisky you gave me was not too good, Gilder."

If the man sensed the suspicion in his voice he gave no sign of embarrassment.

"That's what the other gentleman thought. I guess the whisky's bad around here. I'll ask her ladyship to get some more down from town."

"Where is my mother?" asked Lebanon quickly. "Was she there when – "

Gilder shook his head.

"No, sir, she was in her room."

"What happened?" asked Lebanon curiously.

The man looked at him with a grim smile.

"Maybe you'd like to come and see," he said curtly, and, pulling on his slippers, Lord Lebanon followed him along the corridor, down the broad circular staircase into the hall.

Brooks was there in his shirt sleeves, apparently trying to clear up the mess. A table had been overturned; the edge of the Knole sofa was smashed; a little china clock lay in ruins on the stone surround; and four of the pseudo-wax candles in the great chandelier hung drunkenly and without life. Lebanon stared around.

"Who did this?" he asked, and tried to bring into his tone a note of authority.

"A friend of Dr Amersham's," said Gilder, and there was a note of malice in his tone which Lebanon did not detect.

The floor was strewn with broken glass and was stained; evidently the whisky decanter had been smashed. One of the panels was broken.

"It looks as if a lunatic had been let loose," said Lebanon.

The smile came off Gilder's face. He was momentarily startled.

"Hey?" he said. "Yes, I guess so. He behaved like one, anyway – this friend of Dr Amersham."

It was half-past three. There was a grey light in the east when Willie unbolted and unchained the great door, and stepped out into the cool freshness of the morning. It was very dark and very calm, and the silence made the young man shudder. The late-sleeping beasts of the earth had gone to bed, and the early risers had yet to chirp their first husky notes of salute to the new day. Far across the Priory Field he saw a light, and then remembered that Tilling, the gamekeeper, lived there, just on the edge of the wood, a surly, unfriendly man. He would be up, of course. It was a gamekeeper's job to patrol the estate. Marks Thornton had a fair share of poachers, shrewd, furtive, brown-faced men, with nondescript dogs.

Willie Lebanon grinned in the darkness. To him, at any rate, poaching was no crime. If he were made a magistrate of the county he would never convict a man for taking what, after all, was his own.

He heard Gilder's slow, rather weary step on the stone flags behind him, and the man came up to him. He was smoking a cigar without any evidence of embarrassment.

"Tilling's up late tonight. I suppose he is on duty?"

Gilder did not answer immediately. He puffed steadily at the cigar, his eyes fixed broodingly on the distant light.

"Tilling went to London last night," he said suddenly.

As he spoke the square of light went out, and Lebanon heard the footman make a clucking note of disapproval.

"That fellow is asking for trouble."

"Who – Tilling?"

Gilder did not reply.

"I think you had better come in, my lord. You've only got your dressing-gown on, and the night is chilly."

His tone was quite respectful.

There were times when Lebanon liked this gaunt American. There were times when his very insolent familiarity amused him. He did not resent the cigar or the friendliness or the assumption of equality.

"You're a funny devil," he said, as he followed the footman into the hall, stood by and heard the great bolt shot home and the clang of the chains when they were fastened.

"I have never felt less funny," said Gilder, "or less like a devil."

"Who was it made the fuss?"

Gilder shook his head.

33

"A friend of Dr Amersham," and then he smiled whimsically. "When you come to think of it, he is probably not so much of a friend – "

And then the young man heard the footman's voice change.

"What are you doing down here, miss?"

Willie looked towards the stairs. It was Isla. She wore a thick, quilted dressing-gown. Apparently she was half dressed beneath, for she wore stockings and shoes.

"Nothing," she said jerkily. "Is everything all right, Gilder?"

"Quite OK, miss. Nothing to worry about. The gentleman who made all the trouble has gone home."

He said this with great deliberation, looking at her fixedly. Willie had the impression that he was prompting the girl, or rather pressing upon her an explanation for the disorder which was not only untrue, but which she knew was untrue.

She nodded her head quickly.

"I see." She was still breathless. "He's gone home... I am glad... Her ladyship wanted to see Dr Amersham before she went to bed, Gilder."

He stroked his chin.

"She did... Well, I guess Amersham...the doctor is out. He went out for a stroll, half an hour ago. Queer time for a stroll, isn't it? You can tell her ladyship I'll send him right along if I can find him."

When the girl had gone Lebanon turned his astonished gaze to the footman.

"Did she see it – whatever it was? Miss Isla?"

Gilder nodded.

"I guess she did," he said shortly, obviously in no mood to offer his confidences. "You'd better go to bed, my lord. It's late."

Lebanon did not protest. In fact, he was heartily in agreement with the suggestion, for suddenly he had become shockingly tired and most surprisingly apathetic.

He had been drugged; he knew that, but was very little worried. In that state of exhaustion he was incapable of feeling distressed.

7

Chief Inspector Tanner preserved in his big frame and his super-practical mind just that quantity of romance which makes life endurable. He had faith in many things, practical and material things mainly, but no small part of his life had its basis on the imponderable substance of dreams. He argued that when a man stopped dreaming, he died, and here he was right, for out of his dreams, often wild and extravagant, came many oddly practical solutions to the most mundane of his problems.

He was a fanatical believer in the efficiency of the Records Department, but even here he found the glamour of romance, and he would spend hours in the bureau renewing old acquaintances. Give him a file, a few cross-indexes, a guard book, packed with the photographs of unpleasant people, and he was thoroughly happy. He could sit and ponder and wonder.

Mainly his speculations started off following a conventional path. What had happened to Old Steine? It was years since he had seen him. There he was, the ugly old man, staring from the guard book; a man with a two-card record; burglar, safe blower, suspected murderer. Dead perhaps? Filling a pauper's grave, or dissipated under the hands of a youthful anatomist in some London hospital. Here was Paddy the Boy; good-looking, the same hard stare in his eyes; a burglar who could never resist the temptation of kissing a sleeping housemaid. That had been his undoing. Here was Johnny Greggs, benevolent, bald, smirking at the prison photographer who posed him. Johnny was doing seven and five at Parkhurst, and was lucky to have escaped a bashing. The crime was robbery with violence, and when arrested he had been found in possession of two automatics fully loaded – an unforgivable sin.

Mr Tanner had allowed himself to be led from the path of investigation. He closed the book, and went back to the examination of the MO cards.

Now all habitual wrong-doers are specialists, and the *modus operandi* method reduces their speciality to the measure of a cold-blooded index, and Mr Tanner was inspecting the names and records of all the men who had at any time, since the formation of the criminal index, strangled or attempted to strangle. Not a few of the names he read were men who had taken the nine o'clock walk to the dropping trap. Some of them were in Broadmoor; perverts who had stepped across the border line. In the remainder he could find no parallel to the event at Marks Priory. There was a surprisingly large number of men and women who had attempted or succeeded in snuffing out life with a cord, but examining them one by one he could discover no name and no record which suggested the perpetrator of the Marks Priory murder.

He went down to his room, found Sergeant Totty comfortably installed in his chair, and unceremoniously snapped him out of it.

Sergeant Totty was not romantic in the larger sense. He was an ingenious liar when recounting his own achievements. A harmless liar, because nobody accepted his embroideries as being of the piece; they were tacked on too clumsily. He harboured a grievance against educational authorities which demanded a certain standard by which men who desired promotion should be tested, and he shared with the redoubtable Sergeant Elk, long since inspector and retired, an almost malevolent disrespect for Queen Elizabeth, since it was his failure to furnish accurate particulars of her very full life that had led to his undoing in three separate examinations.

Totty got up reluctantly, went to the window and stared down at the busy Embankment.

Professionally it had been a dull week.

"Who is Amersham?" asked Tanner unexpectedly.

36

"Eh?" Mr Totty was taken aback. "Amersham," he said, "is a town down in Kent."

"Amersham," interrupted Inspector Tanner patiently, "is a town in Buckinghamshire. Your passion for knowing everything will lead you one of these days to being accurate. I am talking about Dr Amersham."

Totty pursed his lips.

"Oh, him!" he said. "You mean that bird down at Marks Thornton. He's a doctor."

"Even that you don't know," said Tanner. "He calls himself a doctor and presumably is a doctor, but whether he is a doctor of music or a doctor of medicine we have no means of knowing."

He took a notebook from his pocket, turned the pages and stopped to read a note.

"He has a flat at Ferrington Court, Devonshire Street," he said. "A block of flats, one supposes."

"It's on the corner of Park Lane," said Totty briskly.

When he was brisk Tanner knew he was wide of the mark.

"That I would be prepared to believe if I didn't know you were wrong," said the big man. "Ferrington Court is an expensive residence for a doctor. He owns a couple of race-horses, too."

"One of them won the other day," said Totty. "Funny enough, I meant to back it."

"None of them has won for two years," said Mr Tanner gently. "I wonder what his antecedents are? And before you make any wild guess about antecedents, I mean what is his dark and gruesome past."

"I hardly noticed the man," said Totty.

"That is not remarkable," said his superior, "since you didn't see him. I'll tell you in case you would like to pose as an authority on the subject: he's been to India, so presumably he is a doctor of medicine. I wonder exactly what he does at Marks Priory, what is his connection with the family?"

"He could have committed the murder," said Sergeant Totty, momentarily alert.

"So could you," said Tanner. "So could almost anybody you can find in the telephone directory."

"I'll tell you what I did notice when I was down there." Totty's voice was very business-like, and Mr Tanner was prepared to listen. "They have a gamekeeper – a fellow named Tilling. He has a face as cheerful as a wet week. I saw him down at the boozer – at the inn, I mean. His hands were on the counter. I never saw hands like 'em: like shoulders of mutton. I mentioned it to the bung – "

"To the what?" Mr Tanner was elaborately puzzled.

"You know what I mean, Tanner – the landlord. And he said that Tilling had killed a dog once with his bare hands – strangled him."

"The devil he did," said Tanner.

Totty preened and smiled.

"I keep me ears open, Tanner. You think I am a dud, but if there is anything going – "

"Of course you keep your ears open. Nature has built you that way," said Tanner. "Strangled a dog? Why didn't you tell me before?"

"To tell you the truth" – Totty was unusually frank – "it went out of me mind. He's got a wife too – a beauty from what I've heard."

"Does that mean she's good-looking or troublesome?"

"She's both. Very fond of the boys by all accounts. There have been two or three fellows having a little sweethearting with her. Good Lord!" His jaw dropped. "Why, Studd was one. Now how did I forget that?"

"The man who was killed – the chauffeur?"

"That's right." Totty was permeating knowledge. "Very funny I didn't put that two and two together. But I am like that, Tanner. I have to get everything right in my mind."

"What else has been simmering in that vacuum?" asked Tanner, impatiently. "I saw the man – a big, sulky fellow; I remember him."

Totty looked up to the ceiling for inspiration.

"That's about all I know," he said. "Oh, yes, he was in London the night the murder was committed. He went up to town with the landlord's son. That's why I didn't go any farther with my inquiries."

"Tilling was in town – we'll check that up. I'll go down and have a little chat with that woman, and in the meantime I'd like to meet Dr Amersham."

He looked at his watch. It was half-past four.

"Want me to come with you?" asked Totty.

"I don't think it is necessary. You stay here and try to think up a little more that you have forgotten. You know where Tilling and the landlord's son went when they came to London?"

Totty tapped his forehead, and smiled slowly.

"Yes, I do," he said. "It's there, Tanner." He tapped his forehead again. "Criminal index. Card index. I never forget anything once it's planted. They came up to see the landlord's brother who has a pub in the New Cut. It was his birthday or something, and young Tom drove Tilling up, and they spent the night in town."

"Check that," said Tanner.

He came to Ferrington Court half an hour later. It was a new block of flats, erected by an architect who had leanings towards the Queen Anne type of building when he was planning exteriors, but went arty-crafty the moment he got inside the walls. The lobby was of marble. The false pillars were neither of Corinth nor Egypt, nor yet Byzantine. There was an elevator with a French gilt door, and its interior was of lacquer in the Chinese manner.

"Dr Amersham? Yes, sir, he's in. Is he expecting you?"

"I hope not," smiled Bill Tanner.

He had stepped into the lift when a newcomer entered the vestibule and hurried across. He was a clergyman, a weak, pale man who smiled benevolently at the elevator attendant and as genially upon Bill.

They went up to the third floor. When the door was opened, Bill followed the clergyman on to the landing. He saw him now at No. 16, which was also his destination.

A young liveried footman opened the door. Evidently the clergyman was no stranger. For some reason he accepted Mr Tanner as accompanying the clerical visitor.

"I will tell the doctor you are here, Mr Hastings," said the man, and left them alone.

"My business is not at all pressing," smiled the clergyman. "So please do not let me interfere. I am the vicar of Peterfield – John Hastings. Do you know Peterfield?"

"By repute," said Tanner politely.

He did not wonder at Dr Amersham knowing a man of the cloth. Amersham, for all he knew, might be a man of deeply religious principles, or this might be an old school friend.

The vicar lowered his head, and spoke in a confidential tone. "I am afraid I am going to be a nuisance to our dear friend Amersham," he said, a note of waggishness in his voice. "It is the village hall – a perfect nightmare to me. We have been seven years, and we haven't completed it yet. The doctor has been awfully kind, and – " He coughed.

The door opened and Dr Amersham came in. The smile with which he greeted the vicar vanished as he saw Bill.

"Good evening, Mr – Tanner, I think, isn't it?"

"That is my name, doctor," said Bill. "You have a good memory."

"A marvellous memory," breathed Mr Hastings. "I had a remarkable instance of that when the doctor came down to Peterfield on rather, shall I say, a vital errand – ?"

"I can give you a few minutes alone, Mr Tanner. Will you come into the dining-room?"

Amersham was brusque, almost rude, in his interruption.

"You don't mind, Vicar?"

He walked quickly through the open doorway, and, when Bill had passed, closed the door behind him.

"Well, Mr Tanner, have they discovered anything about this wretched affair?"

"No, doctor, nothing very important. I wondered if you would be able to tell me something?"

Dr Amersham looked at him thoughtfully, pursed his bearded lips and shook his head.

"No, I don't think there is much that I can tell you. Naturally, it is a great shock to me and to Lady Lebanon – a terrible shock. The man himself – Studd, I am talking about – was not a particularly pleasant person; in fact, I had many rows with him. He was rather impertinent in his manner, and not an especially good chauffeur."

Studd was, in fact, an excellent chauffeur, but the doctor could not forego the disparagement.

"He was something of a lady-killer, too, wasn't he?" asked Tanner.

The doctor stared at him.

"I don't quite know what you mean. Naturally I knew very little about his private life. Was there a woman in it?"

Bill laughed softly and shook his head. There had been something of malice in his question.

"I am not much wiser than you, but I have heard a story that there was some sort of affair between himself and a gamekeeper's wife, a Mrs – " He paused to remember the name. "Tilling, isn't it?"

He saw the doctor bridle. The suggestion was hurtful to his vanity.

"That's absurd!" He almost snapped the words. "Mrs Tilling is quite a – er – nice woman. Studd? Ridiculous!"

"She is rather pretty?" suggested Bill. "At any rate attractive?"

"Yes, I believe she is," said the doctor shortly. "No, Mr Tanner, you're altogether wrong about Studd. Mrs Tilling is a very reserved young woman, and hardly the sort of person – tush!"

Bill Tanner had never heard a human being say "Tush" before, and he wanted to laugh.

"Who told you this?" asked the doctor.

The inspector lifted his broad shoulders.

"It was one of those idle rumours that float around and attach themselves to a listening ear," he said good-humouredly. "But I understand her husband is rather jealous of her. Have you heard that?"

"Her husband's a fool," said the doctor angrily; "a stupid commonplace oaf, and a brute! He has treated that girl most abominably!"

He seemed to feel Tanner's interested inspection, and went on hastily:

"I don't know her very well, of course. I've attended her professionally, One has to depend upon rumour, as you do, Mr Tanner."

Obviously here was a delicate subject to enlarge upon. The doctor was prepared to change the conversation. Bill, on the other hand, would have been glad to hear more.

"I thought you knew her very well," he said, in all innocence. "Otherwise I should not have mentioned her."

"Why should I know her well?" asked the doctor coldly. "To me she is just the wife of one of her ladyship's employees – that and no more. Naturally I take a great deal of interest in the staff – but it is the interest of a doctor in his patients."

"Naturally," murmured Bill. "So in your opinion all talk of any kind of" – he shrugged his shoulders again – "well, any kind of friendship between Studd and Mrs Tilling is absurd?"

"Absolutely," said the other emphatically. "It is the sort of foul rumour that goes round a little village that has no other occupation in life than to gossip – and to gossip maliciously."

Then he forced a smile.

"I expected you to come here with a lot of information to give me about this wretched case. Scotland Yard is not living up to its reputation for sensation."

"We have no reputation for sensation," said Inspector Tanner easily. "We are the most commonplace department of Government. If you want a real thrill you should go to the Treasury! I'm sorry to have bothered you, and I won't keep you any longer from your friend."

He held out his hand.

"Oh, you mean Mr Hastings? Do you know him at all?"

Amersham asked the question carelessly, but the big man sensed a hidden anxiety.

When Tanner shook his head: "A very amusing country parson," the doctor went on. "I've been helping him with his boys' club – by the way, Mr Tanner, is it true that there was a well-known criminal in Marks Thornton on the night of the murder? I heard something about it, and I was wondering whether you were pursuing that line of investigation."

Bill Tanner thought of Briggs and chuckled.

"I wouldn't call him a well-known criminal. He is certainly a well-convicted criminal. No, there's no suspicion attaching to him. He's a forger, and this was about his third or fourth conviction. You may have met him in India; you were there for some time, I understand? A man named Briggs."

Dr Amersham could control the muscles of his face, but he could not control its colour. The red faded to yellow, and presently grew redder still. For a second Inspector Tanner could not believe the evidence of his senses. At the mention of this little forger Amersham had paled. It was unbelievable, but it was a fact, and he was dumbfounded.

"I've never met him," said Amersham slowly, "or even heard of him. Yes, I was in India for five or six years – I suppose you know that? In the Indian Medical Service. It was a dreadful job, and I resigned...the fluctuation of the rupee...and the conditions of the work were..."

He was incoherent, but he recovered himself almost immediately, and again flashed his white teeth in a smile.

"If at any time I can give you information, don't hesitate to ring me up, Mr Tanner. I am usually here, though I spend two or three days a week at Marks Priory. Lady Lebanon and I are writing a book together – this is a secret and I hope you won't tell her, because she'd be rather annoyed – on heraldry. I am rather an authority."

Bill did not ring for the lift, but walked down the marble stairs, and in his mind were one or two problems.

The hall porter in his little cubby hutch smiled at him and tried to catch his eye, but Bill's mind was fully occupied.

Curiously enough, the first of his problems was the "vital occasion" of Amersham's visit to the village church of which Mr Hastings was vicar. He turned that over and disposed of it by the mental promise of further investigation, and came back to Amersham himself. Here was no small problem. Why had the doctor changed colour when Briggs' name was mentioned? What association could there possibly be between a cheap criminal who had spent the greater part of his life in prison for forgery and counterfeiting, and this officer of the Indian

Medical Service? And why had he championed with such vehemence the reputation of Mrs Tilling?

As to this, there was a simple explanation – that the gossip which brought their names together was true. It was not unlikely. Mrs Tilling was, as he had said, a most attractive woman, and, unless he was wrong at every point, Dr Amersham was, to say the least, impressionable.

Tanner stepped out into Devonshire Street, and was looking round for a taxi when he became aware of a man who had been standing on the opposite side of the road. He saw him turn abruptly and become absorbingly interested in the window of a maker of surgical instruments. But he had not turned quickly enough: Tanner had immediately recognised in this man, momentarily fascinated by the gruesome exhibits which filled the window, no other than Tilling the gamekeeper – and he knew that Tilling the gamekeeper had been watching Dr Amersham's flat.

8

He was starting to cross the street towards the man when his quarry, who must have seen him out of the corner of his eye, walked rapidly away. Bill followed at the same pace. Tilling turned into a side street, and by the time his pursuer had reached the corner had disappeared. There was a taxi moving towards the far end of the street, and Tanner guessed that the gamekeeper was the passenger.

He went back to Scotland Yard with a new interest in the Marks Priory case, and was in his room, going through a small private dossier he kept in his desk, when Totty returned.

"I've checked up that statement and it's OK," he said. "Tilling slept at this pub in the New Cut – "

"You haven't had time to go to the New Cut," said Tanner.

"What are telephones for?" demanded Totty.

"Not to make police inquiries," said Tanner sternly.

"As a matter of fact, I know the landlord. Him and me are like brothers," said Totty calmly. "Tilling slept there – at the pub, I mean – and went back in the morning. He's a great friend of young Tom's – "

"Talking of sleep, did you have plenty last night?"

Totty looked at his superior suspiciously.

"I slept very well, yes. Why? I've got no conscience – "

"I know that. You mean you have no bad conscience, but by accident you spoke the truth. Totty, I'm giving you a job after your own heart. Go to Ferrington Court and shadow Dr Amersham. Find out if he's in, and who his visitors are. You can have a talk with his

45

servant – he's got a young footman there – and you might pick up a little information from some of the attendants of the building."

Totty groaned.

"It's hardly a job for a sergeant, Tanner – "

" 'Mr Tanner,' if you please, or even 'sir,' " said Bill. "As a matter of fact, it is a job for an inspector, and I wouldn't trust it to anybody but you. There may be a break in this Marks Priory case, Totty, and I want you to be in it. It doesn't look as if it's going to rain, and, anyway, you can manage to get inside – I've never known you to be uncomfortable if you could help it. If you don't like to go I'll send Ferraby. Nobody would imagine he was a detective – "

"Nobody would imagine I was a detective," said Totty loudly. "I've got nothing to say against Sergeant Ferraby or any other junior officer, but if you want me to do it, I'll do it."

There was one quality in Sergeant Ferraby which was a very sore point with Totty. Ferraby belonged to that select band of public school men who had drifted into police work. The incidents of Queen Elizabeth's reign were no mysteries to him. A charming, well-spoken man, he had shown an aptitude for his work which had earned him early promotion. Secretly Totty admired him, and carried his admiration to the point of imitating him. He had cultivated what Tanner, in his more offensive moments, described as the Oxford and Cambridge accent, and this he employed much more frequently than Mr Tanner was aware.

There was excellent reason for Totty's reluctance, for shadowing is a boring and miserable job, involving hours of patient watching during which time nothing happens. To follow a man in the street without losing him is not as simple as it sounds, especially a man who has at his call the services of a fast car.

When he strolled into the busy vestibule of Ferrington Court it was without any hope of finding a profitable hook-up in the resplendent porter and lift attendant.

If Tanner had been more observant, and had troubled to pierce behind the disguise of gold lace and purple raiment, he would have recognised the attendant as a sometime constable of the Metropolitan

Police Force, one Bould. Totty knew him immediately, and hailed him gratefully as a friend.

"Funny thing, Tanner didn't notice me when he was here this afternoon. What's he after, sergeant? That fellow Amersham?"

"Why should he be, Bouldy?" said Totty, who invariably put a "y" to any name on which a "y" could hang. "Bless my life, it's surprising to see you here. You look like a cinema barker!"

The ex-policeman surveyed the sleeve of his well-fitting coat with a scowl.

"I don't know why they go in for all this fancy stuff in a respectable place like this. It's art, but art never meant anything to me," he said, and then went back to the afternoon visit. "He went up to Amersham's place. I suppose it's connected with that murder down in the country. It's a funny thing, I've been expecting to see the chief inspector here ever since I knew our bloke was connected with the case."

"What sort of a fellow is Amersham?"

Mr Bould shook his head.

"He treats servants as if they was dogs," he said. "A jump-up if ever there was one! And what a gentleman! I could tell you a few things about him," he added darkly.

There was a little office where he sat when the lift was not required, and into this he ushered Totty.

"If you sit there in the corner nobody'll see you when they come in." He indicated a seat. "Amersham? He's hot! He had a party here about – now, when was it? It must have been two months ago. All the other tenants complained... Women, champagne – it was more like modern Babylon than anything else."

"Was it?" said Totty, in a hushed, sympathetic voice, and asked avidly for particulars.

Unhappily, all that was truly Babylonian had happened behind closed doors, Mr Bould being able to supply only such lurid particulars as he had gleaned at first-hand from Joe – Joe being the evening footman who had opened the door to Tanner that afternoon.

"That's his weakness," said Bould, after he had given a "few particulars" which were not wholly satisfactory to the listener, since authentic details were missing.

"Is he in?"

Bould shook his head.

"No, sergeant; he went out about half an hour ago, but he's coming back – he's got an appointment. He's got a young lady calling; he said if she come before he returned I was to put her in a waiting-room. We've got a grand waiting-room – have you seen it?"

"I haven't, and I don't want to," said Totty. "Where's the servant – Joe, is it?"

Mr Bould winked.

"Out! He let him off early tonight."

He winked again, and Totty, who knew the sign language of the lower ranks, realised that the retirement of the servant and the advent of the lady visitor was no odd coincidence.

"Is Tanner after him for something? I shouldn't be surprised if he was," said Bould. "That feller's always seemed suspicious to me – he's got plenty of money – gets it from somebody down in the country by all accounts. He's only here about three nights a week, and then it's parties and theatres – and whoopee! Do you know what whoopee means?"

"I've heard of it," said Totty.

He threw a warning glance and shrank into a heap in the corner. A quick step sounded on the marble flooring of the vestibule. Bould went out quickly, snapping out the light as he did so, and a second later Totty saw the doctor pass, heard an inquiry, and then the slam of the gate and the whine of the elevator as it shot up.

It had hardly gone before Totty heard another step, and, peeping cautiously round the edge of the plate-glass window, he saw a girl, and his mouth opened at the sight of her, for it was the girl he had seen at Marks Priory – Isla Crane!

She was dressed in a long coat and a little black hat pulled down so that her face was not easy to recognise. But Totty never forgot any person he had ever seen. She was a little pale, tired-looking, obviously nervous. Her very uneasiness suggested guilt – though, in fairness to her, it may be said that almost any emotion spelt guilt to Totty.

She looked left and right, and had half turned towards the office when fortunately the lift came down and Bould stepped out.

"This way miss. You want to see Dr Amersham, don't you?"

"If you please," she said in a low voice.

Totty waited until Bould returned.

"That's her," said the attendant. "Good looker! They all are, the girls who come here. If she was a daughter of mine – "

He lifted his eyebrows impressively.

Totty made no comment. There was nothing remarkable in the visit. The girl was secretary to Lady Lebanon, and probably she bore some sort of message from her employer. But she had not come as a messenger. Her nervousness, her pallor, were all significant to this worldly man.

"Is there any way I can have a look into that flat?" he asked suddenly.

Mr Bould's face was grave. The policeman in him urged the instant discovery of pass keys, or at least an entrance into the empty flat next door to the doctor's. There was a convenient balcony which ran along the front of the doctor's apartment and was only separated by an iron bar under which an inquisitive man might duck. But he was no longer a policeman: he was custodian of the welfare of Ferrington Court and all that were accommodated therein, and for that he received a respectable wage which might be jeopardised by an indiscretion.

"Well, I don't know, sergeant," he said, scratching his chin. "If it was an important case, or you had an arrest to make, of course I'd do anything you wanted."

Totty argued for a few minutes, and they went up in the lift together.

Isla Crane had hardly pressed the bell before the door opened.

"Come in, my dear."

Dr Amersham was genial, fatherly, much more of a friend than he had ever appeared in the presence of Lady Lebanon.

"It's terribly good of you to come. Let me take your coat."

49

But Isla had not come to be entertained.

"No, thank you, I'll keep it on. I can't be here for more than a few minutes. How did you know I was in town?"

The doctor smiled as he showed her into his drawing-room.

"I've been on the phone to her ladyship, and she told me you were here. A night off, eh? I hope I haven't spoilt your evening. It is abominable the way you are being kept in that gloomy Priory."

"I am going on to Stevenage in the morning to see my mother," said the girl shortly.

He pushed a chair up for her, but she did not sit down.

"Lady Lebanon told me the hotel you were staying at," he said. "I was fortunate to find you before you went out."

"What do you want?"

Her tone was without friendliness or compromise, and he mentioned this.

"I didn't expect to make a friendly call," she said coldly. "You said you wanted to see me urgently about her ladyship. I shouldn't have come otherwise."

"You're a little hard, Isla. Let me take your coat off."

But she stepped back and avoided his helpful hand.

"Why did you want to see me?"

It was difficult for him to find an approach. The disinterested friend was a role not easily assumed in the circumstances.

"Somebody wants to marry you – do you know that?" he asked, and, when she did not reply: "How does the idea strike you? You'll be Viscountess Lebanon, with precedence over commonplace baronesses and the smaller fry of the peerage. That's funny, isn't it? By the way, you're not to tell her ladyship that I asked you to come and see me."

She shot a quick glance at him.

"Why not, if it concerns her?"

"It concerns you and me – and your prospective marriage. It would be rather a good thing for you, Isla. The boy will make a very good settlement on you, or, rather she will. You don't seem very excited about the prospect."

He saw her moisten her dry lips.

"Lady Lebanon has told me, or rather, hinted to me," she said, "but I don't wish to be married, and I have told her so."

He laughed.

"And I presume she ignored your wish on the matter and went on as though it were all settled? A domineering person, is Lady Lebanon, and rather difficult to resist when she sets her mind upon a thing."

If he expected her to reply he was disappointed. He waited for a second or two, and, when she showed no inclination to speak, he was irritated.

"Why the devil don't you take your coat off and behave like a rational being, Isla?" he said. "You and I are in the same boat. We're both upper servants of the same all-highest. We both draw our salaries and our sustenance by hiding our real feelings – "

"Is there anything more you wanted to say?" she asked. "Because, if there isn't, I'm going."

She half turned, and then, before she realised what was happening, she felt herself jerked round towards him and she was in his arms. They were strong arms; his clasp was not easily broken. His little beard brushed her cheek; his pale eyes held a luminosity which terrified her.

"Isla, there's nobody else in the world but you," he said breathlessly. "I want to be your friend. I want to help you through the rotten time that's ahead of you."

"Let me go for a moment," she said evenly, and he was deceived.

On the wall of the room was a little silver knob, and beneath a neat metal plate, so neat indeed as to disguise from any but the sharp-sighted its utilitarian instructions. Hardly had the arms about her slackened than she drew herself free and flew to the wall. Her thumb touched the knob.

"You'll open all the doors, please," she said, "and then you will go into another room."

Amersham was breathing quickly. He said nothing, knowing the futility of argument in that moment of defeat. He flung open the door of the room, passed through the lobby and opened the outer door with a crash.

"You can go," he said. "I was a damned fool to help you."

She pointed to the door at the other end of the drawing-room.

"Don't be stupid; you're perfectly safe – " he began.

"I'm perfectly safe whilst my hand is on this fire alarm," she said quietly, "because you wouldn't want to be made to look ridiculous."

From the balcony outside the peering Sergeant Totty approved.

"Very neat," he said.

He saw the outer door close on the girl, and watched the doctor come back into the drawing-room and slam the door.

"Very neat," said Sergeant Totty again.

For a little while Amersham paced up and down the room, his hands thrust into his pockets, his bearded chin on his breast. Totty heard the tinkle of a telephone bell, and saw the man go to an instrument on his desk and pick up the receiver. His brow knit in an angry frown and he said something which was indistinguishable. Then he snapped out the lights in the room and went into his bedroom.

Totty passed farther along the balcony. The blinds were drawn, but through half an inch of space at the side he could follow Amersham within a limited range of movement. He saw him open a drawer and take something out, which he slipped into his pocket. What that something was he could not see, but from the movement he guessed it was a revolver or an automatic pistol.

There was another telephone in the room, and to this the doctor went and spoke for a minute or two. Evidently it was a house phone, for the reply came immediately, and Totty remembered that in Bould's office he had seen a small switchboard.

Amersham took his overcoat from the wardrobe, wrapped a white silk scarf round his throat, and the detective made his way along the balcony through the empty flat into which he had persuaded Bould to introduce him, and was in the hall before Amersham came down.

"He's going out," said Bould. "Just now phoned to his chauffeur – there's the car at the door. Half a tick!"

Bould went outside and interviewed the driver of the car.

"He's going down to Marks Thornton," said the porter behind a cautious hand when he returned. "You ought to have a talk to that chauffeur. What he doesn't say about Amersham…! He's a new man, but he's the second Amersham's had in a month."

The lift bell interrupted him. He darted into the elevator, and was gone less than a minute. When he came down Amersham stepped out briskly through the gate and into the street.

Not till the car moved did Sergeant Totty come out.

"Funny devil," he said.

"Seen anything?" asked Mr Bould, who had joined him at the door.

"A lot of things," said Totty mysteriously.

"She wasn't there very long."

"She wasn't there as long as he wanted her to be," said Totty. "That fellow's mustard!"

He stopped at the nearest telephone booth and phoned the Yard. Mr Tanner was not in. He tried him at his house, and was more fortunate.

"I wonder what made him go to Marks Thornton?" asked Tanner thoughtfully. "Obviously he had no intention of going there originally. Where is the young lady staying?"

Totty groaned.

"Have a heart," he snarled. "I don't know everything!"

"What a confession!" said Tanner, and hung up.

The telephone booth was less than a hundred yards from Ferrington Court. As Totty pushed open the door and came out he was conscious that a man was standing half a dozen yards away, watching him intently. His first impression was that it was a local detective, for there had been a number of robberies from call boxes recently. Then suddenly he recognised the watcher, and his mouth opened in surprise. Evidently the stranger intended speaking to him, for he met Totty half-way.

"Your name's Tilling, isn't it?"

"That's my name," said the other. He had a deep rumbling voice, and his normal tone was unfriendly. "Didn't I see you come out of that place?" He pointed to Ferrington Court. "Have you been to see Amersham?"

"Now listen!" Totty was elaborately polite. "You know who I am –
a detective officer. What do you mean by asking me questions?"

"Who was the girl that went in? Did you see her?" He asked the
question eagerly.

"Yes, I saw her."

"Did you know her? Did you see her when you were down at
Marks Priory? She didn't go away with him, did she? I missed her
coming out. That flunkey called a cab for her, and I was waiting to see
him."

"Who do you think it was, son?"

Totty was being diplomatically polite.

"It couldn't have been her, anyway; she's not so tall, and she don't
dress like that. Who was it?"

"My aunt!" said Totty. "Who did you think it was?"

And then the object of the inquiry flashed on him. "I'll tell you
who it wasn't, if you'd like to know – it wasn't your wife."

The man was momentarily taken aback.

"Who said it was, and why should it be? My wife's down at Marks
Thornton. Where's he gone?"

"Who – Dr Amersham? He's gone to Marks Thornton. Now, my
friend, what's the idea? Why are you spying on Dr Amersham?"

"Mind your own business," snarled the man.

As he turned Totty gripped him by the arm and flung him round.

"Politeness costs nothing," he said.

Tilling was evidently surprised at the strength of a man who was a
head shorter than himself and created no impression of robust health.

"I beg your pardon, sergeant," he said, more politely; "but I've got
a bit of domestic trouble on my mind."

"Who hasn't?" said Totty, and let him go.

He watched the gamekeeper till he was out of sight, then he
strolled back to Bould.

"You've no idea where that young lady went, have you?"

"Treen's Hotel, Tavistock Square," said Bould. "That's the address
she gave the cabman."

THE FRIGHTENED LADY

Totty had no desire to interview the girl, but his time was his own. He walked till he found a bus which landed him within a few hundred yards of Tavistock Square. Treen's Hotel comprised two private houses joined into one. A cheap and respectable hostelry in a quiet backwater.

The young lady had not gone to bed, he was told: she was in the writing-room, which was also the drawing-room and the card-room. It was a veritable writing-room at the moment, for she was sitting at a desk, writing a letter, and was alone when Totty walked in. She did not recognise him at first.

"Sorry to disturb you, miss, but you probably remember me. My name's Totty. I was in charge of the Marks Priory case."

She stopped her pen and looked round at him, startled.

"Oh, yes. I remember you, of course," she said. She was a little out of breath. "Is there anything you want to see me about?"

Totty smiled affably, sat down on the edge of a chair, and balanced his bowler hat on his knee.

"I happened to see you get out of a cab and I thought, 'Why surely that's Miss Crane!' I said, 'No, it can't be. What's she doing up in town?' And then I said, 'Well, it must be'..."

She listened to this self-examination with growing confidence.

"How are things at Marks Priory, miss?"

She leaned back in her chair, her hands folded in her lap.

"Very much the same as they were."

"How's Dr Amersham?" he was bold to ask.

She drew a deep breath.

"I haven't seen Dr Amersham for a long time," she said.

He smiled again very benevolently.

"That's funny! I could have sworn I saw you coming out of Ferrington Court."

She sat bolt upright.

"I saw him tonight, but I didn't think it was a matter which really concerned you, Mr Totty. Have you been watching me?"

He nodded.

"I watched you go in, and I watched you come out. And the reason, miss, I watched you go in and watched you come out was that I didn't think the doctor was a nice man to call on after dinner when he'd sent all the servants out."

At first she was alarmed, then he saw a smile on the corner of her lips.

"Thank you, Sergeant Totty," she said. "You were a sort of guardian angel?"

Totty smirked.

"I've got a reputation for it," he said.

The curse of Totty was that he could never resist the temptation to make dramatic revelations. In the past it had many times been his undoing. Here, however, he might secure his effect with little injury to what is commonly known as the public service.

"Yes, miss, and even if you hadn't found the fire alarm I should have been on the spot."

She looked at him with a wondering frown.

"I was on the balcony outside. Do you know anything about him?"

She hesitated, then shook her head half-heartedly.

"No, except that he's a great friend of Lady Lebanon's," she said.

"A little bit gay, isn't he, miss?"

She smiled again, and then, despite herself, laughed.

"He's never made me feel particularly cheerful. By 'gay,' I suppose you mean — "

"Exactly!" said Totty, with a discreet laugh. "I hear there are rumours about him down at Marks Thornton — Mrs What's-her-name — the gamekeeper's wife."

He was watching her closely. Evidently that little scandal had not reached the girl's ears, for she was frankly astonished.

"The doctor... You mean — Mrs Tilling, isn't it? Oh, no, that's impossible!"

Yet she had heard that Mrs Tilling was a lady with a weakness for admiration. Servants talk. Even the sedate Kelver had once indicated by a significant change of subject his mild disapproval of gamekeepers' wives who make friends.

Totty had heard a great deal; she wondered how much. Had he heard Amersham's reference to her marriage? If he had he gave no indication.

"The doctor's taken a trip to Marks Priory tonight." He volunteered the information at the conclusion of an apparently aimless interview.

She was astonished to hear this, and he saw her look at the letter she had half written.

"Are you sure?" she asked.

Sergeant Totty never made mistakes; he told her so. In fact, he lingered for quite a quarter of an hour supplying proof of his prescience and acumen. She was amused, and went to bed that night in a more cheerful frame of mind than she had thought would be possible. As for Sergeant Totty, he strolled back to Scotland Yard to write his report, and was surprised when the officer on the door told him that Tanner was in his room and had been inquiring for him.

"Don't you ever sleep?" he asked, entering the chief inspector's room unceremoniously.

"Well, what have you found?" asked Tanner. "Sit down there, take your hat off – it's usual when you're speaking to a superior in a superior's private room – keep your hands out of my cigarette box, and tell me as many facts as you can, and as few inventions as possible."

Sergeant Totty was tired enough to be explicit.

"A bit of luck finding Bould there. I think I remember him," said Tanner, when his subordinate had completed an unusually lucid account of the night's happenings. "That may be very useful in the future. You haven't discovered much that I didn't know, except a projected marriage which doesn't interest you or me – Tilling was there, was he? I saw him this afternoon."

"He's jealous!" said Totty.

"And he has every right to be," nodded Tanner. "I think that doctor should be told. Get in touch with Bould, and ask him to report to me when Amersham returns. I'll go along and see him. It isn't quite right to leave him in ignorance that he's being watched by a jealous gentleman who once strangled a dog."

"And who strangled Studd," suggested Totty, but Bill Tanner shook his head.

"I doubt it. That man was strangled with a bit of cloth that came from India. If Tilling was the operator he'd have used his hands. No, we've got another line of investigation, and that leads to Amersham. He has lived in India."

He reached out and pressed a bell.

"What do you want? Can I get it?"

"I want Ferraby. He's somewhere in the building."

"What do you want him for?" asked Totty resentfully.

"I'm going to put him on to shadow Miss Crane. If you want the job you can have it. He can pick her up and go back to Marks Thornton and see what line he can get there. Incidentally, he can keep a watchful eye on Mr and Mrs Tilling."

Ferraby came, tall and breezy, a curious combination of the flippant and respectful. When he heard what his task was he brightened visibly.

"Miss Crane! Good Lord, I'd love to!" he said.

"Do you know her?" asked Tanner, in surprise.

"I saw her the last time we were at the Priory," said the young man, and had the grace to blush. "Terribly pretty, isn't she?"

Totty shook his head reproachfully.

"Your mind's not on your work, boy," he said, and he struck nearer home than he could guess, for Sergeant Ferraby's mind had been occupied, to the exclusion of all other matters, by a vision of sweetness which had never left him since. For he was young, and detectives have their strange emotions.

9

On the second day after he had been detailed for his pleasant task he shepherded back his charge to Marks Thornton, and left her reluctantly at the gates of Marks Priory. Isla Crane was completely ignorant of the fact that she was being shepherded at all, and never once had she supposed that within a few yards of her was a Scotland Yard officer watching her every movement.

Ferraby's work was rendered the more difficult because she knew and had spoken to him. He waited till the station fly was out of sight around a bend of the poplar avenue before he returned to the "White Hart," dismissed the carriage which had brought him from the station, and went in to negotiate for a room.

He saw a young man standing behind the bar, and remembered that he had received instructions to verify Totty's rather sketchy inquiry, for he guessed this was "Tom," the son of the proprietor.

After settling himself in his comfortable little bedroom, he strolled down to the bar parlour. Tom was still on duty, and at this hour the detective was the only customer. Tom broke disconcertingly into the amiable preamble of Ferraby's inquiries.

"Aren't you one of those gentlemen from Scotland Yard?" he asked. "You were down with Mr Tanner, weren't you? Is there anything new about the Studd case?"

"Nothing," said Ferraby.

He was a little annoyed to be recognised at all.

Tom took a cloth and mechanically wiped the counter.

"I wasn't here that night – I went to town for my uncle's birthday, and stopped the night."

"You and Tilling?" suggested Ferraby.

The young man grinned.

"You knew that, did you? Yes, we went up together, but Tilling came back early."

"Didn't he stop the night at your uncle's?"

Tom shook his head.

"No, there wasn't any room for him, and anyway he's rather a quarrelsome fellow when he's had a couple of drinks, and I shouldn't have pressed him to stay even if there had been room. No, he came back by the last train. He's got too much on his mind, that fellow, and nowadays he hasn't a civil word for anybody. He was in here at dinner time, and I couldn't get anything out of him but a grunt. Have you got any new clues, Mr Ferraby?"

Ferraby smiled.

"I'm afraid I'll have to disappoint you," he said. "I'm not on business. I'm here for a little rest. We have them at times."

Tom looked at him suspiciously, and was evidently reviewing all the possible circumstances which might bring a detective officer from Scotland Yard to Marks Thornton, for suddenly he asked:

"Perhaps it's over that other case – the fellow with the forged bank-notes. What was his name? Briggs, wasn't it? He was staying here just before the murder, you know; in fact, he was here the night of the murder. Dad and I have often wondered if he had anything to do with it. He didn't look a murderous chap, but judging from the pictures you see in the papers, none of 'em do!"

Ferraby grinned.

"We'll have to make a detective of you," he said, and began a tactful inquiry about the cause of Tilling's unhappiness. There was nothing at all tactful about the young man's response.

"She'd drive any man to drink," he said emphatically. "I don't blame poor old Tilling – he must have a terrible life."

He expressed his opinion of Mrs Tilling in a few frank words.

"Pretty as a picture. She was a lady's maid when he met her. From what I've heard, all sorts of people have been running after her. They say that the doctor – "

He stopped short.

"Dr Amersham? Yes?"

Tom made a little grimace, and rubbed the counter with greater energy.

"No names, no pack-drill," he said. "What's the use of repeating gossip? They'd ruin the reputation of a saint, the people in Marks Thornton."

It is the peculiar delusion of the inhabitants of all English villages that their neighbours are the worst gossipers to be found in the country, and it occurred to Ferraby that the landlord's son might as well be included in the people of Marks Thornton.

He got on the phone that night and reported to Tanner, and in the morning made a long detour that brought him within a hundred yards of the gamekeeper's cottage. Here he sat on a gate, smoking his pipe, and after an hour's wait was rewarded. A woman walked out of the cottage, down the footpath, and, unlocking the gate, came on to the road. She carried a small basket, and was evidently going to the village to shop. As she passed Ferraby she threw a quick glance at him – a not unkindly glance. She was pretty; could, with a little trouble and expense, have been strikingly lovely. And she was well dressed: Ferraby noticed that. Her shoes were smart, her stockings were sheer silk, and of a fairly fine mesh. The close-fitting little hat she wore was not the kind you could buy at the popular stores.

One thing he noticed was a small, diamond-faced watch on her left wrist. She had passed him when he said:

"Excuse me, this is Marks Priory, isn't it?"

She turned back immediately. Ferraby might have imagined that she was expecting him to address her.

"Yes, this is Marks Priory."

There was just a touch of commonness in the voice, but her eyes were fine and alight with life. Her red lips had been made redder by artifice. It was a complaint of the village, Ferraby had learned that morning, that she "powdered and painted."

"This is not the way in." She nodded to the gate. "The main entrance is by the lodge. It's in the village. Shall I show it you?"

Her glance was coyly timid.

"Nothing would give me greater pleasure."

Ferraby felt that undisguised gallantry was called for, and he walked by her side with that slightly proprietorial swagger which the occasion demanded.

Once or twice she looked back as though she were expecting to be followed. On the second occasion Ferraby turned his head too.

"Is somebody calling?" he asked.

"Oh, no." She tipped one well-shaped shoulder in a gesture of contempt. "It's only my husband – I thought he might be following. Do you know anybody at the Hall?" she asked. (Half the village referred to the Priory as "the Hall," Ferraby had noticed.)

"Oh yes, I know one or two people there."

"Her ladyship?"

She looked at him archly.

She was one of those persons who could not suggest an acquaintance between a man and a woman without inlaying that acquaintanceship with a fine filigree of sex. In whatever awe Lady Lebanon might be held by the village, she was just another woman to Mrs Tilling.

"I've met her ladyship – yes."

"Do you know his lordship?"

"I've seen him – yes. In fact, I saw him going up the drive this morning."

She looked at him oddly.

"If you knew which was the drive, why did you ask me to show you the way?" she demanded, and Ferraby took the bold course, and smiled.

"In the first place I didn't ask you to show me the way, and in the second place, if you want to know somebody I suppose you make any excuse for speaking to them," he said, and the answer was completely satisfactory, for she gave a little gurgle of laughter.

"I wondered if that was why you spoke. You'll get me a bad name, but I've got one already, so it really doesn't matter. You don't know Dr Amersham, do you?" she asked with an affectation of carelessness which would not have deceived a probationary policeman.

"I've seen him, and I think I've met him; I'm not sure," said Ferraby.

"He's a very nice man and terribly clever. I must say I do admire clever people; there are so few of them in the world," she said.

She spoke rapidly, stringing cliché to cliché, yet in the definite manner of one who is discovering unrecognised truths and translating them into original language.

"Cleverness always gets me," she prattled on. "I'd rather a man had brains than good looks. The things he knows... Dr Amersham, I mean... They simply astound me. He's been abroad a great deal, and naturally a doctor knows more than any other kind of man – don't you think so, Mr – ?"

"Ferraby is my name. Isn't your husband clever?"

The smile went off her face, and he saw something very hard, something that was almost repellent.

"Him!" she said, and became aware of the scorn in her voice. "He's a very nice man, but rather trying."

She had no reticences; all there was of Mrs Tilling lay very close to the surface. He had the impression that she lived in a glass case, her motives, her acts and her reactions consciously visible to the world.

They reached the lodge gates, and she stopped.

"This is the drive to the house, but I suppose you know all about that," she said. "Are you staying here long?"

Ferraby was good-looking, tall, and though he was not aware of the fact, her physical beau-ideal.

"For a day or two – " he began, and then stopped short and went red.

Isla Crane was walking down the drive, passed him with one quick, surprised look, and went on. That glance told him two things: first, that she remembered him, and secondly, that she was amazed to find him talking to the wife of the gamekeeper. He wanted to run after her and explain, though how she would have responded to that impertinence he could guess when he thought the matter over.

"That is Miss Crane."

Mrs Tilling had not noticed his confusion.

"She's her ladyship's secretary; full of airs and graces, and they say she hasn't got a penny to her name, except what her ladyship gives her. The way some people carry on, you'd think they were the queen of the earth, wouldn't you?"

There was a touch of asperity here, and Ferraby wondered why.

"Would you say she was pretty? I wouldn't. She's not what you might call a young girl…got a good complexion and all that sort of thing. But she hasn't what I call style."

Then, abruptly, she held out her little gloved hand, and Ferraby took it. It was one of those limp handshakes that really worried him. Dr Amersham should have taught her a better.

He was conscious that over a curtain of the "White Hart" somebody was surveying him. That somebody was Tom, who greeted him as he came into the hall of the inn with a broad smile.

"She found you, did she? Bless my soul, she's a one for finding 'em. I keep away from her myself. I'm engaged to be married, and my young lady's very particular."

He bustled round the counter.

"Is it too early for a glass of beer?" he asked.

"It's never too early for me," said Ferraby untruthfully.

He heard a heavy step behind him, and a hand like a log fell on his shoulder.

"Do you know my wife?"

He turned at his leisure, and looked into the dark face of the gamekeeper. An ugly fellow this, in ordinary circumstances; now his eyes were blazing with fury. Ferraby leaned his elbows on the counter, and looked at the man.

"If ever you lay your hand on my shoulder again," he said deliberately, "I'll give you a sock on the jaw! No, I don't know your wife. I met her this morning – if you are Tilling. I walked with her up the village street, and if you have any further questions to ask, ask 'em now before I boot you out of this bar."

The man was a bully, and therefore had a broad streak of pusillanimity.

"I'm entitled to ask, ain't I?"

Already he had wilted perceptibly.

"You're entitled to be polite," said Ferraby.

"I don't want strangers talking to my wife – "

"I'm not a stranger." Ferraby recovered his sense of humour. "I'm a Scotland Yard detective, and therefore a friend of the world."

Tilling was startled, blinked at the young officer, and when he spoke his voice was husky, as that of a man whose deeper feelings made it difficult to articulate.

"Scotland Yard?" he stammered. "I didn't know." And then, quickly: "What have you been asking her?"

10

Before Ferraby could reply the man turned quickly, walked out of the bar and out of the "White Hart."

"Nice fellow, isn't he?" said Tom, and then, charitably: "I suppose it's his wife. What did you think of her, Mr Ferraby?"

"Very charming," said Ferraby, "and very pretty."

Tom nodded.

"Goin' to drive that fellow bats – you mark my words. He'll do something that he won't be responsible for. If I were her, I'd be scared to death. But she isn't. They say he's like a child when she rounds on him. If she was my wife – "

He shook his head ominously.

Ferraby was not a beer drinker, especially not an early morning beer drinker; but the bar parlour offered a favourable post of observation. He stood, glass in hand, watching the village street, in the hope that Isla Crane would return on that side where the "White Hart" was situated. He was desperately anxious to meet her, most anxious at the moment to explain – what needed no explanation – his acquaintance with Mrs Tilling. He told himself he was being ridiculous – and he was right. Isla Crane was probably unaware of the woman's existence, and possibly had forgotten him.

Presently he saw her, and, putting down his glass hastily, wiped his lips and strolled negligently from the "White Hart" towards her. He saw her glance at him, and lifted his hat.

"You don't remember me, Miss Crane?"

She smiled quickly.

66

"I remember you, yes. You are Mr Ferraby. Didn't I see you just now talking with " – she hesitated – "with Mrs Tilling?"

There was a ghost of a smile in her eyes when she added: "Were you pursuing your usual inquiries, Mr Ferraby?" Then, quickly, "Why are you here at all?"

"Pursuing my usual inquiries," he said, and went on glibly: "As a matter of fact, we've got some data to check up about a man who was staying here and who was arrested for being in possession of counterfeit money."

"Oh!" She was obviously relieved.

It occurred to him afterwards that she was as anxious to interview him as he to meet her. He walked with her to the lodge gates and a little way up the drive. About a hundred yards from the entrance she stopped.

"I don't think you'd better come any farther, Mr Ferraby, or we shall believe that it isn't your forger but the Marks Priory murder that has brought you here, and I think that might worry her ladyship."

She turned her head quickly and looked up the drive. Her hearing was more acute than Ferraby's, and she had recognised the step on the gravel. Presently he came into view, a young man in flannels, bareheaded, swinging in one hand a putter, which he raised in salutation to the girl.

"Do you know Lord Lebanon?" she asked in a low voice.

"I've just met him," said Ferraby. "I don't suppose he'll remember me."

"Good morning, Isla." The young man looked quizzically at her companion. "I know you." He closed his eyes tight, concentrating his mind. "You were down with Mr Tanner. Something like Ferret... Ferraby – that's right, isn't it?"

"You've a wonderful memory, my lord," smiled the detective.

"That is the only thing wonderful about me!" said the young man. "And even that gift raises no loud cheers at Marks Priory! What are you doing? Cross-examining poor Isla? It's a wicked shame!" Lord Lebanon was smiling broadly.

"Nobody cross-examined me – not Tanner, or that queer little fellow who was with him – Sergeant Totty, is that his name? – or anybody. I suppose I look rather unintelligent. Have you seen Amersham?"

The question was shot at the girl.

"I didn't know he was here."

"Oh, he's here all right. We ought to have a flag up when he arrives – break it from the mast-head – a green skull and crossbones on a yellow field!"

"Willie!" She was gently reproachful, and he laughed softly. "You don't know our friend Dr Amersham, do you?" he addressed Ferraby.

"I know him slightly."

"That's just as much as you should know him," said Lebanon. "To know him well may be an excellent education for a policeman, but it's a shocking experience for us poor, simple countrymen."

He looked thoughtfully at the detective.

"What are you really here for – is it about that wretched murder?"

"Mr Ferraby says that's not his business at all. There was a forger in the village – "

"Oh, yes, I remember. Where are you staying, Mr Ferraby – at the 'White Hart'? You could have come to the Priory. I'm sure her ladyship wouldn't have objected, and I – "

He saw the girl's eye, and stopped.

"I suppose you're terribly uncomfortable at the 'White Hart'? It's a pig-sty of a place."

"It's a very nice inn, Willie," insisted the girl.

"And I've got the best room," smiled Ferraby, "and a beautiful set of legs on which I can walk out if I feel so inclined."

The youthful face of the young man wrinkled with laughter.

"You don't walk in your sleep by any chance, do you?" And then, with sudden and surprising penitence: "I'm terribly sorry, Isla."

To Ferraby's amazement the girl had gone red and white.

"Are you going up to the house now, Mr Ferraby? I'll go with you."

"No, Mr Ferraby walked as far as here with me. He's going back to the village."

"Then I'll take a stroll to the village, too."

The girl walked on almost without a word of farewell, and Lebanon called her.

"Isla, if you see Gilder hiding behind that clump of bushes, you might tell him I know he's there! He can come into the open; it will save him an awful lot of bother. Probably the grass is very damp."

As they moved off, Ferraby saw to his surprise that the girl had stopped near the bush Lebanon had indicated, and was talking to some invisible person.

"I knew he was there," chuckled the young man, and, taking Ferraby's arm, they strode down the drive together. He was below normal size; his head hardly reached Ferraby's shoulder.

"There are two popular sayings about members of the peerage," he said. "One is that a man may be as drunk as a lord, and the other that he may be as happy as a lord. I've never been drunk, and it's so long ago since I was happy that I almost forget the experience."

He glanced back over his shoulder.

"I suppose you do a lot of watching, don't you, Mr Ferraby – follow people about, shadowing? Isn't that the word? How would you, for a change, like to be shadowed? I can tell you it's an exasperating experience."

"Have you ever been shadowed?" asked Ferraby, in surprise.

Lebanon nodded so violently that his horn-rimmed glasses slipped down his nose. He pushed them back.

"In spite of the warning Isla gave him, I'm being shadowed at this moment," he said calmly.

Ferraby looked back, and sure enough saw a tall man pacing slowly down the drive behind them, and recognised one of the footmen he had seen at the Priory on the occasion of his last visit.

"It's a rum experience, but you get used to it. I'll make a confession to you." He slipped his arm out of the other's, and looked up at him. "Do you know why I asked you to come back with me? To annoy the gentleman who is behind. When I say 'annoy' I mean scare. Unless I'm greatly mistaken, he will have recognised you, and know that you are an officer from Scotland Yard, and that will put the wind up him to an incredible extent. Why it should I haven't the slightest idea, but one has only to mention Scotland Yard in my ancestral home to produce an atmosphere beside which the Chamber of Horrors is a cosy corner! Where is Scotland Yard?" he asked abruptly.

Ferraby explained.

"Near the House of Commons. I think I know the place. One of these days I'll come up and have a long chat with you and that fellow who's in charge of the case. What's his name? Tanner! I could tell him something that would rather amuse him."

They crossed the village street to the "White Hart."

"Having accomplished the last thing in the world they wanted, I'll leave you."

"What was the last thing they wanted?" asked Ferraby.

"To see me in earnest confabulation with a police officer. I have an idea that is what Gilder is paid to prevent, and if I've disturbed his sleep tonight, I've recovered a little of my lost happiness!"

Ferraby stood in the door of the inn and watched the young man along the street. He saw Gilder cross at a respectable distance. Obviously he was keeping his master in sight.

Tom, the landlord's son, had been a witness.

"I didn't know you'd met his lordship." He was obviously impressed by the friendliness the young man had shown. "There's a nice fellow, if you like! But I wouldn't change places with him for a million pounds."

"Why not?" asked Ferraby.

"Because he's not his own master, for one thing. The real boss of Marks Priory is her ladyship, if it isn't the doctor. Lord Lebanon is a bad third. One of these days – " He shook his head gloomily.

"Well, what will happen one of these days?" asked Ferraby after a long silence.

"I don't know. They got Studd; maybe they'll get his lordship. Studd knew too much for some of them, and I've got an idea that his lordship is getting a little bit in the way. From what I've heard from the servants, he's not only given Amersham the rough side of his tongue, but a punch on the nose one night. I'd like to have been there! But it won't make things any easier for his lordship."

He refused to elaborate this mysterious warning. On the phone that night Ferraby repeated the conversation to his chief.

"Village gossip, I should imagine. Anyway, Lebanon's the type that's born to be bossed. In fact, there's no other type. Some are bossed by women, some by thick-headed detective sergeants."

Ferraby guessed that Sergeant Totty was for the moment unpopular with his superior.

11

The evenings at Marks Priory were dull at the best of times. Amersham had gone back to London, so that Willie Lebanon had not even somebody to goad and quarrel with. If the truth be told, he was a little terrified of the doctor, but there were moments when, by some apparently innocent remark, he could irritate Amersham beyond endurance, and, having learned this trick, he never lost an opportunity of practising it.

Isla had gone to bed, and Lady Lebanon flatly refused to play backgammon, and showed no inclination even to indulge in the most innocent of gossip. She was no entertainment at the best of times, and Willie had never been allowed to reach the stage when heraldry interested him.

He was a little apprehensive that evening. He knew from experience that his mother had something to say, and that something was not too pleasant. There was a certain ominous quiet about her that in itself was a preparation for a disturbing pronouncement.

"Who was that man you were walking with today, Willie?"

So that was it! He braced himself for a few unpleasant minutes.

"A fellow called – I forget his name. I met him in the village."

"He was a police officer, wasn't he?"

"I believe he was," said Willie with a carelessness he did not feel, as he took up a newspaper.

"What did you say to him?"

"Nothing at all. I just passed the time of day. He's staying at the 'White Hart.' An awfully nice fellow. He came down to inquire about a forger, or something of the sort."

She bit her lower lip, her dark eyes on her son.

"He came down to inquire about the murder," she said.

"Poor Studd! Really?"

He swung round in the chair on which he was sitting.

"I wondered if he was telling the truth or not. You can't really believe all these fellows tell you. Who said so?"

"He was seen talking to Mrs Tilling and asking her questions. I hope you were discreet, Willie!"

He exploded with mirth.

"Discreet – how absurd! What have I got to be discreet about? I don't know who killed poor old Studd, do I? I may suspect, but I don't know. If I knew, and was absolutely certain, I'd have him shot like a – especially if it was the man I think it is."

Her gaze did not waver; it was almost hypnotic in its fixed intensity.

"You talk about these things very light-heartedly, Willie" – her voice was very steady – "but I hope you realise what it would mean to a person so suspected. The police, even if they did not prove their case, might concoct a story that would send a perfectly innocent man to prison."

"And a perfectly guilty man, too," said Willie, stung to recklessness. "Good Lord, mother, what are you worrying about? Anybody would imagine you didn't want to see the murderer of poor old Studd arrested!"

He saw her stiffen at this, and watched rather than heard the progress of a sigh.

"What did you tell this officer?" she asked.

"Nothing."

He got up quickly and threw down the newspaper.

"He wasn't half as inquisitive as you are. I'm going to bed." As he turned towards the stairs he saw Gilder standing on the lower step, a forbidding frown on his none too attractive face.

"Wait a moment, me lord. *I'd* rather like to know what you told that bird."

"Gilder!" Lady Lebanon's voice was harsh. "Let his lordship pass."

Lebanon was white with fury, did not trust himself to speak, but pushed past the footman and ran up the stairs.

"That was a little careless of you, Gilder."

"I'm sorry, me lady." There was no humility in his confession of sorrow. "But that fellow rattled me today. I thought they'd finished with the inquiry. What has made 'em take it up again? This is one of Tanner's men."

She nodded.

"He's down at the 'White Hart,' isn't he? Do you think the story is true – I mean, about his coming here to conduct inquiries about the forger. There may be some truth in that. It isn't necessarily the other matter which has brought him."

Gilder looked dubious.

"I don't know. He's only a little man, a sergeant. I guess if there was anything important on the big fellow would have come himself. Those kind of people are only sent to make inquiries and to clear up little points. I shouldn't think he's worrying his head about Studd – if I thought he was – "

"If you thought he was, Gilder, you'd be your own careful self."

Lady Lebanon's smile was rare and dazzling. Gilder himself had never seen her smile more than twice before.

"In the meantime, I should like to know just what he's doing and when he leaves."

She took a cash-box from a drawer of her desk, put it under her arm and went upstairs. She was a creature of routine; rose and went to bed almost to a time-table, except on those nights when such upsetting elements as Dr Amersham intruded into the strained serenity of her life.

There was no reason why she should have worried about Ferraby. He was making preparations to leave on the following morning, and, though he would go reluctantly, Tanner had given him specific instructions.

After the last belated customer had been politely ejected from the "White Hart" he went out for a stroll, and he followed the road he had taken that morning, coming at last within sight of the gamekeeper's cottage. There was a light in one of the windows, and he wondered exactly what would be the effect if he passed through that gate and knocked at the door. Perhaps his sulky friend of the morning would make the night a little exciting for him.

He left the gate behind, walked another hundred yards and turned back. As he came near the cottage entrance he was conscious that somebody was there. It was a woman, her shoulders covered by a dark shawl, and she was smoking a cigarette.

"I wondered if it was you," she said.

She spoke in an undertone, as though she feared she might be overheard.

"This is a dead and alive village. I suppose you're bored to death?"

She affected a curiously refined tone of voice which reminded him irresistibly of Totty in his more genteel moments.

"No, it isn't boring. By the way, I saw your husband this morning; he was rather annoyed with me."

She shrugged one shoulder.

"That's nothing new; he's always annoyed with somebody." She looked back. "He's on duty tonight, on the north side of the park. They've had poachers there. If he's doing his work he's two miles away."

His hand was on the gate when, without any warning she rested her palm on his.

"I'm sorry I can't ask you in," she said. "Would you like to come for a walk in Priory Fields?"

He was staggered:

"I'm going to take a walk to the 'White Hart' and then I'm going into bed," he said.

She laughed mockingly.

"Johnny wouldn't hurt you," she said. He guessed "Johnny" was Mr Tilling. "I always take a little walk in the evenings – so long as I keep in sight of the cottage it really doesn't matter leaving it."

Then her manner and her voice changed.

"Who killed Studd?" she asked.

Her tone was almost metallic, and he sensed in her a depth of fury that he had never suspected.

"The dirty, murderous beast?" There was a catch in her voice. "I'm going to find him, Mr Ferraby, and I'll find him before you detectives do!"

She was breathing very quickly; there had been almost a sob in her voice.

"Studd was a friend of yours, wasn't he?"

"He was my lover," she said defiantly. "I'm telling you the truth. He was the only man in the world – "

Again she stopped, finding it almost impossible to control her voice.

"I was going to get a divorce. Johnny's no saint, I can tell you. And we were going to marry. That's the truth. He'd have changed me – taken me away from this beastly village."

She stopped, fought for her self-control and recovered it.

"I was going to tell you that this morning, only I couldn't. If I ever find out who murdered him, I don't care who they are, I'm going to put them on the gallows!"

There was a concentrated malignity in the words that would have shocked him if he were not beyond shocking.

"That's why I hoped you'd come for a walk with me, why I've been wishing and praying you'd come along tonight. I've been watching for you for two hours. You thought I wanted to do a little bit of sweethearting, didn't you? Well, I didn't. I wanted to find out what you knew, and like a fool I thought it'd be easy to get it out of you. But now I know that if you knew you wouldn't tell me – and you don't know!"

There was no sound but the drip-drip of water from the trees. It had been raining heavily earlier in the evening, but the storm had passed.

"He was on his way to see me when he was killed," she went on, more evenly. "That's why he came from the dance hall alone. I'd have gone to the ball, but I didn't want any talk, especially as Johnny was in London for the night."

"He came back by the last train," said Ferraby. "Did you know that?"

She stared at him, unbelieving.

"Who? Johnny – my husband? He didn't come back till the next morning. You're wrong about that."

"He came back the same night," said Ferraby, "by the last train."

He heard the swift intake of her breath.

"My God! Did he?" she said slowly. "I didn't know that."

They looked at one another in the half-darkness. The only light was the oil street lamp that marked the entrance to the village, a solitary outlier of village civilisation.

"Oh, well, that's something," she said at last. "Good night, Mr Ferraby."

Before he could reply she had turned and disappeared into the darkness of the garden. He caught a glimpse of her as she opened the door of the cottage, and then he went on to the inn, puzzled, and the detective in him stimulated by the interview.

He had not boasted vainly about the comfort of his room. It was a large, low-roofed apartment, and if the wallpaper erred on the exotic side, the furniture was old and comfortable, the four-poster bed very promising.

He undressed at his leisure, read for half an hour, and, opening the bottom sash of the windows, drew the almost transparent curtains before them and undressed.

Ferraby was of that age when a man sleeps soundly and heavily. Usually he fell asleep within two minutes of laying his head on the pillow, but tonight a long time passed, and he turned from side to side before he finally dozed. His last recollection was of hearing the village clock strike midnight.

Then he began to dream: an ugly, frightening dream. He was in the drive, talking to Isla Crane, and somebody came behind him and slipped something round his neck.

"Don't be a fool," he said, and put up his hand to loosen it. It grew tighter and tighter; he was gasping for air; his head seemed swollen to an amazing size. He struggled desperately and woke. It was no dream; to pretend he was dreaming was to die. Something was tightly knotted around his throat and was being drawn tighter.

He tore at it, flung himself out of the bed and tugged. He heard the bed castors come squeaking towards him as he pulled the bed bodily in his direction. He clawed at the scarf desperately, but it was immovable, and he was losing consciousness. With one last effort he reached his waistcoat, hung on the back of a chair. There was a pocket-knife there. He fumbled and found it, pulled open the blade and sawed wildly.

He was free from the worst of it now, but that choking thing still encircled his neck. There was a mad singing and a drumming in his ears; he was hardly conscious of what he was doing, but he slipped the keen blade between his throat and the restriction and cut. In a second he was free, lying on the floor, gasping in the night air.

Dimly he heard a quick patter of feet along the passage, and somebody flung the door open and came into blurred view over him.

"Is anything wrong?"

It was Tom's voice. He saw the figure on the floor, put the candle on the chest of drawers and lifted Ferraby into a sitting position.

"What's the matter?"

Somebody else came into the room; it was the landlord. They dragged the young man to the open window and let him kneel there, his arms on the window-sill.

"Light the gas, Tom."

The inn boasted an acetylene gas plant. In the white clear light they surveyed the room. The bed had been dragged from its place in the corner half-way across the floor.

Ferraby came slowly to his feet, his knees almost giving under him, his head still reeling.

"Pick that up for me, will you?"

He pointed to the fragments of a red scarf that lay on the floor, and, dazed as he was, he realised that this was a replica of the scarf which had been used for the murder of Studd. He could see the little metal tag glittering in the bright gaslight.

In a quarter of an hour he was sufficiently recovered to make a careful examination. The scarf had been knotted round his neck and knotted again to the bed-post. His head must have been dragged over by somebody of unusual strength to make this possible. The very awkwardness of his position as he lay had certainly saved his life.

Whoever it was had come through the window; the curtains were pulled aside, and on the damp surface of the ledge he found the print of a boot. A further search revealed a ladder which stood up against the small outhouse of which the leads formed the roof. There was something Gilbertian in the situation when the village policeman was summoned and given particulars of the happening.

When daylight came Ferraby made a careful search of the room, but the intruder had left no clue behind, and the footprint was so indefinite that it was of very little assistance. Tanner was called on the phone and given a brief outline of what had happened.

"I feel rather a fool," said Ferraby apologetically, "looking for a strangler, and all the time he was looking for me!"

"He seems to have been more successful," said Bill Tanner dryly.

The chief inspector made few comments. Almost his first question was to ask if he had seen Amersham.

"No, he's not here; he went away last night."

"He didn't come back to town," said Tanner. "I think you will find he was somewhere in the region of Marks Thornton. Make a few inquiries and return. Bring back the bits of scarf with you."

"The local copper's got them," said Ferraby, ruefully.

"Go and demand them from him. Anyway, it's our case, and if he gives you any trouble ring up the Chief Constable. I hope you're keeping this matter dark, and that the landlord isn't going to talk. The less that's known about this affair the better. If it gets into the press you'll look silly, and you'll have Marks Thornton filled with reporters, and that's just what I don't want."

In point of fact, Ferraby had secured the promise of the landlord that the matter should not even be mentioned. The village policeman was a little more difficult to silence, and Ferraby took the precaution of ringing up the Chief Constable and securing from him peremptory instructions on the subject.

When he returned to town that evening it was to find that Tanner had gone into the country. He naturally supposed that they had crossed one another on the journey; but Mr Tanner's inquiries had taken another direction.

12

He had arrived that afternoon in a pleasant Berkshire village. He might, had he wished, have gone straight to the vicarage of Peterfield and interviewed the mild Rev. John Hastings. Instead, he made a solitary tour, inspected the Saxon ruins which are Peterfield's chief title to fame, the half-completed village hall, and eventually the church itself, where an obliging verger, who was also something of an antiquarian, revealed the beauties of a building which was old when Henry VIII was king. As a great treat he was taken to the crypt and shown certain gruesome relics of the Reformation. There were church books to be inspected and these went back to the year 1400 – Chief Inspector Tanner had an instructive afternoon.

He came back to find that he had missed Ferraby. That young man, a little shaken, had gone home to a less exciting night, but had managed to type out a fairly lucid account of what had happened. Tanner unfastened the little parcel which contained the cut pieces of the scarf. In every respect it matched the scarf already in his possession, that with which the life of Studd had been taken.

Though Ferraby had made a sketch of the bedroom and its approaches, this told the chief inspector very little that was valuable, but the young man had written a postscript on the back of his report.

"You were quite right about Amersham. He spent the night at Cranleigh, about five miles from Marks Thornton. He stayed at the inn and garaged his car there, and spent most of the evening and night at some place I've not been able to discover."

Tanner read and re-read the account, put it into the folder he kept in his desk, and locked the drawer. The Marks Priory case had flamed up into life again; it was now a vital problem, and henceforth would be in the forefront of police investigations.

Though Ferraby was not aware of the fact, a third officer had been sent to the village to pursue a third line of inquiry, and this time the investigation followed a new and a strange avenue, for it concerned the late Lord Lebanon, who had died with mysterious suddenness whilst Willie Lebanon was in India.

By the morning the one officer who had been detailed to keep connection with the mystery of Studd's death had been increased to a dozen. One of these reported the return of Dr Amersham to his flat; another had taken up the inquiry at Peterfield, where Tanner had left off; a third was pursuing patient inquiries at the American Consulate.

It was reported at seven that night that the doctor had left Ferrington Court for Marks Priory. He had left his chauffeur behind and had driven himself. Within ten minutes of learning of Amersham's departure Mr Tanner was in communication with certain key points on the road to Marks Thornton, and at eight o'clock, when the first of these watchers reported the car going south, he left Scotland Yard by taxi for Amersham's flat.

This time he went armed with authority in the shape of a search warrant.

His interview with Bould was a brief one. The caretaker recognised the warrant when it was shown to him.

"I shall have to report this to the doctor, sir, when he comes back in the morning," he said.

"That's all right," said Tanner, "but if by any chance you forget to report it I shall be very much obliged. I shall disturb nothing that I shan't put back."

Totty accompanied him, and, once they were let into the flat with a pass key, they began a systematic and careful search. There was plenty of evidence that the doctor was no anchorite. The flat was luxuriously furnished; the one or two articles of Indian ware which he had evidently brought back from the East were tastefully chosen. His desk yielded to Totty's persuasive key, but they found little that threw light upon the doctor's habits or the source of his income.

They looked for his bank book, but it was not in the flat: there was, however, a bank sheet which showed his balance in the region of £8,000.

Evidently he did a little practice, for in his bedroom they found a medicine bag already packed, and a case of surgical instruments, which apparently had not been used for some considerable time since they were smeared with a preservative grease.

It was Tanner who made the most important discovery. All the drawers of the desk had been taken out and their contents examined. He observed that two of these, those occupying the centre pigeon-hole space, were very short, and did not reach the back of the desk. He felt in the cavity and tapped the back, which sounded hollow. Presently he found a thumbnail groove, and pushed aside a sliding panel. Putting in his hand, he felt something soft, and took out a piece of cloth. He stared at it and whistled.

It was a red scarf, exactly the shape and substance of the scarf that had killed Studd!

He called Totty, and even that man, who was never at a loss for words, stood speechless at this evidence. The same little red tag was sewn in the corner, bearing the identical manufacturer's mark. Apparently it was unused, for the packing creases were still in evidence.

They looked at one another in silence. Then Bill spoke.

"Tomorrow I will ask Dr Amersham to explain his possession of this," he said slowly, "and I don't think he will find it very easy!"

There were two persons at Marks Priory who intensely disliked one another. Mr Kelver, that eminent servant, was too much of a gentleman even to admit his natural antagonism towards Lady Lebanon's maid, Jackson. Jackson, who was no lady, never disguised her contempt for one whom she invariably referred to as "the fossil." Mr Kelver's very politeness was an offence to Jackson; his refusal to lose his temper in any circumstances roused her to a degree almost of frenzy.

The feud dated back to a time when Jackson, out of her kindness, had retailed a long and apparently exciting story of something she had heard at first hand from her ladyship. It was a scandalous something, and Mr Kelver had listened in silence. When the lady's maid had got out of breath and finished, he had said:

"I would rather – um – Miss Jackson, that you did not bring these stories to me. I am not interested in my – um – employer's private life. Members of the aristocracy have certain privileges which to the lower orders may seem – um – peculiar."

The woman's face had gone dangerously red.

"If you're referring to me as one of the lower orders, Mr Kelver – " she had begun.

Kelver had silenced her with a gesture. It was that gesture which she never forgave. Thereafter they were enemies; tacitly so on his part, openly so on the part of Jackson. Mr Kelver was not worried. All his life had been passed in an atmosphere of disapproving lower servants. Almost it added a zest to existence.

She was a privileged servant in that she had the advantage of access to the main building after all the other servants had been locked out. At eleven o'clock, when her ladyship retired, she also was seen through the door by Lady Lebanon herself, and the key turned on her. But those extra hours marked her out as a person of consequence. The staff at Marks Priory had the impression that she was privy to many secrets which were hidden from the rest of the world. They knew that she had the ear of her ladyship as no other servant had, and she was treated with the greatest respect.

To Kelver she was a mischievous woman of uncertain age, and he suspected her, not without reason, of seeking to undermine his authority.

On the night Inspector Tanner made his discovery he was in his little sitting-room, engaged in reading Scott. Probably he was the only man in the world who read Scott and nothing but Scott. Mr Kelver admired the genius of Abbotsford to a degree of veneration, and he was on the last chapter of *The Antiquary* (which he had read fourteen times) when there came a knock at the door, and to his amazement Jackson sidled in.

A glance told him that she was not her usual self. She was flustered, nervous, almost humble in her manner. Her very manner of entry testified to her strange humility.

"You'll excuse me, Mr Kelver, and if you'll let bygones be bygones, because if ever a girl needed a friend I need one now. I do indeed! And I know that a gentleman like you don't bear a young girl malice..."

Mr Kelver might have sniffed at the "young girl" description, but, like a gentleman, he refrained.

She released a turbulent brook of words, and beyond questioning the accuracy of the repeated description of herself as a "young girl," Mr Kelver listened sympathetically. He was not at all sure how the interview might end, and for the moment could hardly be expected to lower his proper reserve.

Her ladyship had been very trying, in fact had been impossible. She had given Jackson notice (Kelver felt a curious sense of complacency at this intimation); she had even struck her maid – boxed her ears, in fact. Mr Kelver, who had often wished to perform the same operation, raised his eyebrows and inclined his head gravely.

"Her ladyship has been like that all day – absolutely unreasonable. Nothing you could do pleased her. Anyway, I was going to give her notice if she hadn't given it to me. I'm tired of this damned house – "

"Miss Jackson!" murmured the shocked Kelver.

"Well, it is a damned house – haunted! I've seen things, Mr Kelver, in the two hours after you've been turned out" (Mr Kelver winced) "that you'd never believe. I've just had a bellyful of it." (Mr Kelver winced again.) "But when I go I shall have something to say, believe me!"

"My dear young lady," said Mr Kelver in his best pontifical manner, "the least said the soonest mended. It takes a lot of people to make a world, and if we all thought alike and behaved alike it'd be a very monotonous place to live in. I have observed that her ladyship is not quite herself today. Something has happened which has upset her. You must make allowances, Miss Jackson, for the peculiar temperament of the well-born. Now, when I was in the service of His Serene Highness, it was not an uncommon thing for him to throw the joint at the chef. I have known that to happen twice – three times."

"I'd like to see anybody throw a joint at me!" breathed Miss Jackson.

Such a possibility made Mr Kelver very thoughtful for a few seconds. He looked at the clock on his mantelpiece: it was not yet ten.

"You're out early tonight," he remarked.

"I've got to go back," she said. "She's got Amersham there, and there's a bit of a row on. She said she'd ring for me when she wants me."

Mr Kelver, always a perfect gentleman, rang his own bell.

"You would like a cup of tea, Miss Jackson? I think your nerves need soothing."

"I'd like a whisky and soda," said that practical woman.

Mr Kelver struggled hard to deny that he had such a thing in his room, but presently produced a new bottle from his cupboard.

There was indeed trouble at Marks Priory that night. Dr Amersham had arrived at nine, in no mood for reproaches, and was, indeed, himself in a frame of mind to reprove.

"My dear lady, I wish you'd decide earlier in the day if you want to see me. I had an important engagement tonight – "

"This is your important engagement."

Lady Lebanon sat stiffly in her chair in the big hall, her pale face a mask, her dark eyes menacing.

"If you have anything more important I shall be surprised to know of it."

He looked ugly for a second, but mastered his anger.

"I suppose it's about this detective. If he was fool enough to get himself half strangled – "

"Who told you?" she asked quickly.

"I heard about it."

"Who told you?" she repeated.

"Gilder. He got me on the phone."

For a long time she looked at him without speaking. Then: "It's not about the detective I wanted to see you; it was on a matter which concerns you."

She took a little slip of paper from the pad in front of her.

"A woman came to see me today, a girl who used to be a waitress at the tea-shop in the village."

She saw his expression change.

"Well?" he asked defiantly.

"Is it true that you have been – paying attentions to her?"

He evaded the question.

"What rubbish! My dear lady, if you listen to these people – "

"Is it true?" she asked again. "Was she a close personal friend of yours – I refuse to put it any more vulgarly than that?"

"I refuse to be catechised."

"I have heard, too, certain stories concerning Tilling's wife."

He laughed, but there was no heartiness in his laughter.

"You could fill a whole day listening to 'certain stories' about her. Surely to God you haven't brought me all the way from London to put me through my paces, as though I were a small boy caught in the act of stealing jam?"

She looked at him for a while, then let her eyes fall to the table. "I suppose it is true," she said. "How beastly, how vulgar! It can't go on, of course."

He pulled up a chair, lit a cigar that he took from his pocket, and waited until it was well alight before he spoke.

"I've been thinking it can't go on," he said coolly. "I've decided I'd like to leave England and live in Italy. For quite a long time I've been doing your dirty work – "

Her chin went up; she hated him for his crudeness. "You've been very well paid for 'doing my dirty work,' as you call it," she broke in.

He laughed.

"Your idea of good pay and mine do not quite coincide. But I won't go into that. My suggestion is that I should leave at the end of the year, buy a villa in Florence, and forget there is such a place as Marks Priory."

She inclined her head.

"Perhaps you will also forget that I have a banking account," she suggested. "That would be a great relief to me."

He smiled at this.

"Not you, but Willie has a banking account, and he very obligingly signs any cheques put before him. No, I don't forget that; in fact, I'm rather depending upon this fortunate circumstance."

The air was electric. She restrained an obvious retort, and touched a bell on her table.

"We can discuss that in the morning," she said. "I don't think either of us is in the right state of mind for argument; it could so easily degenerate into something rather horrible. Amersham, you must stop your philandering. It brings me into disrepute – everybody knows you have the *entrée* here – and it makes you look a fool. You're not a young man."

His vanity was hurt, and showed in the dusky flush that darkened his face.

"The question of my age is immaterial," he said. "It is rather late in the day for you to consider that aspect. And I'm not stopping tonight – in fact, I'm going straight back to town."

"You're staying here," she said, "or there will be no cheque for you tomorrow."

He glowered at her. Dr Amersham had had the training of a gentleman, and if his principles had deteriorated into conventions, to be observed or discarded as opportunity dictated, he preserved certain appearances. He might take money from a woman, but he must not be told he took money from a woman. That was against his rule.

She listened, unmoved, to his immoderate retort.

"I never realised how intensely common you were," she said calmly.

"You'll realise something else," he was stung to reply. "You'll realise that the police have never searched this house, and that if they did the fat would be in the fire. You'll realise you are entirely at my mercy, and that ought to bring you to your senses. I'm going. Perhaps I'll have a little story to tell Inspector Tanner."

She shook her head.

"I don't think so. Nobody would believe you if you told them. Tell them if you dare! Don't forget, Amersham, that you're as deeply in it as anybody. Your trouble is that you always wanted to handle Willie's money, and my offence is that I've stood between you and your shoddy scheme."

He stood there, his eyes glaring at her, and for a moment she thought he was going to strike her.

"All right," he said thickly, "we'll see. I'm not returning."

He passed out along the hall, and she heard the heavy thud of the door as it closed on him. She did not move, staring down the dark passage even after she heard the whine of his car as it left the porch.

"Do you want me, my lady?"

Lady Lebanon looked up. Jackson was on the stairs, and she remembered she had rung for the woman. How long had she been there, and how much had she heard? As though she read the thoughts of her mistress, Jackson went on: "I waited upstairs until I heard the door slam, my lady."

"Very well," said Lady Lebanon. "Yes, I'll be in my room in a few minutes."

Jackson heard the quick patter of feet and looked up. It was Isla.

"What's the matter, Isla?" Lady Lebanon's voice was sharp.

"Nothing."

Isla Crane was not speaking the truth. Something had terrified her.

With a gesture Jackson was dismissed.

"What is the matter?" asked Lady Lebanon harshly, and pointed to a table where a decanter stood.

The girl shook her head.

"I don't want wine – where is Gilder?" she asked.

"I don't know. In his room, I suppose."

"He's gone out." Isla's voice was high-pitched, hysterical. "And Brooks has gone out. I saw them from my window. Oh, God! it's not going to happen again!"

Then, without warning, she collapsed in a heap. Lady Lebanon did not look at her. Her dark eyes came round to the dark passage and the heavy door beyond, and she went swiftly down the corridor, swung open the door and stood, staring into the night. There was no sound, not even the rumble of a distant train. The quietness was almost oppressive. Then, from the black void before her came a scream that struck her cold; a short scream, stifled, that ended with startling suddenness, and then silence fell again. Still she stood stiffly erect, staring blankly into the night, and in her heart a cold terror of premonition.

13

Many are called to the Criminal Investigation Department, but few
are chosen. They are self-called, for most young policemen feel in
themselves the makings of great detectives.

There were little classes held at Scotland Yard for the embryo
detective officer, and it fell to Mr Tanner's lot, since the summer
holidays were on, to deliver lectures on detective work and to
illustrate those lectures from his wide experience. His big room was
set with chairs for the privileged few who were to attend his "class,"
and a blackboard had been wheeled in, on which he was to illustrate
his typical case.

Totty arrived early, saw the blackboard, and would have retreated
but for imperative orders to remain until the chief inspector put in an
appearance. He was sitting at Tanner's desk as usual when Ferraby
came in. Totty had read the "confidential," and looked up with a grin.

"Nearly got you, did they? Well, well, well! I don't know how the
Yard would have gone on if they'd lost its most active and intelligent
officer – so intelligent that he didn't lock his bedroom door – "

"He came through the window."

"Through a trap in the floor!" sneered Totty. "Through a secret
panel, the same as they do in books!"

"Thank you for your sympathy and loving kindness," said Ferraby,
who knew his man. "Where's Tanner?"

"He'll be here in ten minutes. How's the throat?"

"Grand – honestly, I was scared stiff."

"I'd have died," admitted Totty gracefully. "I can't bear being woke up, anyway. What were you doing down at Marks Priory?"

"Looking round," said Ferraby, and then went to the subject which was uppermost in his mind. "That girl's lovely."

Totty looked up, clasped his head, was extravagantly puzzled.

"Which girl?"

"Miss Crane. Unless I'm mistaken, she is the unhappiest creature in the world."

"Oh, that's why you went down!" said Totty scornfully. "To cheer her up. Well, you don't seem to have made a job of it!"

Ferraby had to talk to somebody about the thing that was in his mind.

"They say she's going to marry that fellow," he said savagely.

Totty put down the confidential document which he had no right to be reading.

"Which fellow?" he asked, and, when the other told him: "Lord Lebanon?" he whistled. "She's a lucky girl. She'll be a female viscount – I should say she was lucky!"

"Your ideas of luck and mine are quite different," said Ferraby coldly.

He strolled to the window, looked out on to the Embankment and changed the subject.

"That man Briggs is over at Cannon Row."

"Briggs?"

"The fellow who was pinched for passing slush," elucidated Ferraby. "He wrote to Tanner apparently, and said he had some statement to make about the Marks Priory murder. Tanner thinks he can throw some light on it, and he may – he was in the village on the night Studd was murdered, and he says he saw him."

Totty shook his head and made impatient noises.

"I can't understand Tanner taking any notice of a man like that," he said in despair. "I've had convicts in my office confessing to murders, never mind about throwing light on them. And why? So that they could be brought up for a day's outing from Dartmoor! Convicts' confessions! Lord love a duck!"

He heard Tanner come into the room.

"I was just saying that in my opinion it's a waste of time interviewing a man like Briggs. Let me go over and see him at Cannon Row. I'll get the truth out of him."

"Do you ever say 'sir'?" asked Tanner.

Totty admitted he did occasionally.

"I'll say 'sir' if you want me to say 'sir,' sir," he said with heavy irony. "That man's over at Cannon Row."

"So they tell me," nodded Tanner.

"It's a waste of time. I really am surprised at you – "

"That's entirely my affair," said Tanner.

"I'm only trying to help you, boy," said Totty with the greatest friendliness.

" 'Sir' will do," said Tanner. "In the presence of a subordinate it sounds good." Tanner was almost oracular. "When we are alone I will remember that we were respectively the best and shortest policemen that ever walked a beat together."

"You've said that before," said Totty, "and my reply is, 'I'm still the best.' "

"Are you feeling any the worse for your adventure?" asked Tanner.

Ferraby smiled ruefully.

"I feel an awful fool to go down and make inquiries about a choking and get choked myself. I'm perfectly all right now, but it was a little bit of a shock to my vanity."

"You saw nobody and heard nothing! Didn't catch a glimpse of him?"

Ferraby shook his head.

"No, I must have been sleeping very soundly, and I'm pretty lucky to be alive."

Totty made a disparaging noise.

"They'd never have caught me, boy," he said. "The slightest touch and I'm awake, with all my faculties working at top speed!"

"All your faculties aren't so many," said Tanner. "Now tell me all about the woman – Mrs Tilling."

Even Totty was interested at the recital of those two interviews.

"She knows something, or guesses something," said Tanner. "But I have an idea she may be guessing wrong. You had a little quarrel with the husband, didn't you?"

Totty shook his head.

"It's a funny thing you can't go anywhere without trying to break up a home," he said.

"Will you shut up? You quarrelled with him, didn't you?"

Ferraby smiled.

"Quarrelling with that bird is a normal way of carrying on a conversation," he said.

Tanner rubbed his chin irritably.

"There are too many suspects in this case for my liking. The doctor was in the neighbourhood? Oh, yes, you told me. And you've got no new line about Briggs?"

Totty was looking at the chairs.

"You don't want me to stop for this lecture, do you?" he asked, and, when his chief nodded: "May I ask you what's the good of me taking a recruit's course?" he wailed. "Do you know that I've forgotten more than anybody at Scotland Yard ever knew?"

Tanner looked up in surprise.

"I didn't know that."

"Make a note of it," said Totty. "If I could have passed my examination I'd have been Chief Constable by now. Queen Elizabeth – huh!"

"She wasn't a bad sort," said Tanner loyally.

"The so-called Virgin Queen!" sneered Totty. "That was a bit of a scandal."

"The worst scandal," said Ferraby, "was your saying that she died in 1066."

Totty exploded.

"Does it matter when she died? Would it make me a better inspector if I knew she died in 1815? Anyway, this lecture has nothing to do with history. I don't want to be told how criminals work; I've got it there." He tapped his forehead. "That's where I've got it."

"That's where you've got it," said Ferraby, "and that's the last place in the world anybody would look for it."

"I shan't want you for the moment," said Tanner. "No, not you, Totty – Ferraby. I'll see this man Briggs, and then I'll have the class in."

Totty sighed and elaborately expressed his resignation.

"What's your typical case?" he asked, dropping into a chair and lighting a cigarette.

Bill Tanner thought for a moment.

"Why not take the Marks Priory case? It's fresh in their minds."

"*I* could tell them all about that."

"I wonder if you could tell them all about this?"

Tanner had taken the folder from his drawer and extracted a slip of paper.

"It's a little thing I collected yesterday, which, in conjunction with the red scarf I found in Amersham's desk, are the two most important discoveries we've made."

"May I see the paper?" asked Totty.

"You may not," said the other promptly. "This" – he waved the slip – "is a bit of first-class reasoning and intuition."

Totty was curious, but his curiosity remained unsatisfied.

"It's as clear as mud to me," he said. "Whichever way you turn you get back to Amersham. He was in Priory Fields on the night Studd was murdered; he was in possession of the scarf; he was near Marks Thornton the night they tried to scrag Ferraby – and why anybody should take the trouble of putting him off the pay roll I can't imagine."

Totty leaned forward.

"I've been making a few inquiries on my own. While you were sleeping soundly in your bed, what was I doing?"

"Drinking!" suggested Tanner.

"Toiling and moiling to get the facts," said the indignant Totty. "Racking me brains and getting here, there and everywhere after information. Amersham's on the police records."

Bill Tanner sat up.

"You don't mean that?"

Sergeant Totty smirked at the sensation he had created.

"I found it out myself from the files."

Bill waited breathlessly.

"Driving to the common danger – fined five pounds, licence endorsed."

Tanner sank back in his chair.

"I see – a real hardened criminal," he growled. "Has he ever sold bananas after eight? You make me sick!"

He turned the detached sheets of the dossier.

"Briggs might tell us something."

Totty sneered.

"Him! All he wants is a joy ride. A taxi ride from Wormwood Scrubbs to Scotland Yard is like a char-à-banc excursion for him."

"We'll see. Bring him up."

Totty reached out for the phone, and had his hand knocked away.

"Go down to Cannon Row and bring him over, you lazy devil," he said. "What were you in civil life?"

"I was a soldier," said Totty with some dignity.

He had not far to go. Briggs was outside in the corridor, handcuffed to a prison officer, and he ushered him in. Mr Briggs looked a little healthier than he had when he was sentenced. He was, however, his melancholy self, full of complaints and ready to profit by any opportunity which presented itself. They unlocked the handcuffs, sat him in a chair, and gave him a cigarette. He complained of feeling faint and asked for brandy.

"They never lose hope, do they?" said Totty admiringly. "That's what I like about 'em!"

"Now then, Briggs!" Tanner was brusque and businesslike. "You were in the village of Marks Thornton on the night of the murder, weren't you?"

"Yes, sir." Briggs' voice was a thin wail. He spoke like a man who was suffering. "That's what I made a statement about. I can't help the police the same as I'd like to help them. I've been put inside by perjury, believe me or believe me not, Mr Tanner. I was as innocent as a babe unborn – "

"I'm sure," interrupted Tanner. "Now tell us, is there anything you want to add to this statement?"

Briggs had his story to tell, and he greatly desired that it should not be a short story, that it should last at least the length of time it takes to smoke three cigarettes. Mr Tanner had other views, and presently he came to the story of what Briggs saw as he sat on the stile near Priory Fields. He had seen the murdered man pass and had heard a scream, and then: "I saw a gentleman coming towards me. He was running and out of breath, and when I said 'Who's there?' he said: 'It's all right; it's Dr Amersham.'"

"You're sure of that?" said Bill quickly, and jotted down a note. "You didn't say that in your statement."

"There's a lot of things I didn't say in my statement," admitted Briggs. "To tell you the truth, Mr Tanner, I thought if I put everything in, you mightn't want to see me."

"Wanted the day out, did you? All right! Well, what happened then?"

Tanner had a long experience of criminals and criminals' stories. He knew instinctively when a man of this kind was telling the truth – and Briggs was telling the truth.

Briggs got up from his chair and walked across to the desk. He had a sense of drama, knew that what he was about to say would provide a sensational climax to the interview. For this he was bringing up all his reserves.

"Mr Tanner," he said slowly, "I've got a wonderful memory for voices. The moment I heard him speak I remembered him."

"You had met him before?" asked Tanner in surprise. "Where?"

"In Poona jail," said Briggs. "We were waiting trial together. He was up on a charge of forging a 'kite.' He was an army officer, and he put his name to some other chap's cheque. Bit of a coincidence, wasn't it? I was up on the same charge meself. But he got off; they squared it to save a scandal."

Tanner looked at him incredulously. Dr Amersham a forger? Either he was mistaking the man for somebody else, or – "Are you inventing all this?"

"No, I'm not inventing it," said Briggs; "it's true. If you like to go to the trouble and expense of sending a cable to India, I can give you the date. The fifteenth of November, 1918."

"But Dr Amersham is a man of education, a gentleman, an Army officer – " began Tanner.

"Of course he was an Army officer," said Briggs scornfully. "But I tell you, he forged the name of a brother officer, a man named Willoughby – that's the name, Willoughby. You see if I'm not right. He was dismissed from the Army, and I don't know what became of him after that. They say he married a Cheche woman down in the Madras Presidency."

"A Cheche woman? That's a Eurasian?"

Briggs nodded.

"There was all sorts of scandal about it, but I don't know the rights of it. All I do know is that he was up on this charge, and he was guilty. Leicester Charles Amersham – and I recognised him at once by his voice."

Leicester Charles Amersham! There was no question now – this was the man.

Here was news indeed. Long after the prisoner had been taken away, protesting against the refusal of Tanner to promise a remission of his sentence, the chief inspector sat, his head on his hands, and for once Totty was not flippant.

"I've got to have another talk with Amersham, and I think it's going to be a pretty serious talk," he said at last. "We've got four lines to him from four different quarters – and I wonder what he's after now."

"I'll tell you what he's after," said Totty. "He's after Lebanon."

Bill Tanner pursed his lips.

"Lebanon? Yes, Amersham may be. I always thought there was something queer about him, but I never dreamed he had that kind of record."

"And why the American footmen?" demanded Totty. "Who ever heard of an American footman? It's not natural. He'd be easy, too,

Viscount Lebanon. He's a mug. It'd be like taking money from a child."

It was at that moment that Ferraby came hurriedly into the room. "Well?"

"Will you see Lord Lebanon?" said the sergeant.

Inspector Tanner's jaw dropped.

"Lebanon? That's odd. Yes, bring him in." And, when Ferraby had gone: "What the devil does he want?"

"You'd better let me wait, Mr Tanner," advised Totty impressively. "I've had a lot of dealings with the aristocracy – I know how to treat 'em."

Bill Tanner just looked at him.

Lebanon came in, gazed curiously around the room, deposited his hat, his gloves and his cane on one of the vacant chairs, and looked from Totty to Tanner, not quite sure –

"You're in charge of this case, aren't you?"

Totty would have admitted this by inference, but his superior made the situation clear.

It was no more easy for Lord Lebanon with Tanner than it might have been with his junior. He was ill at ease, shot back an apprehensive look at the door through which he had passed, and out of which Ferraby, at a nod from the inspector, had taken his departure.

"Yes, I remember you, Mr Tanner, and I seem to remember your boy."

Sergeant Totty grew visibly dignified, and was introduced.

"Totty? An odd name, isn't it?"

"An old Italian family," said Sergeant Totty in his most refined voice, and Bill Tanner silenced him with one steely gleam.

The visitor was still uneasy about the door.

"Do you mind seeing if there's anybody outside listening?"

Bill Tanner chuckled. In all the years of his service, and from the thousands, innocent or guilty, who had given him their confidence in that room, he had never heard such a suggestion.

"Of course there isn't anybody listening," he smiled. "People don't do that sort of thing at Scotland Yard."

He had been startled by the arrival of the visitor, the last person in the world he had imagined would come to Scotland Yard, although he had foreseen this eventuality. Ferraby had duly reported the little talk he had had with the master of Marks Priory, and the inspector had formed a pretty shrewd idea as to the position which this unhappy young man occupied in that establishment. Sooner or later friction must come, and somebody would have a story to tell. Was that somebody Lord Lebanon?

"I don't know very much about Scotland Yard. It's a sort of prison, isn't it?"

Totty smiled indulgently.

"But I had to come. I told Mr Ferraby I might. I made up my mind last night."

A thought struck Tanner.

"Are you used to people listening at your doors, Lord Lebanon, or have you any special reason for expecting that to happen here?"

The young man hesitated. It was an awkward position, and an extremely awkward question.

"Well – yes. It is not an unusual experience, and I think it is possible that it may happen here. By the way, is Mr Ferraby a detective?"

Bill nodded.

"I thought he was a gentleman," said his lordship naïvely, and Mr Totty was preparing to make extravagant claims for the gentility of Scotland Yard, but Tanner's scowl stopped him.

"I'll be perfectly frank with you, Lord Lebanon," he said quietly. "In spite of what you told Ferraby I did not expect to see you here. But now that you are here – if I may be allowed to continue in the same vein of frankness – I hope you will be able to tell me something that will clear up one or two little mysteries which puzzle me. You understand I've no right whatever to ask you questions, but since you have volunteered to call I hope you will help me, because I don't know anybody who is better able to assist me in that very difficult task."

He was determined that the visit should not fritter out into a social call.

"There are quite a number of people at Marks Priory who are under suspicion," he went on. "They include – " He hesitated, not inartistically.

"My mother?" said the young man quietly.

That was a good beginning.

Tanner nodded. "In a sense. I think she must know a great deal more than she has ever told us. But I'm thinking more particularly of another visitor – Dr Amersham."

Lord Lebanon smiled grimly.

"He's a mystery man to me, and I don't wonder at his being even more of a mystery man to you," he said. "So far as my mother is concerned – " He paused, evidently seeking some formula to describe her position. He must have failed, for he went on: "You had better know at any rate as much as I know," he said. "I will tell you from the beginning everything there is to be told about Amersham – at least, every fact that I have concerning him.

"I shall be perfectly frank and tell you that I detest Amersham. It is impossible that I should speak without prejudice because I dislike him so much that I find it difficult even to be fair."

He sat down, seemed at a loss as to how he should begin, and speaking slowly and evidently searching at first for words which would not too deeply compromise the actors in this curious drama, he began.

14

"I suppose I'd better begin with my own school days. I was never very strong, and I only spent two years at Eton, and after that I had a tutor and a private coach. My father, as you probably know, was an invalid, and a – what is the word? – recluse. He spent all his life, except one winter when he went to the south of France, which he hated, at Marks Priory, and I saw very little of him even when I was home on my holidays.

"I may say that between us there were none of the affectionate relationships which exist between father and son. I had a great respect for him and was in considerable awe of him, but that is all.

"Marks Priory has always been to me a terribly dull place, and even when I was a boy I hated coming back there. You see, Mr Tanner, I haven't the same pride of family that my mother has and my father had. To them every stone of the Priory was sacred, and the traditions of the family more important than Holy Writ.

"After I left school I spent most of my time with my tutor in Switzerland, the south of France, Germany, and occasionally at one or two English seaside places like Torquay. My father had been in the Army – in fact, the family have always had a representative in a cavalry regiment – and I managed to get into Sandhurst and pass out, I won't say with distinction, but without being an absolute duffer.

"Up to then I had only seen Amersham half a dozen times. He used to come regularly to the Priory, as my father's medical attendant. I know that he had been in India for some years, but I didn't know then that he had left the Army under peculiar circumstances. And when I say 'peculiar circumstances' I mean, of course, that he left under a cloud – in fact, as the result of a very discreditable act on his part.

"I never liked him. My earliest recollections of him were that he was rather sycophantic to both my mother and myself. Then gradually a change came over him, and he adopted a domineering manner, and began to interfere in all sorts of matters which didn't concern him.

"My regiment left for India very soon after I joined it, and I was very glad to get away. My father was desperately ill, and, as I say, I hardly knew him. I suppose it was very undutiful of me, but I never really worried much about him. When I heard of his death I was naturally sorry for mother's sake, but I can't say that I grieved – I'm being perfectly truthful, and I don't want you to think I am any better than I am.

"I was in India when this happened, having a fairly good time. There was plenty of shooting, and if the society was a little boring it was endurable. The only unpleasant thing that happened to me was that accidentally I shot one of my bearers when I was out shooting – he got in the line of fire when I was shooting a tiger.

"Things might have gone on quite normally, because there was no need for my returning to England; my mother, a very able woman, could deal with my father's estate, and all the documents I had to sign were sent out to me. I might have finished my full term in India, but I got a bad attack of fever which happened just after the shooting I told you about, and I was ill for I don't know how long. It must have been fairly serious, because mother sent Amersham out to bring me back.

"I hadn't been brought into contact with him very long before I realised the kind of man I was up against. There was something odd about Amersham, and what made me suspicious was the furtive way he behaved. He saw nobody, hardly left the bungalow and I was surprised to find that on the voyage out he had grown a beard. There had been some sort of gossip about him, but I hadn't paid much attention to it. I didn't know then – but I knew before I left India – about the Eurasian girl – I'll tell you about that later.

103

"The impression I got was that he was afraid of meeting people he had known before. If he went out of the bungalow it was after dark. He even chose a slow train to Bombay because it left after sunset.

"I came home to England and found a state of affairs that was truly astonishing. Amersham was practically the master of Marks Priory, and these two American footmen were installed. Now, the curious thing is, I had seen these footmen before. They had been in either Amersham's or mother's service before I went to Sandhurst. But they had never seemed so conspicuous or so evident as they were on my return.

"Mother had hardly changed, but I found a new-comer at the Priory – Isla. That is the young lady you have met. She's the daughter of a cousin of mother's – very charming, very quiet and rather clever. She acts as mother's secretary, but she is something more than that. My mother is very fond of her. In fact" – Lord Lebanon hesitated – "I'm going to marry her. I have no particular desire to marry her, or to marry anybody, but that is my mother's idea.

"I found a curious tension in the house. Amersham, as I say, dominated the place; the two footmen seemed quite independent of anybody's authority. They were impertinent, though never to me; they did as they pleased, and they were so incompetent that any boy I picked out of my stables would have known more about their work than they did.

"I began to realise there was something wrong at the Priory, some secret that everybody was hiding, but I never dreamed that my return was embarrassing for them until I discovered that I was never free of their observation."

He laughed softly.

"Apparently my illness and the necessity for bringing me home upset all their plans – what they were I don't know. It seemed to me that they were scared to death that accidentally I would come upon the thing they were trying to hide, and even my mother shared their anxiety. It was puzzling, and, I confess, a little frightening but I got used to it after a while.

"The first shock I had was when I discharged Gilder for his incompetence, and discovered at the end of the week that he was still at Marks Priory. I was furious about it, called my mother and insisted that the man should go."

He laughed softly.

"I might as well have insisted that Marks Priory should be razed to the ground! After two attempts of this kind I accepted the position. They were my servants, I paid them, but I had no command over them.

"Really they were not very difficult to cope with, and in many ways they are quite nice fellows and sometimes rather amusing. Amersham is a different proposition. Here is a man who does not disguise the fact that he is boss of my house. He has plenty of money, a car, racehorses – but you probably know this. Now, if Gilder and Brooks, the footmen, are not polite to anybody else, they are very respectful to him. He treats them as equals, and although I know my mother hates that sort of thing, she does not complain, and has never interfered.

"You have only got to realise that my mother is what I would describe as an aristocrat of the old school, who regards servants as inhuman, to understand just what that tolerance means to my mother.

"The man Amersham hated worst of all was Studd, my groom, the poor fellow who was killed. They hardly ever met without snapping at one another, and I think he would have had Studd sacked but for his death. I don't know what he had against him – whether Studd knew something – but whatever it was, was sufficient to make Dr Amersham his enemy. Studd, by the way, was an old soldier, and had been in India.

"As I say, almost the first news my mother gave me on my return was that she wanted me to marry Isla. I've got to marry somebody, I suppose, and it really doesn't matter whom, but one would at least like to make one's own choice! As you know, she is a very charming lady, and was quite a normal individual – until the death of Studd."

Inspector Tanner sat upright in his chair.

"Until the death of Studd?" he repeated slowly. "Then what happened?"

"She changed. From that day on she became – frightened! 'Terrified' would be a better word. She jumps if you speak to her unexpectedly, and all the time she gives you the feeling that she is expecting something ugly to appear. And she walks in her sleep!

"I've heard of people walking in their sleep, but I never saw one till I saw Isla. I was sitting in the hall, taking a whisky and soda before going to bed, and I heard somebody coming down the stairs. She was in her nightdress, and wore nothing else, and I wondered what on earth was the matter, and spoke to her. It gave me the creeps – I don't know whether you have ever seen anybody walking in their sleep – it's weird! As I say, I spoke to her. She made no reply, but came into the hall, searched round as though she were looking for something, and then just as slowly went up the stairs. I got close to her and saw her face. Her eyes were wide open, and she was talking in a low tone to herself. What she said heaven knows. I couldn't distinguish a word.

"That has happened twice to my knowledge. I knew it was dangerous to wake her, and on the first occasion went and found my mother. The second time mother saw her herself and took her back to her room. Mother was awfully upset about it in her way – which is not particularly demonstrative. Honestly, I don't remember my mother ever kissing me in my life!

"Naturally, this sleep-walking hasn't made the prospect of marriage any brighter. One doesn't want to have to search the house in the middle of the night for one's wife."

"Walks in her sleep, eh?" said Tanner thoughtfully. "Does Amersham know?"

Lord Lebanon nodded.

"Of course he knows," he said bitterly. "There's nothing that happens in the house that he doesn't know. He had a draught made up for her, but I don't know whether she took it."

"She's frightened, you say? Of what?"

"Of everything! If a bit of panelling cracks she jumps out of her seat. She will not go out at night; she locks her room – she's about the only person in the house who does. In fact – she's frightened."

Bill thought for a time. Here was an aspect of the case which made it just a little more complicated.

"You were talking about a Eurasian girl in connection with Dr Amersham earlier on in your narrative. What happened in connection with her?"

Lord Lebanon nodded.

"She was a very beautiful girl. I think you ought to know about this. It happened after he came out to bring me home. The girl was found in his bungalow – strangled!"

Tanner sprang to his feet.

"What!" he said incredulously.

He could only stare at the visitor. If this were true then the mystery of Marks Priory was a mystery no longer.

"Are you sure?"

Lebanon nodded. There was a smile of triumph on his face. Apparently he was young enough to get a kick out of making a sensation.

"It's a fact. A really lovely girl – not of the best class, although her people had plenty of money. She was found strangled on the stoep of the bungalow where he was living alone. There was a terrible fuss about it, but they couldn't bring it home to him, though there were signs of struggle in his room. The newspapers said it must have been a native who had a grudge against the girl, but a piece of red cloth was found round her neck exactly the same as was found round Studd's."

"I didn't know of this," said Tanner, after he had recovered from his amazement. "Does your mother know?"

Lord Lebanon hesitated.

"I'm not sure. It is so difficult to find out what she knows. I hope she doesn't. Now, Mr Tanner, I want you to advise me. What am I to do? I suppose you'll tell me that it's quite easy for me to forbid Amersham the house, and legally I suppose that's right. But my mother is a person, too, and it's almost impossible that my instructions would be carried out. Will you come down to Marks Priory as my guest for a weekend?"

Tanner smiled.

"What would her ladyship say to that?" he asked, and the young man's face fell.

"I don't quite know," he admitted with a grimace. "No, that might be very awkward."

"May I suggest," said Bill, "that you yourself take a holiday? There is nothing to prevent your going abroad for a few years."

Lord Lebanon smiled again.

"That seems an obvious solution, doesn't it? But when you say that there is nothing to prevent me you are overlooking such important facts as my mother, for example, and Amersham. Not that Amersham's opinion would matter twopence, but I couldn't go against my mother's wishes. I have already suggested that I should go to America and buy a ranch, and see the second heir to my property."

He chuckled at this.

"Who is the heir?"

"Oddly enough, he's a person who lives in America, and is, I believe, a waiter or something. No, no, I was joking. There is no likelihood of my meeting him – the first heir, or heiress, by the way, is Isla! I didn't know this until the other day, when my mother told me.

"Yes, I did think it would be a grand idea if I went to Canada and forgot there was such a place as Marks Priory, and I've told mother so a dozen times. She says my place is here, and squashed the scheme before it was properly formed."

He got up from his chair and came over to the table. He was not smiling now; rather was there an expression in his face that moved Tanner to pity.

"Mr Tanner, I am a weakling. There must be hundreds of thousands of us in the world – I should say the majority of us. All the strong, silent men of the world seem to be in Scotland Yard!"

He raised a smile at this, but went on more seriously.

"I cannot oppose my will to my mother's. I am entirely and completely in her hands, and to be absolutely honest, I haven't the energy to make a fight."

He spun round suddenly.

"There's somebody at that door," he said in a low voice.

"My dear Lord Lebanon," began Bill, amused, "I assure you – "

"Do you mind looking?"

"Open the door, Totty."

Totty opened the door and nearly jumped. A man was standing outside, his head bent in a listening attitude. It was Gilder, the footman.

"Excuse me, gentlemen!" He walked carelessly into the room. "His lordship went away without his cigarette case, so I brought it up to him."

"Why were you listening at that door?" demanded Bill sternly.

"Say! I wasn't listening. I didn't know exactly which room you were in, Mr Tanner, and I had to be sure if I could recognise his lordship's voice before I knocked."

"Who told you to come up?"

"The policeman on the door, I guess," said Gilder, who was in no measure embarrassed.

He took a cigarette case from his pocket, and handed it to his lordship. Then with a friendly wave of his hand he went out of the room. Bill watched him half through the door, and made a signal to Totty.

"Follow him and see where he goes."

He was amazed at the man's daring. How long had he been behind the door, and what had he heard? The audacity of this act of espionage within the sacred walls of Scotland Yard took his breath away.

"I wasn't so foolish after all," nodded Lebanon. "I thought I'd got away from Marks Priory this morning without anybody knowing, but Gilder is a difficult man to slip."

"How long has this spying been going on?"

"Ever since I came back from India. Possibly before I went away, but I didn't notice it. But that is the sort of thing I've had to contend against since I have been back."

"Does your mother know?"

His lordship shrugged.

"It is very unlikely that she doesn't," he said. "Certainly Amersham knows."

"Where is Amersham now?"

"He was at Marks Priory last night, but he came back to town. Mother mentioned the fact at breakfast, otherwise I should not have known that he was there at all."

Bill went back to his desk, took out a sheet of paper and scribbled a note.

"Can you give me the date of the girl's death?"

"Come down to Marks Priory; I've all the facts there, and you can see my diary."

Lord Lebanon took up his hat and stick.

"You can tell Amersham that I told you, but I'd rather you didn't, because it is bound to make for unpleasantness at home. Come down for a weekend, and I'll tell you something that's even more interesting. Do you know Peterfield? It's a little village in Berkshire."

Tanner looked at him sharply. That certainly was a question which he did not expect.

So Lord Lebanon was not quite such a fool, and he knew his mother's secret too. And probably knew what was still a mystery to Tanner — all that lay behind the Peterfield adventure.

He walked down to the entrance of Scotland Yard with his visitor, and on the way back Totty overtook him.

"I left him on the other side of the Embankment," he said. "I suppose we couldn't pinch him for loitering?"

"You mean Gilder? No, hardly. Anyway, he can do very little harm, unless… I wonder if he heard?"

"About the woman?" asked Totty. "The Eurasian girl? That's a bit damning, isn't it, Tanner? I should think we've got enough evidence to pinch Amersham."

"When you have learned your business as a detective officer, which will be somewhere around 1976," said Tanner offensively, "you will discover – and probably be amazed by the discovery – that there is always sufficient evidence to pinch people, but generally not quite sufficient evidence to convict them."

As he came back he saw a crowd of men lining the corridor and groaned. He loathed lectures, and was less inclined at the moment to discuss the elementary facts of the Marks Priory case than ever he had been in his life. For they were no longer elementary. They were facts for a class in advanced criminology.

He wanted to get away to see Amersham and ask him a few vital questions.

"After the class is dismissed," he said, "go along to Dr Amersham's flat and tell him I wish to see him at Scotland Yard. You can tell him he need not come unless he wishes, but that it may simplify matters if he saw me here. Give him the usual warning – he has probably got somebody pretty high up who will make a fuss if we neglect the rules."

"And if he won't come, bring him?" suggested Totty hopefully.

Tanner shook his head.

"No, we haven't got to that stage yet, though I don't think we're far off."

The class came in, filed into their seats, and Totty called the roll and delivered the preliminary routine lecture, whilst Mr Tanner drew a few lines that represented the rough ground plan of Marks Priory.

His lecture was halting; his mind wandered; he was too near the subject to deliver a first-class narrative. But he could speak very plainly between those four walls, and the lecture developed into a very frank examination of the character of Dr Amersham.

This had not been his original intention, he realised, as the lecture progressed. But the events of the morning had supplied red arrow marks which, with singular unanimity, pointed to Dr Amersham as the guilty man.

"I don't mind telling you that he is under suspicion, and for the following reasons."

A messenger came in with a telegram and Totty took it and opened it.

"There are certain facts which have come to my knowledge this morning," said Tanner, "and which I cannot at the moment discuss. Amersham has undoubtedly a very bad record, and when you come to examine the Studd murder you have to realise, not only that he was in Marks Thornton, but that he was actually in the field and was seen a few minutes after the murder was committed. Everything points to him – "

"Mr Tanner!"

It was Totty's agitated voice.

"Where is the west wing?"

Tanner marked the drawing with his chalk. Totty read out an extract from the telegram.

Bushes fifty yards south of the west wing.

Again Tanner indicated the point.

"Why do you ask?"

Totty did not reply. To his chief's amazement he walked to the blackboard, took the chalk from his hand, and made a big cross.

For a moment Tanner thought he was indulging in an ill-timed joke.

"What is that?" he asked sternly.

Totty's voice was agitated.

"That is where the body of Dr Amersham was found half an hour ago!" he said.

Bill Tanner could only look at him. He took the telegram from the sergeant's hand and read:

Very urgent, very urgent. Body of Dr Amersham found in Priory Field at 11.7 a.m. behind bushes fifty yards south of west wing Marks Priory. Deceased has been strangled but no cloth or rope found. Come immediately. Chief Constable.

15

A gardener, who had been to the village, was walking across Priory Fields to the greenhouses when he had seen something under the shadow of a rhododendron bush. He thought it was some old clothes that had been thrown there, and went closer to investigate, and then he saw...

Here was all that remained of Amersham, his stiff hands clawing upwards at his invisible enemy. Something had been knotted round his neck; the mark of the cloth was there plainly to be seen, but the murderer had waited long enough to remove this evidence.

A doctor had come from the village. Amersham had been dead for hours, he said. He was not prepared to give the exact time.

Lady Lebanon was in her room when they brought the news to her, and she was surprisingly calm.

"Notify the police," she said. "You had better send a telegram to the man at Scotland Yard. What is his name? Yes, Tanner."

The phone message to the county police headquarters had, however, been transmitted to Scotland Yard, and Inspector Tanner did not receive Lady Lebanon's wire till later in the day.

Everything which could be done at the moment was done. The body had not been removed when the squad car came hurtling through the village and up the drive, and stopped to discharge Tanner and his four assistants. The police surgeon and the local doctor were on the spot, and Bill made a brief examination of the dead man's pockets. There was nothing here which at first glance afforded any clue. In one pocket he found three notes of a hundred pounds, in another a passport.

Photographs had been taken before he arrived, and he ordered the body to be removed after he had made a careful search of the ground, without, however, finding any trace of a struggle. But the gravel drive offered information. There were marks of a car wheel which had run off the drive on to the grass verge, had come back to the drive and gone on to the grass for some distance on the opposite side, and had finally come back to the gravel and gone straight-forwardly towards Marks Thornton.

Those wheel marks were very informative, and he read them almost at first glance and, as it proved, without error. Fifty yards from the place where the car had left the drive for the second time, Totty found an accumulation of oil on the ground and the burnt stalks of two matches. One had been lit and had gone out almost immediately; the other had burnt half its length.

With the assistance of Ferraby he went over the grass very carefully. Presently they found a cigarette, sodden with the dew. It had not been lit, and was bent and broken in the middle. They widened the circle, but found nothing new, and Totty carried the cigarette to Tanner. Bill read the words printed on the paper.

"A Chesterford," he said. "A purely American cigarette, though I believe people do smoke them in this country. Keep that, and the matches. Now come up the drive, and see if we can find any foot-prints coming from the grass on to the gravel. If we find them at all they'll be just above the place where the car left the road."

The gravel drive was damp; there had been an hour of rain on the previous night, and though nothing had fallen subsequently the night air had been damp and the roads had not dried. The marks of the wheels were clearly readable.

"Where is the car, sir?" asked Ferraby.

"The Chief Constable says it was picked up in a lane about two miles away. They're bringing it up from the village."

He looked round.

"In fact, there it is. Tell him to stop where he is, Totty. I don't want these tracks to be confused. And have a look at the road and see how far it corresponds with the marks on the drive."

Totty came back, and was able to identify the wheel marks.

"It's the same machine," he said.

"Did you find any footprints in the car itself?"

They had discovered one rather deep indentation, but absolutely valueless as a clue.

"I think I can tell you how the murder was committed," said Tanner. "Somebody jumped on the back of the car here. The car is now closed, but my theory is that at the time the murder was committed it was open. It is so untidily closed that you will notice that all the loose ends of straps are hanging and inside," he pointed, "the metal clips in the roof have not met." He pointed again. "It was at this point that the cloth went round the doctor's neck. This is where he left the drive, and from here on the car makes a pretty erratic course until it stopped on the grass where you found the oil. It must have been there an hour before somebody came and drove it away. That somebody lit a cigarette before he got in. He opened a new packet of Chesterfords – Ferraby has just found a bit of the carton that was torn off – and in pulling out the first cigarette he broke it and threw it away. The second cigarette he lit, after two attempts. He then drove the car back to the place where it was found. The Chief Constable said a policeman saw the machine pass at half-past two, but the hood was up, and he did not see the driver. That pretty well establishes the time. Amersham left Marks Priory soon after eleven. He was killed within two minutes of leaving, and dragged over to where he was found. The murderer then at his leisure came back and disposed of the car. He may have gone to the house – he probably did, but he would hardly hang around for two or three hours for no reason whatever. The man at the lodge remembers hearing a car go out, but isn't sure of the time."

He rubbed his chin furiously.

"Now the question is, why on earth did the murderer leave Amersham's body in Priory Fields when he could have taken it in the car and disposed of it, or at any rate removed him from the scene of the murder – that is a puzzling element."

Later he made a closer inspection of the car, the cover of which had been lowered on his instructions. The clock on the dashboard had been smashed. There were mud and scratches on the windscreen.

"Amersham did that," said Tanner. "When the thing went round his neck he threw up his foot to get a purchase, and in so doing broke the clock. Those are his footmarks you see on the screen."

He examined the carpet and the running-board. On the latter he found a deep, right-angled scratch as though something heavy had been dragged across the rubber.

"That is where he was pulled out of the car and dragged across the grass – there's a distinct track from the place where Totty found the oil to the bushes where the body was found. I'll see all the servants, and, of course, I shall want to see Lady Lebanon and the two footmen. Is Lord Lebanon back?"

"He arrived about a quarter of an hour before we did," said Ferraby. "Isn't that he?"

"Talk to him, Ferraby. I don't want to discuss theories at the moment, and I'm not in the mood to answer questions."

He strode up the drive and into the hall. Lady Lebanon was in her room, the butler said. There was somebody else waiting to see him, very eager and full of information. Miss Jackson was in her most communicative mood, and what she said was so completely interesting that Tanner took her into the grounds, and for half an hour was questioning her and checking her statements.

"Have you seen her ladyship this morning?"

"No, sir," said the maid. "I went to her room, but she wouldn't let me in – told me to get out of the house as quick as I could. In fact, she ordered a fly up from the village to take me."

"When was this?"

"At nine o'clock this morning. She gave me a month's wages, but she was so anxious to get rid of me that I thought I'd stay."

She smiled triumphantly.

"I know when people want me out of the way."

"This was before the body was discovered?"

"Yes, sir. She is so careful with the wages, I thought, 'Well, this is very funny, taking all this trouble to get me off by the ten o'clock train. I wonder what's up?' So I missed the train," she said.

"Have you looked into her room at all?"

"No, but I do know this – she hasn't been to bed all night. Her evening shoes are all wet. I found them in her dressing-room, and there was mud on her evening gown. Mr Kelver took her some coffee, and said the bed hadn't been slept in – you ask him, sir."

"I have no doubt I shall ask him," said Tanner grimly. "Had you heard of this murder before the body was found?"

She had not.

He went back to Totty.

"Walk down to the bushes where the body is, and see if you can find any marks of a woman's high heels. Have a good look round where the car was standing, and make another examination of the drive lower down – say at a point exactly opposite where the car was left. I particularly want evidence of a woman having been near the place either where the car was or in the vicinity of the spot where the body was found."

He went back to interview Kelver, who was waiting for him in the great hall. The place was familiar to him, but he needed reminding. Kelver volunteered all the necessary information. He had the manner and language of a guide, and even the event of the morning had not disintegrated the solid dough of his pomposity.

Yet he was perturbed, had taken a decision himself, and was waiting for a favourable opportunity to communicate his plans to his employer.

"This is the lounge, sir. It was originally the entrance hall, or, as they called it, the Prior's Hall. Some years ago the late Lord Lebanon had it converted into its present appearance at the cost of some thousands of pounds."

The room was a little cheerless by the light of morning. Lady Lebanon's neat desk he knew. The two footmen were waiting expectantly, standing with their backs to the small anthracite stove in a corner of the room, and were prepared for him. He was conscious that they were watching his every movement, and did not doubt that their stories were already cast-iron and unbendable. He called the taller to him.

"You're Gilder?"

"Yes, sir." Mr Gilder was very suave, entirely self-possessed. "I have had the pleasure of seeing you before this morning – in fact, I only arrived just a little ahead of you."

Tanner ignored an alibi which was by no means waterproof.

"How long have you been here?"

"Eight years."

Tanner nodded.

"You were here in the days of the late Lord Lebanon?"

"Yes, sir."

He was smiling as he talked. One might have imagined that he was participating in a very amusing ending to this little talk.

"A footman?" said Tanner.

"Yes, sir," said Gilder.

"Scotland Yard has been making rather a quick investigation about you Mr Gilder. I've just had the result of it. You have an account at the London and Provincial Bank, haven't you?"

Gilder's smile broadened.

"That's very clever of you to find out. My opinion of Scotland Yard has gone up. Yes, I have."

"Very unusual, isn't it, for a footman to have an account at a London bank?"

Gilder's face puckered.

"Some of us are thrifty."

"A pretty substantial balance, I hope?"

"Three or four thousand pounds," said the other coolly. "I've speculated rather wisely."

Tanner had expected at least a little confusion at the revelation of his discovery, but the man was imperturbable, perfectly calm. A dangerous man, this. He did not underrate him. It occurred to him that one who had at some time or other survived the stringentness of an American third degree examination could hardly be expected to sag beneath the milder methods of Scotland Yard.

He called the second man to him, and the big American loafed up, his hands in his pockets.

"You're an American citizen, too?"

"Yeah," drawled the other, "but I haven't got a banking account. Some of us American citizens have lost a whole lot of money lately."

"Have you been here long?"

"Six years."

"As a footman?"

Brooks nodded.

"Why is a man like you in service?"

"Well, I guess I am naturally servile."

Was he laughing? He was certainly as unperturbed as his companion. A tough-looking man; there was the scar of an old wound on his face. Tanner remarked on it.

"Oh, that was done some years ago. I got it in a rough house," he said. "A feller landed me with an ash can!"

"You were a footman then, I presume?" asked Bill sarcastically.

"I guess I was."

The detective turned to Gilder.

"Do you know this house very well? Lady Lebanon sent a message to say I might see over it. Perhaps you could show me round?"

"Sure!" said Gilder.

Tanner dismissed them, and turned to the waiting and interested butler.

"What do they do?"

"They wait on her ladyship, his lordship and Miss Crane," said Kelver.

"Where is she?" asked Tanner quickly.

"She's on the lawn, sir. The poor young lady is rather upset, which is natural. It is, I might say, a climax to a very unhappy period for her."

Tanner did not ask him to elucidate his cryptic reference, and Mr Kelver seemed a little disappointed.

Ferraby came in at that moment, and Tanner drew him aside.

119

"Go and find this girl Crane; have a talk with her and see what you can discover. She probably knows more than she'll be prepared to tell you at first, but you've got to work at her and get facts."

When he had gone: "You heard nothing last night?"

Kelver shook his head.

"No scream or shout or anything?"

"No, sir."

Tanner was not quite convinced.

"You remember the night the chauffeur Studd was killed? You heard nothing then?"

"No, sir. If you remember, I told you when you were here at the time."

Bill nodded. He remembered asking the question.

"Were there any visitors here last night, in this room – none of the servants, for example, told you about somebody calling late?"

"No, sir. Pardon me, sir, I thought I saw you speaking to her ladyship's maid, Delia Jackson." He looked round and lowered his voice. "She was discharged this morning. Possibly she might tell you – she has access to this part of the house – and a discharged servant, though naturally spiteful and not always accurate, may furnish you with information."

"Thank you, I've seen her."

Kelver, standing at the foot of the stairs, glanced up and saw somebody who was invisible to Tanner.

"Her ladyship, sir."

Lady Lebanon came down, very calm, normally self-possessed. The dark shadows under her eyes supported Jackson's story. But if she had not slept her voice was without a tremor, and from that one might have imagined nothing unusual had happened to disturb its harmony or quiet.

"Have you all you require, Mr Tanner? Kelver, you will arrange for Mr Tanner to see the servants, and give him whatever assistance you can. Will you finish your inquiries today?"

She asked this almost carelessly as she went to her desk and sorted the letters that had been placed upon the pad.

"I don't think so," said Tanner.

He was watching her closely. Here was a new type, a kind he had never met before, not to be stumped by threats nor cajoled by promises. If he could make her speak it would be the crowning achievement of his career.

"I've ordered you rooms at the 'White Hart,'" she said. "It is a comfortable inn, though I understand from the village policeman that one of your men had a very unhappy time there."

He nodded.

"You told me I might look over the house."

"Certainly. Brooks will show you round."

She stood meditatively by the desk, her white fingers outspread upon the blotting-pad.

"The man seems to have been killed in the park," she said and Tanner almost gasped.

"The man?" he repeated.

She moved her head impatiently. "Dr Amersham."

Here was a new type indeed, not to be dealt with by ordinary methods. To her Amersham and all he stood for was just "the man." He had been killed in the park – an item of news, more or less interesting to the general public, but of no especial importance to her.

"Yes, he was killed in the park," said Tanner when he had recovered his breath. "This house stands in the park. It is quite possible somebody in this house may have heard sounds, if there was anything to hear."

She nodded slowly.

"That would be very interesting to find out," she said.

She pressed a bell on the table, and almost immediately Brooks came in.

"Show Mr Tanner round the house," she said.

16

There was somebody waiting to see her, and no better indication of her character could be afforded than that within a minute of Tanner's leaving to make his inspection she should be admonishing a nervous little decorator for certain mistakes he had made in his drawings. Mr Rawbane, architect and authority on heraldry, stood nervously by her desk.

"I thought perhaps you'd rather the matter stood over for a day or two," he said. "It was a great shock to me – this dreadful affair."

She looked at him coldly.

"Mr Rawbane, there are dreadful affairs happening somewhere every day, but we have to live our lives and attend to our business."

She pushed a drawing towards him. He hardly saw it. There were three water budgets on a field azure and a stag at gaze, which formed no part of the Lebanon quarterings. He squirmed and agreed, was anxious either to talk about the tragedy of the morning or to be gone. At last she closed the portfolio and handed it to him, and he, who had already forgotten the instructions she gave, returned eagerly to the matter which was uppermost in his mind. She stopped him.

"I am not asking you to discuss Dr Amersham," she said. "It is very sad, and we're all dreadfully sorry. His death is quite unimportant to the world – will you remember that, Mr Rawbane? But these arms stand for eternity."

Kelver showed him out, and hurried back in time to catch her before she went up to her room.

"When are these detectives going?" she asked, one foot on the stairs.

"They gave me the impression they wouldn't be leaving for some considerable time, my lady," said Kelver, and then, as she made a move: "If your ladyship will pardon me, I did wish to speak to you on a rather unpleasant matter – unpleasant for me, that is to say," he added quickly. "Tomorrow is the end of the month, and I would like your ladyship, with all due respect, to accept my notice from that day."

Her eyebrows went up. From the concern she showed it might have been imagined that this was the day's chiefest tragedy. For she knew what was coming, had been expecting – and dreading – the news he was to give her.

"Your ladyship is aware," he went on nervously, "of the very distressing happenings – sensational, if I may call them so – that have brought us a great deal of undesirable publicity."

Mr Kelver in such moments as these was pompous to an unbelievable degree. Yet, curiously enough, she could take a reasonable view of his agitation. It was as one aristocrat speaking with another.

"But it is hardly an affair of yours, Kelver," she said gently.

"Pardon me, my lady." Mr Kelver was nearly firm. "I realise that it does react very disagreeably to your ladyship and to his lordship; but it also has a detrimental effect upon myself. In all the years of my service I have never had my name associated with matters which were – your ladyship will pardon me if I describe them as being of vulgar public interest."

The logic was irresistible. They were meeting on common ground – the aristocrat of the servants' hall and the aristocrat of Marks Priory. She could see his point of view, but felt called upon to contest his argument.

"How are you affected?"

Kelver spread out his white hands.

"Ladies and gentlemen, my lady, shrink from contact with matters which have been the subject of public discussion, and they look askance at an upper servant who has figured even indirectly in" – he found it difficult to say – "a police case – two murder cases, my lady.

123

I have to be worthy of my past. Your ladyship will remember that I had the honour for many years to be the butler of His Serene Highness the Duke of Meklstein und Zwieburg, and that I was for many years with His Grace the Duke of Colbrooke."

There was nothing more to be said.

She could perfectly well understand his point of view, and was genuinely grieved. If it was in her to be apologetic for all that had happened at Marks Priory, she would have apologised.

"Very well, Kelver. I'm sorry. You will be rather difficult to replace."

He inclined his head slightly. He had no doubt as to that, but was grateful to have a public acknowledgment of his indispensability.

"Where is his lordship?" she asked.

"He is in his room, my lady. He has just come in from the park."

"Tell him I want to see him."

Willie Lebanon came sheepishly, a little fearfully. He had screwed up his courage before, and found it grow loose under the steady disapproval of her dark eyes. But he swaggered into her presence with an air of assurance which he could not feel.

"I say, isn't it a terrible thing – " he began.

"Where did you go this morning, Willie, when you left the Priory in your car?"

He licked his lips.

"I went up to town, mother."

"Where did you go?" she repeated.

He tried to smile it off, but the smile died.

"I went to Scotland Yard," he said doggedly.

"Why did you go to Scotland Yard?"

He avoided her gaze, and when he spoke he was a little disjointed of speech.

"There are things happening in this house that I don't understand, and I got scared, and – well, I damned well wanted to go, and I went!"

"Willie!"

He wilted. "I'm sorry, mother, but really you treat me as if I were a baby."

"You went to Scotland Yard! That was very tiresome of you. If there is anything the police should know, you may be sure they will know it without your help. It was very ill-bred of you, and you have hurt me very much. Did you tell them anything about Amersham?"

That was the real question she was asking. She knew that he had been to Scotland Yard – Gilder had told her. He could not tell her what this embarrassing son of hers had revealed to the detectives.

"No," he said sulkily; "only that he was a queer bird and I didn't understand him, and I told them there were a lot of things that I didn't understand in this house. I don't understand these damned servants; I don't understand Gilder."

He flung himself down on the settee petulantly.

"I wish to God I'd never come back from India."

She rose from her chair and came towards him, standing over him, a rather terrifying figure.

"You will not go to London again unless you ask me, and you're not to speak to the police about anything that happens in this house. You understand?"

"Yes, mother," he growled.

"I'd like you to conduct yourself with a little more dignity," she went on. "There is no necessity for a Lebanon to make friends with policemen and people of that sort."

"I don't know," he said sullenly. "They're as good as I am. All this family nonsense… You know that fellow Gilder came up to Scotland Yard after me, and followed me back to the Priory? He was in a car, too."

"He did it on my instructions," she said. "Is that sufficient?"

He laughed helplessly.

"Yes, mother."

Then, as he rose:

"Don't go; I've some cheques for you to sign."

She took a flat book from a drawer and opened it. He came reluctantly to the desk, took up a pen and dipped it in the ink. They were blank cheques, as usual.

"Isn't it rather stupid? You never give me a cheque to sign with any figures filled in. I do feel I ought to know something about – "

"Sign four," she said calmly. "That will be sufficient. And please be careful not to blot them."

If he had followed his own inclination he would have taken the ink-well and emptied it on the book, or he would have sent the cheque-book flying out of the nearest window; but under that steady stare of hers he could do nothing but sign, grumbling the while.

It didn't matter very much, he comforted himself. He was a rich man, and she was the most careful of managers. He was anxious to get out of doors, to join Tanner and that odd little detective and Ferraby, and when she released him he almost ran from her presence.

She was half-way up the stairs when she remembered something with a shock and gasped. How careless of her! How criminally negligent! She came quickly down the stairs, glanced left and right, went straight to the drawer of her desk, unlocked it with trembling hands, and took out a small red bundle. Her hand was shaking as she opened the top of the anthracite stove and dropped the deadly clue on to the coal, pressing it down with a short steel poker. She saw the little metal tag in the corner, and shivered. To have left that in the drawer, where a prying police officer could find it! It was madness. When she sat down on the chair at the desk she was shaking from head to foot.

She crossed again to the stove, wondered which was the damper, and pulled a rod at random before she resumed her place at the desk. She was waiting for the inevitable questions, and had framed in advance answers most satisfactory to herself and least informative to the police.

It was no new experience to Lady Lebanon. All her life she had been pretending and interpreting and striving to hide one secret after another. But now she felt she was facing the supreme test, and that on its outcome depended life itself.

126

17

Sergeant Totty was amusing, was lazy, was difficult, was many things that a sergeant of detectives should not be, but he was an excellent bloodhound. He found the first impression of a high heel on the very edge of the drive; the second within a few feet of the car.

He found something else: a tiny silver-topped bottle, half filled with a powerful aromatic fluid. This was an accidental discovery and was at a point nearly fifty yards south of the place where the car had stood. Near the bushes where Amersham was found he could see nothing, neither shoe-marks nor any other indication. But on a bare patch, where the grass grew sparsely and it was a little muddy, he found not only the marks of a heel, but of a pointed foot, sole as well.

He was in the midst of his investigations and glanced round to find he was being watched by an interested American footman.

"Looking for clues, Mr Totty? I guess that's the mark of her ladyship's shoe. She was around here this morning."

"She didn't leave her room this morning, my boy," said Totty.

"Is that so? Well, I wasn't here myself and I'm only depending on what these servants tell me. They saw her leave her room, and Brooks saw her leave her room, and I dare say other people did."

"Why here?" asked Totty, and then he was suddenly inspired. He made an elaborate search of his pockets. "Have you got a cigarette?"

Gilder felt in the inside of his jacket, produced a silver case, opened and offered it.

"They're Chesterfords," he said calmly. "The same as you picked up this morning. As a matter of fact, I smoked one just before you cops arrived – I was rattled."

"How do you know I picked it up?"

"You didn't pick it up. Mr Ferraby found it." Gilder smiled broadly. "I'd be a good detective, Mr Totty. I not only find clues but I can make 'em!"

Totty thought it beneath his dignity to reply. He continued his search, moving down across the broad meadow to a belt of trees that ran parallel with the road. Presently he got to a point where he had a clear view of the gamekeeper's cottage. He was turning back when he saw a small camp stool under a tree. The thin grass about it was littered with the ash of pipe tobacco, and on one side of the stool he saw lying on the grass a half-smoked pipe. He saw, too, a tiny knot of unsmoked mixture and at least a dozen burnt matches. Somebody had sat here, watching. There was the mark of nailed boots.

Then he made another discovery. The grass that ran behind the trees was long, and in this he found a double-barrelled gun. It could not have been there more than twenty-four hours, for there was no rust on it. Both barrels were loaded he found when he broke it. Slipping the cartridges into his pocket, and after another search, he came slowly back to where he had left Gilder. The footman was not in sight, but walked out of the main entrance to greet him.

"Hullo, sergeant!" he began, and then his eyes fell upon the gun, and the whole expression of his face changed. "Where did you get that?" he asked.

"If there's any questioning to be done, I'll do it," said Totty curtly.

He inspected the barrels more carefully; the gun had not been fired; there was no fouling nor was there any scent of smoke.

"Do you know this?" he asked.

"It looks like one of the gamekeeper's."

"You don't know this, I suppose?"

Totty took the pipe from his pocket.

"No, sir, I don't remember it," said Gilder stolidly. "I don't smoke pipes myself. Maybe, if you analyse the ashes you'll find another clue, Mr Totty. I seem to remember reading in a book – "

"Where is Mr Tanner?" asked the sergeant sharply.

Tanner was upstairs. He was still making his search, and it had not been unprofitable. He had passed from room to room under the guidance of Brooks. Lord Lebanon's apartment was small, more modernly furnished than any other. The biggest room was that occupied by Isla Crane, a gloomy panelled apartment with raftered roof. It must have remained unchanged for two hundred years. There was little furniture: a big four-poster bed, a dressing-table, a settee and a few chairs emphasised its bareness.

"It's the old lord's room," explained Brooks. "That's what it's called, mister. Full of ghosts. It's the one room in the house that gives me the creeps."

Tanner passed slowly along the wall, tapping panel by panel, and Brooks watched him curiously.

"There are plenty of secret panels in this house, but none of them practicable, I guess."

"You've been on the stage, haven't you?" asked Tanner.

"Yeah, two years on the road. How did you guess that? Oh, 'practicable.' You can't forget those words. Once a pro, always a pro, eh?"

If there were secret panels here Tanner could not discover them. There were many that sounded hollow.

"Which is Lady Lebanon's room?"

"I'll show you."

Brooks waited till he was out and locked the door. Her ladyship's apartment was on the other side of the passage, more cheerful than the old lord's room. There was a desk here, and two or three Persian rugs, and the bed and the fittings were modern.

Tanner made a very careful general survey before he proceeded to a closer inspection. He saw a loose red cover on the desk. He picked it up; it was an ABC time-table.

"Does Lady Lebanon travel a great deal?" he asked.

"Why, no, but she asked Gilder to go up to town and I guess she was looking up a train."

"Gilder went by car and returned by car," said Tanner. "Think up another explanation."

There were a few papers in the waste basket. He scooped them up and put them on the table, looking at them one by one. There was nothing at all of interest until he came to a half-sheet of note-paper on which a few figures were scribbled in a column:

'630, 83, 10, 105.'

They had been scrawled in blue pencil, and a blue pencil was on the desk. At first they puzzled him, and then he realised that they had some connection with the ABC and that they referred to trains which left at 6.30, 8.3, 10 and 10.5. He puzzled over this. Why four trains? And to what destination did trains leave at 10 and arrive five minutes later? The solution came to him instinctively. There were two trains jotted down here, one that started at 6.30 and arrived at 8.3, and one that started at 10 and arrived five minutes later, and that was hardly possible. He put the piece of paper in his pocket. There might be a perfectly simple explanation for the note, but it was his experience that those matters which were susceptible to a simple explanation were difficult to explain when the screw was applied.

10–10.5. Of course, a Continental trip. There was a boat train that left at 10 in the morning. Where would it arrive at 10.5? Aix-la-Chapelle? Somewhere between Paris and Dijon? Some place short of Chambéry? He could not fit in the times.

"Here is a room that perhaps you ought to see, captain," said Brooks, as he swung along the passage. "It's a guest-room, where Dr Amersham used to stay when he slept here at nights."

Tanner stopped dead.

"What room is that?"

He pointed to a door which Brooks had passed without notice.

"Oh, that's the lumber-room."

"I'd like to have a look at it," said Tanner.

"Say, captain, there's nothing there," protested the man.

"There's something there you didn't want me to see," said Tanner calmly. "That is why you started that bright line of talk about Amersham's room. Open it."

The man stood squarely before him, his thumbs in his waistcoat pockets.

"I haven't got the key of that room. If I had it wouldn't be worth looking into. There's a lot of old junk – "

"Go and get the key."

"You'd better ask her ladyship for it. I don't carry keys around," replied the man sulkily. "Nobody guessed you wanted to look in an old lumber-room."

"I guessed I did," said Bill, "and I generally guess right."

He tapped the panel of the door. It sounded unusually solid.

"You like a nice heavy door for your lumber-room, eh? Afraid of the furniture walking out?"

He bent his head and listened, but there was no sound from inside.

"All right, we'll pass that – but we're coming back."

Brooks went on, silenced by something. He threw open the door of Amersham's room and jerked his head to the interior.

"There's nothing here, but maybe you'll think it's worth looking into."

There was literally nothing of Amersham's personal belongings, Tanner discovered. Coming out of the room he saw Totty with a gun under his arm.

"Can I see you for a minute?" said the sergeant. He came into Amersham's room and closed the door. "I found this," he said, and gave a brief account of his other discoveries. "It's the gamekeeper's gun and probably his pipe."

"What made him leave them behind?" said Tanner thoughtfully. "Let me see the cartridges."

He inspected the shells and handed them back.

"Rather heavy shot for a gamekeeper to use, and fatal, I should guess, if it was fired at poachers. Tilling, of course. The position tells you that. He was sitting there, watching his cottage, and I can pretty well guess who he was looking for. Then something happened that made him drop his pipe and his gun – what was it?"

"I've sent down for him," said Totty, and the big man nodded his approval.

"About that cigarette, Totty. It's as clear as daylight that Gilder was getting his story in first. That fellow's got a nerve! He's not satisfied with giving an alibi to himself, but he hands one to Lady Lebanon. She must have gone down when she heard about the murder – and that was long before the body was found. Why didn't she go to the place where the body lay?" asked Tanner. "Why did she wander fifty yards south and never go near the bush where they found Amersham? Shall I tell you, Totty? Because she didn't know he was there. And she didn't know he was there because she couldn't see, and because nobody knew he was there. She thought he was there and she was looking for him."

He looked up at the ceiling, his chin in his fingers.

"The question is, was Gilder there? I don't think he was. At least, she didn't see him. He may have come on the scene a bit later, or he may have been there all the time unknown to her. I'll be interested to hear what Mr Tilling has to say."

"It's a funny sort of place," said Totty.

"It doesn't make me laugh," said Bill.

There were three separate telephone services in Marks Priory each communicating directly to the outside world. This was rather unusual in a big house, which generally has a central switchboard.

In Mr Kelver's pantry was one instrument, and this Tanner used to get in touch with Scotland Yard. He came through to one of his office searchers.

"I want a list of every train that leaves any station in England at six-thirty and arrives at its destination at eight-three, and I want another list showing the trains that leave at ten o'clock, either in the morning or night, and arrive at ten-five the same day or the following morning. I don't know what stations they go from; you've got to find that out."

What was Lady Lebanon's plan? Where did she intend going in the wild panic following her discovery? The body had not been found till just before eleven o'clock in the morning but the murder must have been committed at least twelve hours before – and she knew, and was planning – what? A getaway? That was hardly likely. She was not that kind, unless for the moment she was overbalanced by the horror of her discovery.

He was on his way back to the hall to interrogate Lady Lebanon when Totty met him with a startling piece of information.

"Tilling's not in Marks Thornton," he said. "He left early this morning, and nobody knows where he's gone."

Tanner whistled.

"Does anybody in the house know?"

"No; I've spoken to his lordship, but he had very little to do with the man. I asked him to see his mother, but she knows nothing either."

Tanner considered this.

"Who told you about Tilling leaving early this morning?"

"His wife. Rather an affable young lady." Totty straightened his tie.

"Don't allow her to be too affable," said Tanner. "I'll see her. Is she here?"

"No; I asked her to come to the hall, but she wouldn't. I'll tell you something, guv'nor; this girl knows a lot. She's as jumpy as the young lady outside."

"Miss Crane – she's jumpy too, is she?"

Totty's lips curled.

"Ferraby's doing his best to soothe her nerves, but he hasn't got far."

"Very well," said Tanner. "Show me the way to the cottage."

They crossed Priory Fields, passed the bushes where the body had been found, through the gate and up the flagged path of the little garden before the cottage. As they came to the door it was opened. Tanner remembered the woman, though he had only seen her once. Her face was white and drawn. Here was another who had had little sleep on the previous night. She looked at the chief inspector fearfully, hesitated a moment, and then invited him in a husky voice to come in. He followed her into the pleasant little parlour.

"It's about Johnny, isn't it?" Her voice was strained. "I don't know where he is. He left very early this morning."

"Where did he go?"

She shook her head.

"I don't know…he didn't tell me very much."

"What time did he come in last night?'

Again the hesitation.

"It was early this morning. He came in and went out, and that's all I know."

Tanner smiled benevolently.

"Now, Mrs Tilling, let me hear a few facts. And please don't be too careful. You're not shielding anybody – you are just laying suspicion on them. What time did your husband come in? Were you in bed?"

She nodded.

"He woke you? What time was it?"

"About one o'clock," she said. "I heard the water running in the kitchen – the tap's just behind my bed – in the other room I mean – I got up to see what it was."

Then without warning, she dropped her head on her arm and began to sob.

"Oh, my God! Isn't it awful? Both of them. Amersham too!"

He waited till she was calmer.

"Mrs Tilling, you'll be doing me a great service, and probably doing yourself one, if you tell me exactly what happened last night. You've a lot to tell which you haven't told. When do you expect your husband back?"

"I don't know," she said, with a catch in her voice. "I hope I never see him again."

"Where has he gone?"

"He didn't tell me."

"You heard the water running. What was he doing?"

He saw her lips close tightly.

"Was he washing?"

"It was nothing – just a scratch," she said quickly, and tried to make her statement more innocuous. "He got into some holly bushes."

"Where was the scratch, on his hand?"

"Yes, there weren't many."

"Both hands?"

She did not answer.

"Did you lend him something to bind them up? Come, come, Mrs Tilling. He was hurt, wasn't he, and you helped him? Did you have to bind up his hands with a bandage or something?"

"No, he used a handkerchief. The cuts weren't bad."

"Had he been fighting?"

She dropped her eyes.

"I suppose so," she said, after a while. "He's very quarrelsome."

"Now tell me this: before he went out did he change his clothes?"

She looked from side to side like somebody trapped.

"Yes, he did."

"Where are the clothes he took off?"

Inspector Tanner had intuition which made a great deal of his investigations appear to be guesswork. He progressed from step to step, taking advantage of every slip that his victims made. Invariably he started with no predetermined course of examination – his questions arose out of answers, and were invariably successful.

It was a long time before Mrs Tilling would tell the story, and when she did it was worth hearing.

18

At half-past one (evidently she was not quite sure of the time) she heard her husband come in. She was awake, and not, as she first said, in bed at all. It struck Bill that she was expecting somebody, for she admitted being in the drawing-room with the lights out. The blinds were up, and she saw Tilling come quickly through the gate, and went out to meet him.

He told her nothing of what had happened except that he had had a little fight, and she asked him if it was with Dr Amersham – (Tanner passed this statement without probing too deeply), but he protested that he had not seen Dr Amersham. His coat was torn; the velvet collar of it was hanging, and there were wounds on both hands as if he had been fighting with a wild animal.

She put some iodine on his hands and bandaged the worst of the cuts with a silk handkerchief. He had changed "into a pepper and salt suit," and had left the house at half-past three, wheeling his bicycle. She produced coat and breeches from the out-house, and the coat gave evidence of hard usage. There was a smudge of blood on the front which probably came from his hands; two buttons were torn off and a third was hanging.

"Was his face damaged at all?"

"Yes, it was," she admitted, "but there was no cut – only a bruise. He was terribly upset, and wouldn't give me a word of explanation, except that he'd had a fight with some poachers and he'd lost his gun."

Bill checked and re-checked the story, and was leaving when he had an inspiration.

"Did he give you any money before he left?"

She was reluctant to answer this question, but presently she produced four new five-pound notes.

"I'll take the numbers of those," said Tanner. He saw they were consecutive. "Had he any more?"

"Yes, he had quite a big lot that he took these from. He said he'd be back in five or six weeks, and that's all I know, Mr Tanner. I'll swear he didn't kill the doctor. He's a bad-tempered man, but he's not that kind. And he didn't kill Studd, either. I asked him before he went, and he went down on his knees and swore he'd never seen Studd on the night he was murdered."

"How many pipes had your husband?"

She was surprised at the question, but gave a satisfactory answer.

"Only one – he stuck to one pipe until it was burnt out, and then bought another."

He was very "particular" about his pipes, and paid good prices for them.

He checked the time again.

"He left at half-past three."

"You're sure of the time?"

It might have been later, she thought. Her clock had stopped on the night before, and she had not thought to look at her watch, so that she depended on a recollection of the church chimes. Apparently she had forgotten the diamond watch she wore, or possibly it was a better ornament than a timekeeper.

Clear of the cottage, Tanner handed the numbers of the notes to Totty.

"Go down to the bank in the village, and see if you can trace those notes, where they came from, and if they've ever passed through any account at Marks Thornton. Take a squad car. I shall want you, so hurry. And, Totty, get through to the Yard; ask them to issue to the press an inquiry addressed to all tobacconists who may have sold a briar pipe to a man between eight-thirty and ten. It's a patent pipe called the 'Orsus.'"

"You mean Tilling's?"

Tanner nodded.

"A man who loses a favourite pipe invariably buys one like it. Arrange to examine all answers to the inquiry, and tell them to get me a full description of the man who purchased it."

The mystery of the time-table was a mystery no longer. He hurried back to the house, overtaking Ferraby and Isla. She was calm now. Whatever inquiries Ferraby had made must have been of the gentlest character.

"She says she knows nothing, and yet I'm sure she knows a great deal," said Ferraby, who followed him into the hall.

He was troubled, for he was taking a personal interest in the case of Isla Crane.

She waited until Tanner had gone before she found the young detective.

"He frightens me," she said, in a low voice.

Ferraby smiled.

"Mr Tanner? He's the nicest man in the world."

She turned her head. Her hearing was very sensitive. "I think he's calling you," she said.

Lady Lebanon found her there, sitting on the big Knole couch, her head in her hands, and just at that moment Isla was in her mind.

"Isla!"

The girl sprang up.

"Do you want me, Lady Lebanon?"

She heard a little laugh behind her. Willie Lebanon was standing on the stairs.

"I say, all this 'Lady Lebanon' stuff is rather stupid, isn't it? Why not something more friendly? Why not something reasonable?"

He caught his mother's eyes and stopped.

"Where have you been, Willie?"

"I've been trying to work up an interest in police investigation," he said flippantly. "Nobody seems particularly anxious to employ me as an amateur detective. They're all so busy chasing shadows – "

"There is no need for you to interfere with them," she said sharply.

He half turned to go, changed his mind and came back.

"I'm not sorry about Amersham," he said stoutly. "I'm telling you the truth, mother, although I know it annoys you. Naturally, one hates to see a fellow go out…but he was an awful outsider, but I'm relieved, and that's the truth."

"You may go, Willie."

Her voice was like ice, but still he waited.

"They asked me if I'd heard anything, and I said 'Yes.' I hadn't, of course, but I thought maybe they'd take a little interest in me, but, bless your heart, that fellow Totty tied me up in knots in two twinks! If only somebody thought I was important enough to take me into a nice, quiet room and quiz me – that's an American phrase, mother dear – "

"Willie, when you've finished being stupidly sarcastic, I'd be glad if you'd go. I want to speak to Isla."

He could not contend against a direct order, and lounged out of the room, a very bored and discontented young man.

She went to the great archway which commanded a view of the corridor, listened a moment at the foot of the stairs.

"What is the matter with you?" she asked quickly. "Tell me, before this man comes back. My God! What *is* the matter with you?"

Isla was interlacing her fingers one in the other, her bosom was rising and falling quickly.

"Nothing," she blurted. "What did you think was the matter with me?"

She rose from the settee again and walked across to the desk where Lady Lebanon was seated.

"I opened the drawer of your desk this morning, and I found a little red scarf with a metal tag on the corner," she almost wailed.

Lady Lebanon's face hardened.

"I don't think it ought to be there. It was stupid of you to keep it there."

"Why did you open the drawer of my desk?"

The older woman carefully articulated every word.

"I wanted the cheque-book," said Isla impatiently. "Why do you keep that scarf there?"

Lady Lebanon's lips curled.

"My dear child, you're dreaming. Which drawer?"

When the girl pointed, she unlocked and pulled open the receptacle.

"There's nothing there. Isla, you mustn't let these things get on your nerves."

"These things!" The girl was almost hysterical. "How can you speak so lightly about it! A man killed like a brute!" Her voice was trembling. "I hated him. I loathed him. He was always so beastly with me – "

Lady Lebanon came to her feet.

"Always so beastly with you? What do you mean?" she asked. "Made love to you?" incredulously. "Amersham?"

The girl's gesture was one of utter helplessness. She walked back to the end of the couch, and leaned on it, her head on her arms.

"I can't go on staying here," she said. "I can't do it."

Again Lady Lebanon smiled slowly.

"You've been staying here for quite a long time," she said. She searched methodically for a letter on her desk, and presently she found it.

"I sent your mother her quarterly cheque on Monday, and had such a charming letter from her this morning. The two girls at school are so happy! She said how wonderful it was to feel safe and secure after the hard time she's been through."

The hint was too plain to be mistaken. Isla Crane had pitied this hard woman; for the moment she hated her. It was wicked of her to throw this reminder in her face, and tell her in so many words that her mother's and her sister's happiness depended upon her complaisance.

"You know that I wouldn't be here a day if it weren't for her and the girls," she breathed. "She doesn't know what I'm doing – she'd rather starve."

Lady Lebanon listened again. It was the sound of Tanner's voice.

"For heaven's sake don't be hysterical," she said. "I'm doing you a great service."

Again she pronounced every word with the greatest care.

"When you are Lady Lebanon you will find me very broadminded about your married life. You understand that? Very broadminded."

Isla looked at her puzzled. It was not the first time she had used that very expression. What did she mean? But her ladyship offered no elucidation.

"I saw you outside with a young policeman. I hope you weren't in a state of nerves when you were talking to him?"

"He's very nice," said the girl wearily. "In fact, much nicer than I – "

"Than you deserve? Don't be silly. I'm sure he's very agreeable. He talks well. He must have been to a good school."

Isla had the name of the school, and her ladyship lifted her eyebrows.

"Really? Quite an interesting public school – not of the first class perhaps, but I have known quite a number of very nice creatures who went there. In the police force – how absurd! That's the war, I suppose. What is his name?"

Isla was in no mood for small talk, but the young police officer occupied a distinct territory of her mind.

"John Ferraby," she said, and saw Lady Lebanon's eyes open wider.

"Ferraby? One of the Somerset Ferrabys? Lord Lesserfield's family? The man who put the leopards in his quarterings – quite without authority?"

"I suppose so," said the girl listlessly. "Yes, he comes from Somerset."

Lady Lebanon looked at her with a speculative eye. The thought that went through her mind was happily for Isla Crane, unexpressed.

"There's no reason why you shouldn't know him, though you mustn't speak to him about Amersham. Made love to you, did he?"

Isla turned impatiently.

"He's dead now. O God, how awful!"

"If this young man should ask you questions – "

The girl turned quickly.

"He hasn't asked me anything. We were talking about people we know. Mr Tanner will ask me questions. What am I to tell him?"

"My dear, you will tell him just what it is necessary he should know."

Then Ferraby came in.

"Oh, I beg your pardon, but Mr Tanner was looking for you. I'll tell him you're here."

"Don't go, Mr Ferraby. I'll see Mr Tanner."

She gathered up her letters at leisure.

"My niece was telling me you are related to the Lesserfields."

Ferraby was a little embarrassed.

"Well, yes – he's a sort of relation of mine – very, very distant. One doesn't worry about that sort of thing."

"You should," she said sharply. "It's the finest thing in the world to be a member – even a cadet member – of a great family. To know that your stock has continued in authority through the ages, and will go on through thousands of years. Where is Mr Tanner?"

"I left him in the butler's room. He was telephoning to town."

She smiled graciously.

"I will even go to the butler's room," she said.

Ferraby was impressed.

"Good Lord!" he said, half to himself. "She belongs to the Middle Ages."

"She belongs to this age," said the girl ruefully.

"How odd!" He shook his head. "Lesserfield quite impressed her – of course I know him; he's a perfectly stupid ass, and even more broke than I am."

There was a silence; she looked up to find his eyes fixed on her.

"Do you mind if I ask you a question?"

She shook her head.

"What makes you so nervous?"

Isla tried to fence.

"I told Lady Lebanon that you didn't ask me questions."

"And I let you down? Well, it was quite friendly. Why are you so jumpy?"

"Am I?" she asked innocently.

142

"You are. All the time you seem to be looking round as though you expected a bogey man to appear out of one of your secret panels – I suppose there are secret panels in this old house? What are you afraid of?"

She forced a smile.

"Of the police," and, when he shook his head: "What happened last night I'm afraid of really."

He was not satisfied.

"You've been like this for a long time, haven't you?"

"Who told you that?" she asked quickly.

Then the police officer in him took a holiday.

"I wish I could be of some service to you. Do you think I could be?"

She looked up at him; there was a hint of suspicion in her gaze.

"I suppose you want me to confide in you – officially?"

He should have said "yes." It was his job to worm out every little secret she had, but he knew he would hate himself.

"You're not my idea of a policeman," she said unexpectedly.

"That's very rude or very complimentary," he said. "You're not really afraid of me – you can't be."

"Why not?"

It was a staggering question which he could not answer.

"I'm not afraid of anything," she went on, and looked round quickly to the stairs. "There's somebody there," she whispered. "They're listening."

He ran to the stairs and looked up. There was nobody in sight, and he came back to her, more thoughtful than ever.

"Are all you people afraid of being spied on? When Lord Lebanon came to Scotland Yard this morning he had the same fear. There's something in this house that's got you all down. What is it?"

She did not answer.

"What is it?" he asked again, and when she shook her head: "What is the secret of Marks Priory?"

Her smile was entirely artificial.

143

"That sounds almost like the title of a sensational book, with Mr Tanner as the hero." And then, seriously: "Is he very clever?"

"Tanner? Rather – the cleverest man at Scotland Yard. He's got an uncanny instinct for the truth."

There was a silence.

"Whom does he suspect?"

He laughed at this.

"Everybody, I should imagine."

Then, to his surprise, she came quickly towards him and gripped the lapel of his coat. She was agitated; he could feel her trembling.

"I want to ask you something... Suppose one knew who committed this horrible murder...and didn't tell the police... I mean, kept it to oneself... Is that an offence?... I mean, is it...would it be a crime?"

He nodded.

"Yes, the person who knew might be charged with being an accessory."

He was sorry he had said this when he saw the effect upon her.

"Whoever knows ought to tell," he said gently. "It might be easier to tell me."

She took hold of herself again.

"I don't know," she said jerkily. "Why should I know? You think because I'm jumpy... These things don't get on your nerves! I suppose a case like this really doesn't matter to you. Isn't that strange?"

"This case matters," he said quietly, "quite a lot."

It was on the tip of her tongue to ask why, but she knew the question was unnecessary.

"I suppose you've got a very matter-of-fact name for this dreadful thing – Case No. 6, or something like that?"

It was a pitiful attempt to banter him and bring the talk to a lighter tone. He shook his head again.

"No; to me it's the Case of the Frightened Lady."

"You mean me?" she said breathlessly.

"Yes, I mean you."

Then she saw him sniff, and asked:

"What is it?"

He looked at the floor, under the desk, behind the sofa.

"Something's burning. Can't you smell it? Has somebody dropped a cigarette on the carpet?"

"I hope not. If Lady Lebanon knows there will be trouble," she said.

Then he saw the stove, went to it and lifted the top. Lady Lebanon had not pulled the damper as she had imagined. She had still further deadened the fire, and only now had it slowly burnt through to the top stratum, and that was where the smell came from.

"Somebody's been burning stuff here," he said, peering down. "A piece of cloth – I can still see the fibre. You can smell it now, can't you?"

She stood stiffly at the foot of the stairs, her face set.

"No, I don't smell anything." She spoke in so low a tone that he could hardly hear her.

Totty came in at that moment. He, too, sniffed.

"Come here and look at this."

Totty crossed to the stove.

"Looks like a bit of linen."

As Ferraby was about to move it with a poker: "Don't touch it," said Totty excitedly. "Do you see that little piece of metal where the corner was? It's melting, but you can see it. Where's Tanner?"

He looked at the girl. She was struck speechless. Too well she knew the significance now of that pungent smell of burning cloth. That was where it had gone. She had seen it in the drawer that morning. Lady Lebanon must have forgotten until the last moment, indeed, till the police were in the house, to destroy that terrible piece of evidence.

Then she found her voice.

"Mr Tanner is in the butler's room," she said, and, turning, ran up the stairs.

19

Tanner came in haste and made his inspection. The burning coal had consumed the scarf, but the fairy-like gossamer of its fibre was still visible. The contour of the metal tag corresponded with the coal on which it rested, but the fact that it was a tag, similar to that which had been found about the throat of Studd, about the throat of Ferraby, and in Dr Amersham's desk, was beyond dispute.

Her ladyship had followed him at her leisure, and found him alone.

"Something burning in the stove?" she asked lightly. "Probably it's silk. Yes, I think it was. I was making a doll's dress last night for the village bazaar. I found the cuttings on my table, and burnt them."

"These were not cuttings," said Tanner quietly. "These were of a piece. I suggest these remains are of a scarf, an Indian scarf, probably red; it has the manufacturer's trade mark sewn in the corner. I suppose you've never seen such a thing? But Dr Amersham did."

She looked at him quickly.

"I don't understand you."

"I found such a scarf in Amersham's desk when I searched it last night," said Tanner.

He went to the door; Ferraby and Totty were within call, and he gave them instructions, which were audible to her ladyship.

"Nobody must come into the room while we're talking."

"Does that mean I'm a prisoner?"

"It means I don't want to be interrupted."

She sat down and folded her hands on the writing-table before her.

"You want to ask me some questions? I'm afraid I am not going to be of very much assistance to you."

"I'm hoping you are," said Tanner. "I shall not only ask you questions, Lady Lebanon, but I shall tell you a few facts of which you believe and hope I am ignorant. That amuses you?"

"Don't grudge me a little amusement on this horrible day," she said.

He admired her. He had met many men and many women, but none like the cultured and delicate woman who held such complete control of herself and her circumstances, possibly of her fate.

"There is a room upstairs, Lady Lebanon. Your man could not open it for me. He called it a lumber-room."

"Then it must be the lumber-room," she said lightly.

Bill shook his head.

"On the first floor, in one of the best positions in the house? That's a queer place for a lumber-room."

She shrugged her thin shoulders.

"We call it the lumber-room. Really it's a store where I keep one or two valuables."

"Have you the key?"

"I never open that room."

The metal was in her voice again.

Interruption came. The stairway leading into the hall was unguarded. Lord Lebanon came down and overheard the last words. For the moment she did not see the young man.

"Mr Tanner, I'll tell you the truth," she said. "It was the room where my husband died. It hasn't been opened since that day."

"Oh, I say, mother! Do you mean the room with the heavy door, Mr Tanner? Why, I've seen it open lots of times."

She fixed him with her menacing black eyes.

"You're quite mistaken, Willie. That room has never been opened, and you have never seen it open."

"Well, I'd like to see it opened," said Tanner.

"I'm afraid you can't."

"I'm sorry, but I must insist."

147

"Be reasonable, Mr Tanner." She was amiable, unresentful. "What is there in that room that could interest you? There's nothing there but a few old pictures. I should have imagined that the scope of your inquiry lay outside the house."

"The scope of my inquiry, Lady Lebanon, lies just where I want it to lie," said Tanner sternly.

"Really, mother – "

This time their eyes met.

"Would you mind leaving us for a little while, Lord Lebanon? You will find my entertaining sergeant in the corridor."

He waited for the young man to disappear.

"Now, Lady Lebanon, you realise, of course, that I can get a search warrant?"

She stiffened at this.

"It would be outrageous if you did," she said, haughtily. "No magistrate in this county would grant such a thing." And then, with a change of voice: "Do I understand you want to ask me something? What is it about?"

There was nothing to be gained at the moment by pursuing the question of the closed room. It would be a simple matter to obtain a search warrant, and he had already made a request to London for that instrument.

"Curiously enough, I want to speak to you about the murder of Dr Amersham," he said.

When Bill Tanner was conducting an examination he was a restless man. He paced from the stove to the centre of the big room, passed round the Knole couch, walked to the foot of the stairs, and from the foot of the stairs to the entrance of the corridor, and possibly this was the most unnerving feature of a cross-examination which in the annals of Scotland Yard remains a classic.

"That is why I am here," he repeated. "For no other reason, except to investigate the murder by strangulation of Dr Leicester Amersham."

"I think I have told you – "

148

"You told me you know nothing whatever about it, but I haven't that illusion. Lady Lebanon, when did you last see Dr Amersham alive?"

She was not looking at him now. The crucial test had come.

"I didn't see him this morning – " she began.

"That I realise," said Tanner patiently. "He wasn't alive this morning. The medical evidence is that he was killed last night, probably between eleven o'clock and midnight. When did you last see him alive?"

"Yesterday morning – or it may have been the day before. I am not quite sure."

She had hardly said this before she knew she had committed a stupid blunder.

"He was here at eleven o'clock last night, probably until within a few minutes of his death," said Tanner. "He was here in this room, talking to you."

Her chin went up.

"You've been talking to my servants?"

The very fatuity of the charge almost upset Tanner's gravity.

"Naturally I have been," he said. "You don't think that's very remarkable, do you, Lady Lebanon?"

"It would have been a little more decent if you had come to me first," she snapped.

"Well, I have come to you." Bill Tanner's smile was very sweet, very disarming, but it did not disarm Lady Lebanon. Rather was she raising her defences with all the reserves she could summon. "And you tell me it was yesterday morning you saw him, or it may have been the day before. Here is a man murdered – rather an impressive fact."

She frowned.

"I don't quite follow you."

"If you had a friend who, soon after you saw him, met with a fatal accident, wouldn't you say immediately; 'Why, I was speaking to him only an hour before!' That is what I mean by an impressive fact."

"Dr Amersham was not a friend," she said in a low voice. "He was a self-willed man who saw nobody's but his own point of view."

149

Tanner nodded.

"So the fact that he was murdered within a few hundred yards of this room really doesn't matter?"

Again she stiffened.

"That is a little insolent, Mr – Inspector – !"

"Tanner," said Bill. "Yes, I suppose it is. Doesn't it strike you, Lady Lebanon, that your own attitude is peculiar? I don't say arrogant. I am a detective officer, investigating the murder of Dr Amersham. You tell me you cannot remember when you saw him last, although he was with you up to a few moments of his death. You suggest you cannot fix the time, because he was not a friend of yours, but just a self-willed man. That seems a little inadequate, doesn't it? If he wasn't a friend, what was he doing here at eleven?"

"He came to see me."

"As a doctor?" She nodded.

"At your request?"

She thought before she answered. "No, he dropped in."

"At eleven o'clock at night?" Tanner was incredulous.

"I had a touch of neuritis in my arm."

"But you didn't send for him? He just guessed you had neuritis, and drove down from London in his car to treat you? Did he write a prescription?"

She did not answer.

"He left you at twelve and drove down the Long Avenue – isn't that what you call it? Half-way down somebody jumped on the back of his car and strangled him as he sat at the wheel."

"I know nothing whatever about that," she said quickly.

"They found the car from which he was evidently dragged abandoned at the other side of the village."

These unnecessary details maddened her. She had gone over every aspect of the case, not once but a hundred times.

"Really I'm not interested," she was trapped into saying, and Bill Tanner was genuinely shocked.

"Lady Lebanon! You've known this gentleman for years; he was a constant visitor – your own doctor and friend, and you're not interested in his brutal murder?"

She drew a long breath.

"I'm terribly sorry, of course. It was an awful thing to have happened."

He was a long time before he asked the next question; her nerves were on edge.

"What did Dr Amersham know?" he asked.

She shot a quick glance at him, and shook her head.

"What did he know?" repeated Tanner. "Your last words to him as he left the room were these."

He took a notebook from his pocket, and considered it with great deliberation.

"You stood there" – he pointed to a place near where she was sitting – "you spoke in an angry voice. You said: 'Nobody would believe you if you told them. Tell them if you dare! And don't forget that you are as deeply in it as anybody. You've always wanted to handle Willie's money.' "

He closed the book with a slap.

"Those may not have been the exact words, but they are the sense of the words. What was he deeply in?"

She did not answer.

"What did you dare him to tell?"

For the moment she was stricken dumb, devastated by the accuracy of his information; and then it came to her whence it had been obtained, and her pale cheeks went pink with fury.

"Jackson told you, of course – my maid." She spoke rapidly. "She is an utterly dishonest and untrustworthy girl, and I've discharged her. If you listen to discharged servants Mr Tanner – "

Tanner waggled his head wearily.

"I listen to anybody – that's my job. How long was your husband, the late Lord Lebanon, ill before he died?"

She was not prepared for this sudden and violent change of angle, and had to think.

"Fifteen years,"

"Who attended him?"

"Dr Amersham."

The words came reluctantly. Out came Tanner's notebook again.

"Although he was ill so long, he died rather suddenly, didn't he? I've got the particulars of the certificate here. It is signed by Leicester Amersham, LRCP, MRCS."

The book went back to his pocket. She wondered what would be the next question he would ask, prompted by its pages.

"During his illness you administered his affairs, you and Dr Amersham?"

She nodded.

"I found his name on a number of leases he signed under a general power of attorney."

She felt on safer ground now, and had the impression that the crisis of the examination was past.

"Yes; my husband liked the doctor, and he did help to administer his estate, as you say."

She waited. Tanner was looking at her, and when he spoke his voice was quiet, almost pleasantly conversational.

"Why did you marry again?"

The full significance of the question did not at first reach her. Then she came to her feet.

"That is not true!" she breathed.

"Why did you marry again, at Peterfield Parish Church – and marry Leicester Charles Amersham? The ceremony was, I think, performed by the Rev. John Hastings."

She swayed for a second, and then very slowly sat down.

"Who told you that?"

Bill Tanner smiled.

"A certain register of marriages told me that. I inspected it at Peterfield. I was a little curious, to tell you the truth, Lady Lebanon, as to why the Rev. John Hastings and Dr Amersham should be on friendly terms – they were so unalike – and I rather gathered that the friendship was based upon a service which Hastings had rendered. I took the trouble to go down to Peterfield. Why did you marry him three months after your husband died, and why did you keep the marriage a secret?"

There was a small crystal jug of water on her table. She poured a little into a glass with a steady hand and sipped it, and Bill waited, curious and expectant.

"The marriage was forced on me," she said. "Dr Amersham was an adventurer of the lowest kind. He was a penniless doctor in the Indian Army. He blackmailed me into marriage."

"How?"

A twist of her shoulder was the only answer.

"What hold did he have on you? You know you can't blackmail people unless you know something to their detriment. Had you broken the law?"

"I'll not answer." Her mouth closed like a trap. "I refuse to answer. I know that he had – he was a thief and a forger; he was kicked out of the Army."

Tanner nodded.

"He may have been all those things, but he was here last night at eleven or twelve. He threatened you, and was killed a few minutes later, and you're not very interested!"

Her face flushed again.

"Why should I be? I'm glad he's – " She stopped suddenly.

"You're glad he's dead?" suggested Tanner. "And now you remember something, and you aren't so glad?"

She muttered a sentence which he could not hear. He thought she said that he was absurd, and was probably right.

He waited till he saw her grow tense again, and then: "As to your first husband, Mrs Amersham – "

Her head came up at this.

"I shall be glad if you will call me Lady Lebanon." And then, with a little laugh which was not altogether forced, she dropped back into the chair. "You said that to annoy me. I'm beginning to understand your methods, Mr Tanner."

"Who saw the late Lord Lebanon after his death?" Bill went on relentlessly.

"Dr Amersham."

"Did you?"

"No, nobody but Gilder and Brooks – they did everything."

"I see. And the doctor signed the certificate. The truth is that he died, and nobody saw him but Amersham, Gilder and Brooks. Amersham was considerably interested in his death."

He saw her start.

"I'm bringing no accusation, I'm merely stating facts. He blackmailed you because he knew something. I'd like to know whether he started blackmailing before or after your husband's death. That would be interesting to know."

"I have no doubt there are many things that it would interest you to know," she said, with a touch of her old hauteur.

Tanner nodded.

"Yes; I'll tell you one at this moment. I'd like to know why it was necessary for you to get your gamekeeper out of the way this morning, why you gave him a considerable sum of money – I must confess I don't know how much – which you drew two days ago from the banks in Marks Thornton in order to induce him to go. I have traced the notes, of course."

Her dark eyes did not leave his.

"That is the first time I have heard that he had left the estate," she said. "I certainly gave him money, for a purpose which was entirely his own affair. I know nothing more."

"Then I may be able to give you a little further information tonight," said Tanner.

He looked at his watch, and was surprised at the length of time he had been at Marks Priory. It was already growing dark, and there was a lot of work to be done in the village.

"This morning my interest in this case was academic, Lady Lebanon, except that I was interested in Dr Amersham. Now I am very interested in you and in this house."

He walked to the desk and held out his hand.

"And in the room which you say is never opened. Have you the key?"

She did not appear to hear him, and then, with sudden geniality: "Oh, well, Lady Lebanon, I'm probably worrying you unnecessarily, but I should have liked to have seen the room. I am an inquisitive man, and I have an idea – I may be wrong – that Dr Amersham's hold over you had something to do with that room. Now, am I not right?"

"No," she said. "It had something to do…with my past."

He shook his head smilingly.

"It took an effort for you to say that, and it isn't true. You are one of those people one reads about – blood proud." He frowned. "By the way, you must be a Lebanon yourself?"

The effect upon her was wonderful. In that brief second of time her face grew radiant, almost beautiful.

"How amazing of you to realise that!" she said softly. "Yes, I am a Lebanon. I married my cousin. I go back in direct line to the fourth baron."

He shook his head.

"Amazing!"

"The family comes from most ancient times, Mr Tanner. Before there was a history of England there was a history of the Lebanons, and it will go on! It must go on. It would be wicked if the line were broken!"

She was a being exalted, rapt. He could only gaze at her in astonishment.

"Amazing!" he said again, and she smiled.

"You said that before, Mr Tanner."

He went to the corridor entrance, and called Totty.

"I think I'll leave you for tonight. But I'm afraid I shall return to be a nuisance to you in the morning."

He was at the foot of the stairs, and happened to look up. Out of sight of any but himself he saw Isla Crane standing. She had her finger at her lips, and beckoned him urgently. Carelessly he walked up the stairs, and she gripped him by the arm.

"You're not going, Mr Tanner?" Her voice was quavering. "For God's sake don't go tonight! Stay!"

The hand that gripped his arm convulsively was shaking. He went slowly down the stairs.

"I will have a car to take you to the village – " Lady Lebanon began.

Bill was smiling at her.

"I wonder if you'll forgive me changing my mind. I've decided to stay at Marks Priory tonight – it's a whim of mine. I hope you don't mind, Lady Lebanon?"

For a second he saw the fury blaze in her eyes, and then, turning abruptly, she walked out of the room.

"What's the idea, Mr Tanner?" asked Totty.

"I'd like to be able to give you an answer, Totty, but I'll be able to tell you better in the morning," said Chief Inspector Tanner.

Totty drew a long breath.

"If it's your idea of spending a happy evening to stay on in this bogey house, very well and good! But it's not mine, Tanner!"

"Mister Tanner," corrected the chief inspector. "It sounds better – even in a haunted house!"

20

A police motor-cyclist, smothered with mud, delivered a flat package to Bill Tanner before dinner. Apparently all over the kingdom trains started at six-thirty in the morning and arrived somewhere at eight-three. He went through them carefully and marked the first, with the absolute assurance that he was right. It was a train that left Horsham for London Bridge, and Horsham was within a cycle ride.

The trains that left at ten and arrived at ten-five the following morning or the same day were few, and none of them was a Continental train. There was one that left London at ten in the morning and arrived at Aberdeen at ten-five. He consulted a work of reference. Lady Lebanon had a small shooting lodge ten miles out of Aberdeen, and that was undoubtedly Tilling's objective.

He telephoned instructions which were to be transmitted to the Aberdeen police; he was too late, but he was not aware of this fact. A telegram had been delivered at an intermediate Scottish station, which had resulted in a lumbering and rather perturbed gamekeeper leaving the train and doubling back via Edinburgh to Stirling.

There was other information. Only one person had bought a pipe of the brand he had described. A tobacconist near King's Cross Station had hardly opened his shop before a man, easily recognisable from the description as Tilling, had come in and made a purchase.

Totty had spent a completely satisfactory evening in the servants' hall, where he was regarded with the right amount of awe to which his position and his achievements entitled him.

Here he found a new life, a life of which Lady Lebanon knew nothing: human beings with theories and facts, sometimes curiously near the truth. Here were men and women who had known Studd and had liked him, who regarded him as a human being and not as a figure in a case; who remembered his good humour and his peculiar weaknesses, of which they spoke with the greatest discretion, although there was a kitchen-maid who mentioned Mrs Tilling with a sniff.

They were all pleasurably terrified and more pleasurably reassured by the presence in the house of Scotland Yard officers. Totty became godlike, hinted rather than told of his many successes in the art of detection, and so far relaxed – or Ferraby's statement was a libel – as to hold the hand of a pretty housemaid under the table during high tea.

There were evening newspapers containing a garbled account of the crime, and mentioning the fact that Chief Inspector Tanner had taken charge. To Totty's annoyance no mention was made of him.

He was surprised to find how few of the servants had ever seen Amersham. Their information about him was at second-hand, and mainly supplied by Studd, who had been brought into contact with him.

They liked Lord Lebanon, were afraid of his mother, and their attitude towards Isla, for some reason, was one of pity.

Mr Kelver, who had presided at high tea, verbally requested Totty to come into his sanctum.

"I wouldn't discuss matters with the servants if I were you. They're unreliable, and it is a great mistake to give them a sense of importance, Mr Totty."

Totty inclined his head gravely, and since Mr Kelver was not only himself refined but an inducer of refinement, Totty drifted insensibly into the intonation of the aristocracy.

"Yes, yes, I suppose so."

He had a little affected laugh when he spoke in this strain.

"A nice old house, Mr Kelver."

"Yes, it is quite old – historic. Queen Elizabeth lived here for a year."

Totty was instantly attentive.

"Go on!" he said, looking round with an added interest. "Did she die here?"

Mr Kelver not only knew where she died, but he knew the date of her death. It was the first time that Sergeant Totty knew that such a thing had really happened. Hitherto he had regarded these incidents of the great queen's life as the inventions of vexatious examiners, intended to trap the unwary.

"You've got two very fine, strapping footmen," he said.

"As you say, very strapping," said Kelver, strangely sardonic. "I have very little to do with them."

He had seen Dr Amersham but had no knowledge of his character, except what he had learned from Studd.

"He was not a very nice gentleman, according to poor Studd; but then, as I said to him so often, it takes a lot of people to make a world."

"True, true," agreed Totty. "I suppose nothing unusual ever happens here? You never had a barney?"

Mr Kelver was puzzled, and his visitor hastened to explain. Apparently there had been some sort of disturbance, and after Mr Kelver had expressed his reluctance to discuss his employer's affairs, he proceeded to discuss them.

"There was one morning when it looked as if there'd been a free fight," he said in a hushed voice. "Mirrors were broken and chairs smashed and wine glasses thrown about the floor, and Gilder the footman had a black eye; and I am told, although I have only got the word of poor Studd to go on, that Dr Amersham was a little the worse for wear the next day."

He went to the door, opened it and looked out, closed it and went on in a lower voice.

"There's something happening in this house, sir, which I cannot fathom. His lordship is treated as though he had no existence; his wishes are ignored, and in my opinion he's nothing better in this house than a prisoner."

He made this dramatic statement and stood back to watch its effect, and Totty's reactions were perfectly satisfactory.

"They never let him out of their sight," said Kelver. "I can tell you this: I've had instructions, which I very much resent, though they were given to me by her ladyship, that I am to listen to any telephone calls he makes. If he has a servant he trusts, that servant is discharged. He has engaged three valets to my knowledge, and each man has been discharged on some excuse or other. The only man with whom he was friendly was Studd, who, I believe, would have done anything for him." Again he paused dramatically.

"Studd was murdered! I've never expressed my opinion before, and I trust, Inspector Totty – am I right in saying 'Inspector'?"

"Perfectly right," said Totty gravely.

"I trust this will go no farther. There is something in this house, some dreadful force, which is beginning to get on my nerves. I would gladly sacrifice a month's salary to leave tonight."

Totty leapt to his feet. Kelver stood, open-mouthed. There was no mistaking that sound. It was a scream – a woman's scream of fear. In two strides he was at the door and had flung it open.

A low passageway ran towards the house, and on the left a flight of stairs leading by the servants' stairway to the upper hall. He heard the swift rush of feet, and Isla Crane flung herself down and would have fallen, but Totty's arm slipped round her and caught her up.

She was on the point of collapse, so far gone in fear that she could hardly speak.

"What's the matter, miss?"

She looked fearfully at the stairway, and shrank farther back. "Somebody following you? Catch hold of the young lady, Mr Kelver."

He leapt up the stairs, and stopped on the fourth step. Gilder stood on the landing above, glaring down.

"Anything wrong?" he asked in his deep, rumbling voice.

"Come here! What's the matter with the young lady?"

"I don't know what you mean, sir. I heard somebody cry out and I came to see what was wrong."

He came slowly down, reached the passage and stood, staring gloomily at the girl. She had recovered a little.

"I don't want you," she said tremulously. "Go upstairs – I don't want you…don't you hear me?"

"Is anything wrong, miss?" he asked.

"No… I'm all right. I…" She could not finish.

Then she turned to Totty.

"I want to go back to my room. Will you come with me?"

He went before her up the stairs, but she said no other word, and, going into the old lord's room, she closed the door almost in his face and locked it.

Gilder was watching him.

"The young lady's a bit nervous," he said.

"Do you know what frightened her? And take that grin off your face, will you?"

"If I didn't smile, mister," said Gilder coolly, "I'd go bats in this house. It doesn't seem unnatural to me that she's upset. We all are. You don't want me, do you?"

Totty did not answer. He went back to the butler's room and found the agitated Kelver helping himself to a small glass of brandy; his hand so shook that Totty could hear the rattle of glass against glass before he came into the room.

"What do you think she saw?" asked the puzzled Totty.

"I don't wish to think about it at all, Mr Totty. Will you help yourself to a little Napoleon brandy?"

Totty never drank before a certain hour, and that hour had not yet struck.

He found Tanner in the small drawing-room, where a writing-table had been placed for him. This room had the advantage that it contained one of the three telephones which served Marks Priory.

"It's a mystery to me," said Totty. "She saw something. Of course, it might be the American footmen she's scared of."

Tanner shook his head.

"By the way, Lord Lebanon is going down to the village. I'd like you to go down with him. You'd better take a gun, if it's only for the moral effect, but I'd much prefer you'd take your little rubber truncheon. I don't think anything will happen, but you never know."

"What's the idea?" asked the startled Totty. "Why is he going to the village?"

"He wants to see Mrs Tilling, and I prefer he should go by the road. He's only just heard about Tilling's disappearance and he's a little concerned. I'd much rather he went by the road than across Priory Fields. If you're scared I'll send Ferraby."

Totty was hurt.

"Have you ever known me to be scared?" he demanded. "And what is there in the park that's likely to touch a couple of men? You're getting romantical, Tanner."

" 'Sir' will do," said Tanner. "No, I'm not romantical, but I don't want you to be too confident, Totty. There will be considerable danger in the park, and be prepared for it."

In spite of his experience, Sergeant Totty felt a cold shiver run down his spine.

"You're not half putting the wind up me," he said truthfully. "Is there a hiding place in the park? Do you think this fellow's still there?"

Tanner nodded.

"He's still on this estate," he said seriously. "Ferraby can go with you – "

"Don't be silly," snorted Totty. "When I get to the point when I have to go out with a battalion I'll chuck the police and join the Army."

"Don't forget that Lord Lebanon is in your charge," said Tanner as he was leaving the room. "If anything happens to him you're responsible. You may take a gun but you're not to use it unless you find that scarf round your throat, and then I rather fancy you won't have time."

"Are they going to do anything to him – Lebanon?" asked Totty.

"I don't know. Nothing will happen to either of you if you carry out my instructions. I'm very serious about this, Totty."

The sergeant found the young man waiting in the hall, fuming at the instructions which Tanner had issued.

"I don't mind being treated as a baby by my revered parent," he said, "but when you fellows from Scotland Yard get this nursemaid habit – well, it's a little trying."

Nevertheless, he was glad of the company, for he liked Totty. They walked down the dark drive, Totty alert, his eyes roving from shadow to shadow, and shooting the ray of the electric lamp which he carried from bush to bush. In his imagination he saw lurking shapes in every hollow. Once he thought he heard a stealthy footstep behind, and stopped and turned. He could have sworn he saw a figure melt into the bushes, but when he shot his light up the drive there was nothing visible.

They had reached the road, and again Totty was sure that he heard somebody moving on the other side of the hedge parallel with the path they followed. It was impossible to see through the thick box hedge, but where it thinned he unexpectedly jerked his light round, and this time he was certain. He saw something move quickly out of the range of the light. Somebody who was walking inside the grounds, under those very trees where he had found Tilling's gun and camp-stool. In spite of his natural courage, he felt unpleasantly damp behind the ears, and was glad when they came to the cottage.

Lord Lebanon was less perturbed and infinitely more intrigued.

"Somebody following us, really?"

He would have pushed through the hedge if Totty had not pulled him back.

"You stay here, young fellow!"

"Who the devil is it?" demanded his lordship.

Here was a question to which Mr Totty could make no very satisfactory reply. He followed Lebanon through the gate, keeping an anxious eye to his right, turned towards the belt of trees, his ears strained to catch any sound. He waited at the gate till he heard the door open to Lebanon's knock, and then he followed the young man inside.

The call brought no satisfaction to him as a detective. Lebanon's visit was one of sympathy. He wanted to know whether the woman had money, and questioned her closely about the gamekeeper. Mrs

Tilling was nervous, and for once in her life reticent. She was obviously overwhelmed by this unexpected visit, and for the most part of their stay was tongue-tied.

"You knew poor old Amersham, didn't you?"

She nodded.

"They say all sorts of odd things about you." His lordship at least had no reticences. "Of course, I don't take very much notice of them."

Totty was surprised that she did not even protest her innocence. "Quite an odd person," said Lebanon as they were walking back, "and rather pretty, don't you think? They say the most terrible things about her, but I don't suppose they're true. I wonder what's happened to her husband – she oughtn't to be there alone."

Totty was absorbed in his own thoughts. He was walking close to the hedge, and again he was conscious of the invisible shadow that paced by his side. Once he heard a small branch break under the feet of the unknown. It broke with a loud crack which made him jump.

"Somebody is there," said Lebanon in a low voice. "Let's get over and chase him."

"Let's leave him to do the chasing," said Totty.

His lamp was going left and right like a lighthouse as they walked up the drive. Somebody was behind them. Twice he turned without warning and flashed his lamp backward, yet saw nothing. But he could hear. The shadow was keeping to the grass, but once he had to cross a path which ran at right angles to the drive, and Totty heard the scrunch of his feet on the gravel. He saw Lebanon up to the door, waited for him to go in, and went back the way he had come. He took the grass verge and moved stealthily, keeping close to the trees. Suddenly he saw something, and whipped out his gun.

"Stand where you are, unless you want a bullet in your stomach," he said and turned on his lamp.

In the circle of light stood Ferraby.

"Don't shoot, colonel," he said cheerfully. "I'm both a friend and a comrade."

"Was it you?"

"Was what me?" demanded Mr Ferraby.

"Have you been following me?"

"In a sense I have been following you, and in a sense have been keeping level with you," said Ferraby coolly.

"Were you the fellow on the other side of the hedge?"

"I was. I didn't realise you were so nervous, Totty, and why on earth did Tanner trust you with a pistol? I hope it isn't loaded."

"What were you doing?"

"Carrying out my instructions," said Ferraby, as he lit a cigarette. "My instructions were to shadow you both. There's a Latin saying, of which you've probably heard, which means 'Who shall have custody of the custodian?' or words to that effect."

Mr Totty was reasonably annoyed, a little relieved, too.

"If Tanner can't trust me – "

"Whom does he trust?" said Ferraby. "You'll probably find there's an officer watching me, only I'm not so sensitive as you are. What happened at the cottage?"

"Nothing."

"Is the beautiful lady in a state of nerves? By Jove, I shouldn't like to be in that cottage alone at night! On the other hand, I shouldn't relish the job of guarding it."

As they strolled towards the house, Totty graciously condescended to accept a cigarette.

"What's Tanner's idea? The worst thing about him is that he gets mysterious. I've noticed it in other cases. He puts all the facts together, and doesn't let you know what's going on till the case is over. It's getting on my nerves, Ferraby, all these squawky women – "

"Which squawky women?" asked Ferraby quickly.

"That young lady of yours, Miss What's-her-name."

"Miss Crane? Has there been any trouble?"

He was so palpably agitated that Totty felt revenged. He told his companion his experience, and Mr Ferraby was visibly affected.

"There is something in this damned house that's scaring them – either in the house or in the grounds. What's inside that room that they wouldn't open for Tanner? I listened today, and I'll swear I heard sounds. It sounded like somebody crying. I told Tanner and he just said 'Very likely.' What do you think Miss Crane saw? My God, it's awful! She ought to go away. I wonder if Tanner wouldn't think it was a good idea to send her to town to her mother till this case is settled."

Totty looked at him severely. They stood in the half-light of the porch, finishing their cigarettes before they went into the hall.

"Are you in love with this woman?" he demanded in his most paternal manner. "If you are, forget it. She's above you, my boy; she's meant for another. The wedding bells will toll when the young lord leads her to the altar. She loves you heart and soul, but yet she will not falter – a bit of poetry that I learnt many years ago. It's curious how it comes back to you."

Ferraby scowled at him.

"That you've any poetry at all in your soul, even doggerel poetry, is the most important and most revolting discovery I've made today," he snarled.

"Jealousy," said Totty complacently.

The police cyclist, his inner man refreshed, was waiting in the shadow of the porch. Totty did not notice him till his companion had gone. He was waiting for a dispatch to town.

"It's a funny thing, sergeant," he said, "but the moment you get down to the country it always seems like half-past twelve. Have you ever noticed that?"

"I notice everything, constable," said Totty.

"Who's that young fellow that came out and talked to me – a boy? You walked up to the door with him a little while ago."

"That young boy was Lord Lebanon – Viscount Lebanon," said Totty impressively.

"Oh!" said the unimpressed constable. "He talks very ordinary. Quite a nice fellow. As a matter of fact, I knew he was somebody important. He asked me a lot of questions about the work. He hasn't half got a good opinion of Mr Tanner."

"Did he mention me?" asked Totty anxiously.

"To tell you the truth, sergeant, he didn't. He was only out for a minute, then he went indoors again."

166

Totty found Tanner where he had left him. He was finishing his report to the chief constable, and folding it in an envelope.

"Is that messenger waiting – good. Well, how is Mrs Tilling?"

"She seems pretty scared, chief – " began Totty.

"You see too many talkies, Totty. Will you be kind enough not to call me 'chief.' If you feel you must be very precise you can address me as 'chief inspector,' but even that isn't necessary. Scared, is she? Humph!" Tanner bit his lip thoughtfully. "I wonder…"

"I'm wondering a bit too," said Totty. "There's no doubt at all that her husband's the murderer. I suppose they'll get him by tonight?"

"Her husband is not a murderer, but I have great hopes that they'll get him by tonight," said Tanner. "Here's the murderer." He held up his sealed envelope. "I think I've all the facts here, and the sequences, and I'll be very surprised if I'm wrong. And I don't mind telling you, Totty, that this is the most interesting case I've ever been engaged in."

21

Tanner looked towards the door, took two steps and flung it open. Gilder was standing on the threshold; he was carrying a little silver tray with a pot of coffee on it.

"Here's your coffee, captain," he said.

"How long were you waiting there?"

"Just arrived, sir, when you opened the door. In fact, I was wondering whether I'd knock on the door with my forehead, or kick," said the man good-humouredly.

Tanner pointed to a table.

"Put your tray down there," he said.

He shut the door on the servant, opened it quickly to make sure he was not still there, and closed it again.

"Lebanon was quite right – they do quite a lot of listening at Marks Priory," he said. "This door isn't too thick, either."

"Why don't you pinch him?" asked Totty.

"There's an excellent reason," said Tanner. "I've an idea that if I pinched him there'd be a lot of trouble. As it is, the need for a little private spying is seriously embarrassing that gentleman, the more so as his companion hasn't got half his wits, and Gilder has to do most of the delicate work."

He glanced round the room with a wry smile.

"A queer place, this, or, as Lebanon says, 'odd.' I'd give a lot of money to have the case finished and be out of it."

He took up the envelope.

"Give this to the courier – no, I'll give it to him myself."

Totty followed him out to the porch. The messenger hastily threw away a half-consumed cigarette and saluted.

"This is for the Chief Constable. Put it in your pouch and be very careful. You ought to be in London by eleven, and the Chief Constable will be waiting in his office for you."

The man wheeled his heavy cycle on to the drive, and with a splutter the machine started gathering speed as it flew down the drive.

He had turned the first bend, and only the dim reflection of his lights could be seen, when suddenly Tanner heard a crash, and the lights suddenly went out. The next second he heard a yell, and raced down the drive, Totty at his heels. There was shouting and a sound of struggle. When they came to the spot the cyclist was on his knees, the machine sprawled at one side of the road. Totty flashed on his lamp. The messenger's face was white; he had lost his cap and his hair was dishevelled. They assisted him to his feet and Tanner gave him a quick examination. No bones were broken, but he was badly shaken and bruised.

"There was a rope across the drive or something," he said shakily. "When I fell somebody jumped at me and tried to put something round my neck."

Totty flashed his light around. There was no sign of the assailant.

"What sort of man was he?"

"I don't know. I couldn't see; my light was out. He must have been pretty strong, for he half lifted me up. I punched him, but I don't think I hurt him."

Totty searched for the obstruction and found it. A rope had been tied from tree to tree breast-high, and had broken under the impact.

"You don't know which way he went?"

"No, sir."

The messenger limped over to his cycle, and with the aid of Totty's light made an examination. Nothing more serious had happened than a smashed lamp, and even this could be rectified with Totty's torch, which he strapped to the handlebar.

"You're not hurt – you're sure?" said Tanner.

He went over the man's limbs and found nothing broken.

"I'm all right, sir; I can get on. Gosh! I'd like to have got that bird!"

"You say he tried to put something round your neck? Perhaps he dropped it."

But when Totty went back to the house and got another torch there was no sign of the red scarf, and no evidence that would connect anybody with the attack.

"Is the letter all right?"

The man felt in his satchel and then made a discovery. The strap that held the pouch was half cut through, obviously by a sharp knife.

"That's what they wanted, eh?" said Tanner. "Quick workers here. All right, my son; stick the letter in your pocket, and explain to the Chief Constable why you had to double it up."

The man buttoned the letter into his hip pocket and started. They followed him at a distance down the drive and saw him turn on to the main road.

"He's safe now," said Tanner. "Quick workers, eh? Would you believe it? I think I was wise to send Ferraby with you – there might have been bad trouble."

Totty, who was prepared to reproach his superior for an act derogatory to his dignity, thought it discreet to drop the subject.

When they got to the Hall a curious thing happened. The big room was empty. They had hardly entered before Gilder came in. He was like a man who had been running, and obviously he was out of breath. His thin hair, usually brushed so neatly over his forehead, and his unpleasant face bore a curious, strained expression.

"Hullo!" said Tanner. "What's been happening to you?"

The man swallowed something.

"I fell asleep in my pantry – a fool thing to do – and had a bad dream."

"Is it damp in your pantry?"

Tanner was looking at his boots. They were wet, and sticking to his heels were two or three tufts of grass. The man looked from the boots to the detective and grinned.

"I went out for a smoke a while ago," he said.

He was moving off when Tanner called him back.

170

"You didn't dream about bicycles, by any chance, did you – motor-bicycles for choice?"

Gilder shook his head.

"No, sir, I dreamt about" – he considered – "earthquakes."

"I can almost admire that fellow," said Tanner when he had gone.

"What, Gilder?" said Sergeant Totty incredulously. "Did you see his boots?"

"I did, and you didn't till I called attention to them," said Tanner.

He sat down at Lady Lebanon's desk, picked up a pencil and nibbled at it.

"Mrs Tilling is a bit of a problem. In fact, I think she's our biggest immediate problem."

He got up and began to pace the room.

"Get the squad car," he said suddenly; "go round to the cottage, pick her up, take her to the 'White Hart,' and say nothing about it to anybody. We've got two men staying there, haven't we? Well, you can tell one of them to keep an eye on her."

"Suppose she won't leave the cottage?" said Totty.

"You will pick her up in your arms very gently, almost tenderly," said Tanner, extravagantly sarcastic; "you may even let her head rest upon your shoulder; you will carry her with the greatest care down the garden path and chuck her into the car. There is a time when there should be an end to all politeness. You may even hit her on the head, but take her to the 'White Hart.' "

Totty drifted out to the garage, found the chauffeur of the service car and drove with him to the gate of the cottage. The gate was open, though he distinctly remembered bolting it when he left. The second little gate was also wide open, and when he got to the door he found it ajar.

"Look here, sergeant" – it was the police chauffeur – "that window's been smashed!"

Totty put his light on to the window. Two panes had been broken; the window itself was open. His heart beating a little faster, he went into the dark passage and advanced carefully.

The sitting-room door was ajar, and when he went in he saw that the table had been overturned. Every picture on the walls had been smashed, and a broken chair which had been thrown on to the sofa was apparently the instrument used.

The next room was a bedroom. There was nobody here, but again he saw signs of destruction. The bed had been thrown bodily on to the floor; a wash-stand had been overturned, and the carpet was littered with scraps of broken water jugs.

These were the only two rooms disturbed, as far as he could see, but the back door was wide open. There was no sign of Mrs Tilling. He was contenting himself with a cursory examination from the doorstep, and was turning back into the house, when the chauffeur behind him said excitedly:

"There's somebody lying up there, near those fruit trees."

At the back of the house was a kitchen garden, and beyond a tiny orchard. Totty directed his light again and saw something huddled on the ground. It was a woman; he ran forward and bent over her. She was breathing. A woman without speech, terrified to the verge of madness; a woman who, when he lifted her up, could only stare at him, glare at him, and move quivering lips that made no sound.

He remembered Tanner's ironic instructions as he lifted her and carried her in his arms round the cottage through the gate into the car. She was moaning, and half-way to the inn began to make incoherent sounds. Fortunately there was nobody about at that hour of the night, and with the help of the landlady and a maid they got her into a room, and Totty went down to the phone and rang up Tanner.

"She's not injured at all?"

"Not so far as I can see, but she's as near to dead as makes no difference," said Totty. "It must have happened a few minutes before we got there. There was a candle in the bedroom, and the wick was still smouldering."

Tanner was so long silent that Totty thought he had left the instrument, and called him.

"All right, I'm just thinking." Tanner's voice was impatient. "Quick workers! Get a doctor for the woman – "

"I've done that. You ought to know me better, Tanner." Mr Totty was reproachful. "I thought of going back to the cottage and seeing what I could pick up."

"Come back to Marks Priory. You'll find nothing at the cottage, not even a thick ear. I'll phone the Chief Constable and get him to send some of his mobile police to take charge of the place. You're sure she's not hurt? By the way, that candle wick isn't very reliable. I've known extra long wicks to smoulder for sixteen minutes, especially if the candles are cheap."

Another long pause.

"Come back."

Totty stayed at the "White Hart" long enough to instruct one of the Scotland Yard men who had his lodgings there, and who had been detailed for an entirely different duty that night. Before he left the inn Ferraby had joined him and heard the story at first hand. He whistled softly.

"Poor little beggar! We look like having an exciting night. Look at me – the Wild West *in excelsis!*"

He opened his coat. Strapped about his waist was a pistol belt, from which two automatic holsters depended.

"Tanner's idea – you know him. Gives you a couple of guns and spends an hour telling you not to use them. Anyway, they feel grand, but who I'm going to shoot, and why, I haven't the slightest idea."

"If you get a chance of shooting you'll be lucky, my boy," said Totty, ominously. "It'll be like hitting back at a streak of lightning."

"I owe that streak of lightning one, anyway," said Ferraby between his teeth. "I haven't forgotten a certain four-poster in this hostelry, which was pretty near to being a gallows." Then earnestly: "I wish to heaven she was out of it!"

"Mrs Tilling?"

"Mrs Tilling! No, you know who I'm talking about – Miss Crane. She doesn't belong to this horrible atmosphere. I've tried to persuade Tanner to send her up to town."

"What did he say?" asked Totty curiously.

Ferraby chuckled in spite of his annoyance.

"He said if everybody who was in danger at Marks Priory had to go up to town, we'd have to hire a motor-bus. There's something in that room they won't open – Tanner's right there. I can't pass the door without my heart going into my mouth. There was a light in there tonight – I saw it from the outside of the house. It was only there a minute, and then it went out again. And I'll swear nobody went in through the door."

"Who's got the next room?"

"That was Amersham's room; it's a spare," said Ferraby as they drove back to the Priory. "Lined with panels; probably every panel's a door."

"What's on the other side?" asked the interested Totty.

"Miss Crane's room. I've been talking with Kelver, who knows something about the house. Out of curiosity he measured up the passage one day, and compared it with the width of the room, and said there was about three feet unaccounted for, and those three feet are between Miss Crane's room and the room that Lady Lebanon refuses to open. There must be a passage there."

He leaned over and spoke to the chauffeur.

"Stop for a minute. There's the room – the fourth window from the top of the porch on the right, and if you look – it's got tiny panes, like one of those old dungeon windows – my God!"

The window was suddenly illuminated. The glass was opaque, and it was impossible to see through it. It shone whitely, tiny squares of diffused light.

Ferraby leapt from the car, and Totty followed. They ran across the grass till they were immediately under the window. Presently they saw a shadow, a grotesque, shapeless thing. It moved slowly, took strangely unnatural shapes – and then the light went out.

22

They stared at one another in the darkness.

"A nice place, I don't think," said Totty, breathing heavily.

"Lend me your light."

Ferraby took it from his hand and put it on the wall. There was no window immediately beneath the mystery room, and apparently there was nothing here except the solid red brick wall of the building.

Then Totty heard an exclamation.

"Look at this!" whispered Ferraby. He was tracing a brick course with a pencil. "That's not mortar, that's iron painted like mortar! There's a door here."

He pulled a knife from his pocket – that blade which had once saved his life – opened the blade and picked at what appeared to be an ordinary-looking half-brick. His search was without success until he pressed it to test its stability. There was a click as the brick fell down like the lid of a box. In the cavity behind was a straight glass handle. Ferraby gripped it and turned, but nothing happened. He tugged again, but if there was a door here, as evidently there was, it had been fastened on the inside.

"Doing a little building, gentlemen?"

Ferraby spun round. He saw the figure which had come noiselessly behind them, but would not have distinguished him but for the voice.

"What have you found?"

Mr Gilder was interested, peered over their shoulders. As the light revealed the handle they heard him gasp.

"Well, I'll go to hell!" he said, and his profanity was so sincere that they knew the discovery was as much of a surprise to him as it had been to them. "Well, I'll be damned!" he varied his prophecy. "I have never seen that."

Ferraby pushed up the lid; it fastened with a click.

"Is that so?" half whispered Gilder.

"There was a light in that window just now," said Totty. "Who went into that room?"

Gilder looked up.

"Brooks, I guess," he said readily. "Her ladyship's got a lot of letters there that she doesn't want the police to see – private letters, which is to be expected in a lady, and naturally she wants to remove 'em before Mr Tanner makes his search. I guess it was Brooks. Anything happening down at the village, gentlemen?"

"It's very quiet," said Totty, "very, very quiet. If you want any further information you'd better read the morning newspapers. They won't know anything, either. Where is her ladyship – gone to bed?"

"No, sir. The last time I saw her she was playing backgammon with his lordship in the saloon – you gentlemen have not seen the saloon. It's about the only place in the house that's got any privacy today."

Ferraby had seen it. Isla had shown him over the lower floor. It was a small, rather dismal and cheerless apartment, which the Louis Quinze furniture did not brighten.

The common room seemed quite cheerful to the two men when they came in out of the night. Gilder brought them each a whisky and soda, made up the fire, for the night had grown cold, and went off, as he told them, in search of Brooks.

Tanner was on the phone to the Yard, and was telling the Chief Constable a great deal more than he intended telling him on the phone. The situation was a little urgent, and he could not wait for the arrival of the messenger before requesting certain assistance from headquarters.

He finished his work in the small drawing-room, turned out the light and joined Ferraby. Totty had gone upstairs to test the door of the mystery room, and came down with a negative report.

He expected to create a sensation by the story of the light, and was disappointed at the calm way in which Tanner received the news. That was the chief inspector's exasperating way.

"I know. I've seen it twice. As a matter of fact, Ferraby told me before he told you. It's very odd of him, but that's what he did. The door in the wall is interesting. I suspected it, of course, but I couldn't find it. When you come to think of it, there had to be a door in the wall, or my theory was a wash-out. Totty, go and find Lord Lebanon and ask him to come and be sociable. That young man has only told half his story, and I have an idea that the other half is likely to be even more interesting."

Totty found the youth alone, throwing dice on to a backgammon board.

"Hullo! I thought you were in bed. Do you play backgammon? I'll play you for money or love – and I'll beat you. That is why my mother will never play with me."

"I haven't played it for years," said Totty, who had never played it at all. "The chief wondered if you'd like to come in and have a chow."

"What's that? If it's a talk, I'd love it. If it is something to eat, I'm not hungry. I've been reciting 'Casabianca' to myself for the past half-hour just to hear the sound of my own voice. My mother is writing letters."

He took Totty's arm in his.

"Do you know your grandfather, Mr Totty? If you don't you ought to be very thankful. I know my great-grandfather and my great-great-grandfather and innumerable ancestors, and I wish I didn't. My dear mother sets great store by what is known as 'the line.' I hoped, when you told me this morning that you were a member of an old Italian family, that you were lying. I am sure you were. I'll bet you don't even know your own father?"

Totty protested indignantly.

"I'm disappointed," said Lebanon. "I should like to meet somebody who admitted they had been found on a doorstep! When are you fellows going away? I think I'll come to Scotland Yard with you and have a bed in Mr Tanner's office. I shall feel safe then."

"You're safe anywhere, my lord," said Totty graciously, and added: "If I am about."

"I don't think you'd be much use," said the frank young man. "Personally, I'd prefer to rely on Tanner. You're too near my size for me to respect you. Little men don't respect little men. It's the big fellows they secretly admire."

By this time they had got to the common room. He greeted Tanner with a nod, and repeated his suggestion. Bill laughed good-humouredly.

"Scotland Yard would be a fine lodging for you; at any rate it would be near to the House of Lords. By the way, have you taken your seat?"

Lebanon shook his head, chose a cigar almost as large as himself from the box, and lit it.

"No, mother's not keen on my going in for politics. I've got a complete list of the things she's not keen on my doing. They'll make a fine book one of these days. I'm rather glad you're staying tonight." He looked round and lowered his voice. "Her ladyship isn't quite as glad! She gave me a fearful ragging, and said I was responsible, which of course was ridiculous."

"Where is Miss Crane?" asked Tanner.

Lebanon made a little face.

"She's gone to bed, I think. She's not terribly sociable. I'm going to have a very dull time when I'm married. She's awfully kind and all that, but we have nothing in common."

Here one member of his audience was entirely in agreement.

Lebanon sat up and grew more confidential.

"I'll tell you who are sick about your staying – those two fellows."

Gilder came through the door, apparently concerned in replenishing a fire which he had made up only a few minutes before.

"I don't want you, Gilder."

"I was going to look at the fire, my lord."

"What time do you go to bed?" asked Tanner.

The man he addressed did not answer.

"Gilder, Mr Tanner is speaking to you."

Gilder looked round with an affected start.

178

"I beg your pardon. I thought you were addressing his lordship. I have no regular hours, Mr Tanner."

"Do you sleep in this part of the house?"

Gilder smiled.

"When I sleep I sleep in this part of the house," he said.

Brooks came ambling down the stairs. There was about his movements a great weariness.

"It sounds as if you don't sleep very well."

"On the contrary, sir," said Gilder, with extravagant politeness, "when I sleep I sleep most excellently well."

Brooks was standing, an interested spectator, his big jaws working. He was a chewing-gum addict.

"Do you want anything?" asked Tanner.

Brooks turned his head slowly in the direction of the questioner.

"I just wanted to see if Gilder wasn't getting into trouble," he said lightly.

Tanner got up from the settle on which he was sitting.

"I'm not quite sure whether you're being flippant because I'm an unimportant visitor, or whether that is your natural manner."

Gilder hastened to explain.

"Mr Brooks comes from America, the home of the free, from the wide open spaces where men are men," he said elaborately.

He turned and fiddled with the fire. In two seconds Tanner was behind him, gripped him by the arm and spun him round.

"When people get fresh with me I sometimes put them in a space which is neither wide nor open, and certainly isn't free!"

He saw the look of resentment in the man's eyes, and went on: "Suppose I took rather a dislike to you two men, and I decided you knew a great deal more than you were prepared to admit about these murders? Suppose I were to hold you as accessories, and take you down to the station – tonight? You aren't smiling."

And here he spoke the truth, for the two men were unusually glum.

"That would be a little embarrassing, wouldn't it?"

Gilder was taken aback, a little alarmed, if his eyes told the truth.

"Why, I shouldn't like to put you to that inconvenience, chief."

"It's no inconvenience at all. There are forty men in this park," said Tanner slowly, "all trained, skilled officers from Scotland Yard. They arrived by motor tender five minutes ago, and this house is surrounded. There will be no murder at Marks Priory tonight."

He spoke slowly. Totty stared at him, his mouth open.

"And it would be a very simple matter to find the necessary escort for you. Have you any doubt on the subject?"

He took a whistle from his pocket and put it to his lips. Ferraby, watching, thought Brooks was on the point of dropping from fear.

"No, chief, there's no reason why you should go to extremes," said Gilder. "If I've said anything I shouldn't have said, I beg your pardon."

He looked at Lebanon, who sat, gaping from one to the other.

"Can I do anything for you, my lord?"

"Get us some whisky and soda, will you? You can go, Brooks."

Brooks went up the stairs again a little unsteadily.

"Phew!" said Lebanon. "Is that true? Forty men? I say, what organisation!"

"To be exact, there are thirty-six. I'm counting the chauffeurs," said Tanner.

He walked round the back of an old couch, leaned on it and looked down at the master of Marks Priory.

"When you were at Scotland Yard this morning you rather suggested that you yourself were in some danger, Lord Lebanon. Did you mean that? Have you had any sort of threat, or has anybody attempted to hurt you?"

Lebanon looked up in surprise.

"I didn't know that I'd suggested that," he said. He thought a while. "Lots of things have happened – odd little things that hardly seem worth talking about, but I think I can say that nobody has attempted my life." He smiled. "If they had I should certainly have died!"

Tanner now came to more delicate ground.

"Did you ever see your father?"

"Of course," said the other, surprised. "Not in recent years. He was a hopeless invalid. But when I was a boy – he was an ever so much bigger fellow than me, and terribly strong. There's a legend round here that when he was young he lifted a farm wagon out of a ditch."

"Have you a picture of him – a photograph? Is there one in the house?"

"No, I don't think there is," said the other slowly. Curiously enough, I came upon an old snapshot taken of him in his invalid chair. I don't remember who took it, but it was between the leaves of a book in the library. I showed it to mother, and she tore it up without even looking at it."

"That was a queer thing to do, wasn't it?" said Tanner.

Lebanon smiled.

"Yes – well, mother is a little odd. It was, I admit, an awful-looking picture of him, but can you understand it?"

Bill laughed.

"If it was an awful-looking picture I can well understand it," he said. "Was he clean-shaven, or did he have a beard, or what?"

"He had a beard – not as I remember him, but I'm talking about the photograph."

"Can you remember any other strange things happening which affected you?"

Lord Lebanon put down the magazine, the pages of which he had been turning.

"You want something really sinister, something that sounds like a page torn from a story? Well, I'll tell you. There have been two occasions when Gilder has brought me a whisky and soda, when I have remembered drinking it – and little more. The last time I woke up in my room, in the dark. I was in my pyjamas, and I should probably have turned over and gone to sleep again but for the fact that I had a perfectly splitting headache. I rang the bell, and when Gilder came up he told me I'd fainted, which was ridiculous – I've never fainted in my life."

"What do you suggest happened to you?" asked Tanner.

Lebanon shook his head.

"I don't know, but it happened twice after I'd had a drink. Naturally I remember the more painful episode. There was a sequel to that. When I came down in the morning it looked as though a bull had been let loose in this very room. The furniture was smashed, and there was every sign of a real wild party."

"I heard about that," said Totty.

"Amersham was in it, and so were the two footmen. I'd hate to think that mother was in it, and really I can't imagine her in any situation that was undignified."

Gilder came in with the drinks. They were already poured out. He handed a glass to Lebanon and to the three men.

"Can't you bring me a decanter and a siphon?" asked the young man angrily. "You aren't even civilised, Gilder."

The man took no offence. He merely grinned cheerfully.

"I thought you'd like a quick drink, my lord. I'll remember the decanter in future."

He took the tray out, closing the door with a thud.

"I wonder if you've ever in your experience visited a household like this?" said Lebanon, and took a sip.

Before Bill could reply he made a wry face.

"Taste this," he said.

Tanner took the glass and drank a little. Overriding the taste of the malt was a harsh, bitter taste.

"Well, is yours like that?"

Tanner took a sip of his own; it was quite normal. "It's rather queer we should be talking about what happened to me," said Lebanon.

He looked round for some handy receptacle. On the table was a small bowl filled with roses, and into this he carefully poured the drink and set down the empty glass.

"That's exactly the stuff I drank on the night of the party," he said.

On the other side of the door Gilder was standing. He found it a little difficult to hear, for the wood was thick. He hoped that Brooks was listening from the stairs. It was not a moment to miss any scraps of information.

He heard a step behind him: it was Lady Lebanon. "What are they talking about?" she asked in a voice little above a whisper.

He moved away from the door. His deep voice carried too far.

"I don't know, my lady," he said.

"Do you think we could get rid of these men?" she asked anxiously.

He shook his head.

"I'm afraid not. There are forty new men come down by tender from Scotland Yard. They're in the grounds somewhere. I haven't told Brooks; he's getting restless. He says he's going to quit. These detectives are frightening him."

She looked at him with a little smile.

"Do they frighten you?"

He shook his head.

"No, nothing frightens me. I'm in now, and I'll go through with it."

"Tell Brooks there will be a thousand pounds for him if we get this thing over without a discovery," she said.

He shook his head again, dubiously.

"Do you think we shall? Brooks has got cold feet. Say, I'm getting a little bit worried about him. Shoot him over to America – that's my advice. If he loses his nerve he's going to be a whole lot of trouble to me."

He crept back to the door and listened. There was no sound, not even the murmur of voices. He looked round for Lady Lebanon, but she had gone. Turning the handle he walked into the common room. As he surmised, it was empty. He heard voices from the end of the corridor. Lebanon was identifying a portrait that hung on the wall: an ancient Lebanon who bore some resemblance to his father.

Gilder looked at the glasses. One was suspiciously empty. He picked it up and turned it upside down, and a drop of moisture came from it. That glass was Lebanon's: there was a tiny red ink mark on the stem which none of them had detected. He looked round, saw the bowl of roses, lifted it gingerly, and sniffed. Whisky! So that was what had happened to Lord Lebanon's nightcap.

Walking to the foot of the stairs, he whistled softly, and his stout companion came down. Gilder pointed to the glass.

"He didn't drink that stuff," he said.

Brooks breathed heavily.

183

"Of course he didn't drink it. You made it too strong. I told you he'd taste it."

"He was getting used to it," said Gilder gloomily. "Has he been talking?"

Brooks nodded.

"Yeah. Kelver must have told that little runt about the rough house, and Tanner got him to talk about it. He knows he's being doped. Do you realise, what that means?"

"Sure I realise," said Gilder coolly.

"Did you speak to her?" asked Brooks anxiously.

"Yes. There's nothing to worry about."

Brooks exploded.

"Sez you! There's a hell of a lot to worry about. There are all these English cops, and that bird Tanner's wise to what's happening here. If the truth comes out we're in a jam – we might get a lifer for this. Where are they?" He looked round.

"They're going up the hall staircase to his lordship's room, I guess – I heard him say 'wireless,' and that's the only wireless in the house – s-sh! Here's one of them."

It was Totty. He stood for a moment in the doorway surveying them.

"The brothers Mick and Muck," he said sarcastically.

"Is there anything I can do for you?" asked Gilder.

"There's a lot you can do for me, boy," said Totty. "I suppose you'll be up all night?"

Gilder smiled.

"If you'll be up all night, sir, I shall be up all night."

"Does it ever strike you fellows that you might be getting yourselves into a bit of trouble?"

Brooks paused at the door, a tray in his hand, and looked anxiously at his companion, but Mr Gilder was smiling.

"Man," he said oracularly, "is born to trouble as the sparks fly upward."

23

Gilder was a type that baffled Mr Totty: he was so offensively unimpressed by the majesty and power of the law. Moreover, he was perhaps the one man in the world who had ever made Sergeant Totty feel small, and that admirable man resented the painful experience.

He was not interested in wireless, but for some reason or other he hated being alone. For this night the regulations which governed Marks Priory had been relaxed. The doors between the servants' wing and the main hall had been left unlocked. Mr Kelver was probably awake. Totty was on a mission of discovery, and had passed the door of the saloon when he heard his name called. It was Lady Lebanon.

"Won't you come in, sergeant? Has Mr Tanner gone to bed?"

"Not yet, my lady."

He was flattered at the invitation.

"Do you mind my cigar?"

She hated cigars, and even Willie was forbidden to smoke in the saloon, but she was graciousness itself, went out and found an ashtray for him, and suggested the most comfortable chair.

On her knees was a small velvet box.

"My cash-box," she smiled, when she saw Totty's eyes on it. "I always take it up the last thing every night."

"Very wise of you, my lady. You can never be sure that there isn't a tea-leaf – a thief around."

"You're a sergeant, aren't you, Mr Totty?"

"Temporarily," said Mr Totty.

"And Mr Tanner is – ?"

"Chief inspector. There's practically no difference between us," said Totty loftily. "It's merely a question of rank."

She inclined her head.

"Will you forgive me if I ask you whether you receive a very large salary? I suppose you do. Yours must be very important work."

He was quite prepared to explain how important, but she went on: "I should so much like to know what is happening," she said, "and what the police think about this case. I suppose there are things arising every few minutes – clues, or whatever you call them?"

"Any number," said Totty.

"And when you make a new discovery you tell Mr Tanner? And what does he say?"

Here Totty could not be perfectly truthful. He had a poignant memory of a number of things that Tanner had said when he had taken "evidence" to him.

"Usually," he admitted, "he says he's known all about that for a week. There's a lot of petty jealousy in the service."

"I suppose he does place a lot of reliance on you?" she insisted. "Somebody said you were his right-hand man."

Totty smirked.

"He was very curious" – Lady Lebanon spoke slowly – "rather stupidly, I thought, about the room I didn't want him to see. Do you remember?"

Totty remembered, and was on the point of blurting out his discovery, but she gave him no chance.

"Suppose you went to him and said: 'I've seen this room, and there's nothing there but a few old pictures'?"

All that was vain in Sergeant Totty went out at that moment. He became his cold, practical, not over-intelligent self.

"That would satisfy him, wouldn't it? He does take a lot of notice of what you say?"

He did not answer.

"Suppose you say," she went on silkily, "that there is nothing in that room? It would save me a lot of trouble."

"Quate!" said Totty.

She opened the little box and he heard the rustle of paper. Very deliberately she took out four notes. From where he stood he recognised them as being for fifty pounds each.

"One feels so perfectly helpless" – her well-bred voice droned on – "I mean, when one is battling against trained and skilful men from Scotland Yard. Very naturally they see something suspicious in the most innocent actions, and it's nice to know one has a friend at court."

She closed the box and got up. The four notes dropped on to the chair where she had been sitting.

"Good night, Sergeant Totty."

"Good night, my lady."

She had reached the door.

"Excuse me" – he held out the notes to her – "you have left your money behind."

"I don't remember leaving any money behind," she said deliberately. She did not look at the paper in his hand.

"This may remind you," he said. "You never know when you may want this money."

She took it from him without confusion or embarrassment.

"I was hoping you might want it," she said. "It's a great pity."

He followed her out into the corridor, watched her with a smile of triumph till she passed out of sight, and then he swaggered back into the common room and found Tanner sitting alone.

"It's a great pity," he repeated.

The chief inspector looked up.

"What's a great pity?"

"That I don't want two hundred pounds that her ladyship offered me."

Bill Tanner frowned.

"What do you mean?"

"She doesn't want that room opened, that's what I mean."

"Oh! I never imagined she did."

And then he connected Totty's statements.

"She offered you money?"

"She left it behind on the chair, which is exactly the same thing."

187

"What did you say?"

Mr Totty drew himself up.

"What did I say?" he said sternly. "I told her she mustn't do a thing like that; that I was a sergeant and would probably get a promotion out of this case – in fact, I have been practically promised, haven't I?"

"No," said Tanner. "Stick to the facts. What did she say then?"

"What could she say?" said Totty. "She burst into tears and went upstairs."

Tanner was impressed.

"That sounds like a lie, but there's probably a bit of truth in it. She doesn't want the room opened? Well, we'll open it tomorrow."

"And I'll tell you what you'll find," said Totty confidentially. "Stacks of bootleg booze! I got it from the first. Why American footmen?"

Tanner looked at him admiringly.

"You're about the worst detective I've ever met," he said. "If it wasn't for your qualities as a faithful hound you'd make a good postman. Why American footmen? I'll tell you why – because they have no friends in England and no families. She's taking no risk of their discussing her private affairs."

"They're using this place as the headquarters of a gang – " began Totty.

"Gang my grandmother's aunt! Motion pictures are your ruin, Totty. Why do they want a gang when they have all the pickings in the world? Lebanon paid over three hundred thousand pounds in death duties, which means that young man has quite a lot of money."

Totty coughed and changed the subject.

"Where's Ferraby?" he asked.

"I don't know – dodging about the house somewhere."

The police officer in Sergeant Totty came suddenly to the surface.

"What about those forty men who are in the grounds?" he said. "Have any canteen arrangements been made for them?"

Chief Inspector Tanner came close to his side and lowered his voice.

"There are not forty men or women or children in the grounds, so far as I know. Keep your big mouth shut, will you?"

Sergeant Totty inclined his head gracefully. He could take a hint.

"What's the idea?" he said in the same tone.

"I'll tell you the idea, Totty." Tanner's voice was little above a whisper. "I want all the murders of tonight to be committed inside this house."

The little detective went cold.

"How many do you expect?" he asked.

"I think you will be the first," said Tanner.

He was feeling rather pleased with himself for the moment, and when Inspector Tanner was pleased with himself his sense of humour took curious shapes.

The old lord's room was a place of fear to Isla Crane. She could never remember any occasion when she was so tired that she could fall immediately to sleep. Night after night she had sat up in her bed, her hands clasping her knees, listening. There were calm nights, when the only sounds which broke the silence were the crack of the age-old panelling and queer rustlings that might have been mice, or the touch of ghostly hands. There were nights when the soughing of the wind added a new terror to the hours of darkness.

Once, when the electric light plant had failed, she lay and quaked till daylight, and thereafter she always had a small night-light by the side of her bed. It was a place of ghosts, of ugly memories, and had frowsy auras that seemed to cling to the wall like fungi. At the best, and on the hottest days, there was a queer, musty smell about the old lord's room.

Tonight it was full of strange sounds of movement; whispering voices came to her from the dark. Once she thought she saw a panel move, and heard a floor-board creak outside the door. She had heard all these things before, and should have been immune to fear.

She had a mother and two small sisters, and she was paying for their happiness. If somebody would take her away – but it must be somebody who could supply the comforts which Lady Lebanon would instantly cut off. It never occurred to her that her ladyship would not dare cut the allowance.

John Ferraby…? He was filling her imagination. A detective? Lady Lebanon had said it was queer, and had suggested the war to explain his peculiar occupation. What was his salary? It all came back to money; everything did. She liked many people, but she liked Ferraby so well that he could occupy hours of her thoughts. It wasn't so ridiculous as it might seem…

She wondered in what style he lived, whether he had any private income – everything came back to money. She wanted to marry Willie Lebanon less than he wished to marry her. Yet she liked him, and was terribly sorry for him at times. Perhaps if he were married Lady Lebanon would retire and give the boy an opportunity… She shook her head. That wasn't Lady Lebanon's way, and she didn't like Willie well enough.

She turned from side to side in the bed, pulled the covers over her shoulders, threw them off again. Presently she felt drowsy and began to dream. But when she dreamed it was of things that she had put out of her thoughts in her waking moments. All the pigeonholes of her mind were opened, and the things she wanted to forget crept out. How stupid of Lady Lebanon to leave the scarf in the drawer! At any time that big man might search the desk, and if he searched the desk he would find it. What had induced her to leave that damning evidence for the most careless of searchers to find?

The scarf should be burnt. She did not realise she was out of bed. As she turned the key in the lock of her door, she did not feel it. She had her consciousness only in her dreams; was obsessed by one idea – the scarf must be burnt, that little red scarf with the metal tag.

Bill Tanner heard the click of the lock as he was giving his final instructions to Ferraby. He walked quickly to the foot of the stairs and looked up, raising his hand to caution the two men.

"Quiet!" he said.

They stood motionless, silent. The white figure came slowly down the stairs. Isla was staring ahead of her; her hands were outstretched as though she were feeling her way along some invisible wall. She was talking, very quietly, very slowly.

"It must be burnt," she said.

Totty opened his mouth to speak, but Bill's glare silenced him.

She reached the bottom step, walked uncertainly towards the desk.

"It must be burnt," she said, in that monotonous tone which is the sleepwalker's own. "You must burn that scarf."

She fumbled at the drawer. It was locked, but in her imagination she opened it.

"The scarf should be burnt – you murdered him with that – I saw it in your hand when you came into the house – you murdered him with that. It must be burnt."

She was moving towards the stairs again. Ferraby took a step towards her, but Bill grabbed him and threw him back. Slowly she went up, Tanner behind her. He saw her go into her room; the door closed softly and the lock snapped.

"You murdered him with that."

Whom was she addressing in her dreams? Mr Tanner had a very good idea.

24

He heard another door open. Lady Lebanon came out. She was still dressed.

"Was that Isla?" she said. "Miss Crane?"

He nodded.

"Was she walking in her sleep – how distressing! Where did you see her?"

"She came down to the hall," said Tanner.

Lady Lebanon drew a long breath.

"She's rather *distraite*. I think I ought to send her away into the country for a month. When she's like that – "

"Have you seen her?"

Lady Lebanon nodded.

"Yes, twice. The trouble is, she talks the most dreadful nonsense when she's in that condition. Did she speak at all?

"Nothing that I could hear," said Bill untruthfully.

He thought she was relieved. She was entitled to be.

"Good night, Mr Tanner. I will speak to Isla later. It isn't advisable to wake her up immediately, but unless she is awakened she may walk again."

Bill Tanner went down into the hall, a very preoccupied man. His two subordinates had been impressed. Totty was unusually silent, and did not offer a ready-made theory.

"Get on to the inn and find out if that woman is calm enough to be questioned – Mrs Tilling."

When Totty had gone: "What do you make of it, Ferraby? She knows who committed the murder, obviously."

Ferraby turned a glum face to him.

"I'm afraid she does, though of course she may be dreaming. After all, she knew that scarf had been burnt, and she may have guessed it came from that drawer. You can't hold it against people what they say in their sleep."

"I'm not holding anything against the young lady. You can set your mind at rest," said Tanner testily.

Then he put into words the question that Isla had asked herself.

"Have you got any money? No, I don't mean in your pocket. Have you any private means?"

The young man flushed guiltily.

"I've three hundred a year."

"Splendid," said Tanner. "That's exactly three hundred a year more than I've got. You're rather keen on her, aren't you?"

"Who – Miss Crane? Good Lord! How absurd! I couldn't – "

"Don't dither," said Tanner kindly. "I know you can't raise your eyes to the old squire's daughter. I've read about such things in books and seen them in plays. But it strikes me that she might be happier in a South Kensington flat than she could possibly be at Marks Priory. You'll excuse me if I help forward your little romance. But I'm in a romantic mood tonight."

"She'd never think of me in that way – " began Ferraby.

"You say that because you're very young, and you make the mistake of classifying women into social strata, and believe that each stratum has its own peculiar code. Women are all women – never forget that, Ferraby. When the Lord created Eve he practically finished his job, and there's been no change – a little general improvement perhaps. But you'll discover, when you learn to think, that the only difference between a twenty-thousand-a-year girl and the office stenographer is that one pays more for her clothes. If you don't mind my being indelicate, I would say that if you saw them in their underclothes you wouldn't know the difference, because they all wear the best that money can buy, for some reason which I've never been able to fathom."

Ferraby stared at him.

"I didn't realise you were an authority on the subject."

"I am an authority on most subjects," said Bill.

He took a cigar out of the box which Gilder had left, pinched it and smelt it.

"If this hasn't been poisoned by the wicked footman it ought to be good," he said.

"What was wrong with that whisky he brought to Lebanon?"

"Doped," said Bill. "I think I know the drug that was used."

"Why?"

"Lebanon thought that they had something on tonight. He didn't mention who the 'they' were, but we can guess that too. Apparently they're in the habit of giving him queer-tasting drinks when they want him out of the way. I wish he had drunk it."

Ferraby's eyes opened.

"But why?" he asked again, and he was concerned that Tanner laughed.

"Because if he were out of the way it would save me a lot of embarrassment tonight. In the morning the Chief Constable is sending me three people who can clear up this mystery more effectively than I – I asked him to send them down, and they'll be here by ten."

"Somebody from the Yard?"

"I'll not satisfy your curiosity – think over all the people I'm likely to send for: it will keep you awake tonight."

Totty came back at that moment. The woman was sleeping.

"That's satisfactory," said Tanner. "Any other news?"

"Yes; they've pinched Tilling at Stirling. He left the train at Edinburgh, but the police picked him up, and they're detaining him."

" 'Detain' is a better word than 'arrest.' Where are those liveried cut-throats?"

"They're in their pantry," said Totty. "I heard them talking together. You mean the Americans?"

"I wonder what they talk about," said Tanner, and smiled. "If they only knew it, this is very nearly their last night at Marks Priory."

"Are you taking them?"

"I don't know yet; it all depends," he said, and began to search for a pack of cards, for he had a weakness for patience.

Gilder and his companion had a great deal to talk about. Brooks did most of the talking. The tall American slumped in his chair, a neat whisky at his elbow, a half-smoked cigar in the corner of his mouth.

"Ah, shut up," he growled at last. "You make me ill! Don't you think I'm worried too? She was walking in her sleep tonight, that girl – and she was talking, and talking a whole lot that didn't help us any."

He looked thoughtfully at the other.

"Brooks, I'm going into her room tonight and take her out."

Brooks stared aghast.

"With the detectives in the house?"

"With all Scotland Yard in the house," said Gilder grimly. "I'm not going to take any more risk – not that kind of risk anyway."

Brooks shook his head in awed admiration.

"Have you told the old woman?"

"To hell with the old woman!" rumbled Gilder. "She doesn't mean a damn thing to me tonight."

He got up, opened a drawer of a little chest, took out a flat leather case, unstrapped it, and pulled back the flap. There was a neat kit of tools here, and after careful scrutiny he selected a pair of long, thin-nosed pliers. He tested them on a piece of wire, then, going to the door, took out the key and put it on the outside. Inserting the nose of the pliers, he turned it and locked the door. Another twist of his wrist and it was unlocked.

Mr Gilder was a careful man with considerable foresight. There was not a lock in the house that he did not oil once a week, for he took no chances.

Restoring the key to the inner side of the door, he put the pliers in his pocket.

"Where are you going to put her?" asked Brooks.

"In my room," said the other curtly.

"Suppose Tanner – "

"Oh, shut up, will you! You're fording the river before it starts to rain. You'd better go back home, Brooks."

"I guess we'll both be lucky to go back home," said the other gloomily.

"Listen!" Gilder laid his big hand on the man's knee. "You've had a pretty easy job, and you've been well paid for it. When you told that bull you hadn't saved money you were lying. I don't say you've got enough to live on for the rest of your life, but you've got the makings."

"I'd give a thousand dollars to be back in Philadelphia," said Brooks.

"You can get there steerage for a hundred and fifty," said the practical man.

He looked at his watch.

"Time's getting on. I'll go along and see if they want anything. Maybe they'll go to bed – even Scotland Yard men must sleep sometimes."

He peeped into the room from a place of observation which he had used before, a convenient slit in the panel, which did not owe its existence to accident. Tanner was playing patience at one table, Totty was manipulating a pack of cards at another. The other detective was not in the room.

He strolled back along the passage and up the stairs. As he turned into the corridor he saw somebody going into Isla's room. It was Lady Lebanon, and he drew back out of sight.

It had taken a long time before Isla's drowsy voice asked who was there, a seemingly interminable time before the door was unlocked. She went in, and closed the door behind her. Isla was sitting on the bed, her head drooping, only half awake.

"Is anything the matter?" she muttered.

Lady Lebanon shook her gently by the shoulder.

"Wake up, Isla."

She looked at the little night-light.

"Do you always sleep with that?" she asked. "It's very bad for you."

"Lately, yes."

She saw a silver box on the table by the side of the bed, and the woman opened it, and looked disapprovingly at the contents.

"Cigarettes – do you smoke?" and, when the girl nodded: "I don't like it very much in a woman," she said. "You're comfortable here?" She looked around. "I have only been through this door twice in the past five years."

Isla shuddered.

"I loathe this room," she said vehemently.

The cold eyes of the woman were on her.

"You've never said so before. One room is as good as another, and this was once the best room in the house. There used to be secret doors here, but I think my husband had them screwed up. The man who planned this room lived a hundred years ago," she went on.

Her mind went instinctively to The Line.

"He was rather eccentric. He never saw anybody. They used to pass his meals through a panel somewhere." She felt along the panelling. "And there used to be a passageway here, in the very heart of the wall."

She followed a train of thought which was very easy to follow: The Line that led back to the great men of the house.

"Courcy Lebanon – that was his name. He married one of the Hamshaws. Her mother was a blood relation of Monmouth." She sighed. "That branch has died out," she said in a whisper.

Then, with an effort, she tore herself from the past.

"I shouldn't sleep with a light; it's very bad for you."

The girl's head was drooping again.

"Isla! I'm sorry, but you must wake up." She shook her less gently. "You must wake up, Isla."

The girl's head drooped to her shoulder.

"I'm awfully tired. I'm half asleep now."

Yet she heard the click of the lock as it turned.

"Why did you do that?" she asked.

"The Priory is full of strange people, and there are others in the grounds," said Lady Lebanon. She sat down on the edge of the bed. "You walked in your sleep tonight." It was almost an accusation.

Isla stared at her.

197

"Did I? I wish I didn't. I never did that before – " She stopped suddenly.

"Before what?"

"Before that dreadful night." Her voice was shaking. "When the furniture was broken and Dr Amersham… I thought he was killed."

She covered her face with her hands.

"If you hadn't come down you would have seen nothing," said the older woman harshly.

Then suddenly she leaned over towards the girl, and there was an intensity and an emotion in her voice that Isla had never heard before.

"Isla, anything may happen tonight. I may be – " She did not finish her sentence. "I hope it can be avoided, but I must be prepared. I want you to marry Willie – do you hear? I want you to marry Willie."

There was desperation in her tone. The hand that gripped the girl's arm tightened painfully.

"I want you to marry him today – this morning."

Isla Crane looked round at her, dazed. "Today? That's impossible! I couldn't marry at such notice. I – I haven't really thought of it seriously."

"You can marry today," said the woman doggedly. "I've had the licence for a week."

"He'd hate it. Does he know?"

"It doesn't matter whether he knows or not," said Lady Lebanon impatiently. "He'll do as I tell him. Willie is the last of the Lebanons – do you realise that? The last link in the chain. A weak link. There was another weak link – Geoffrey Lebanon – weaker than Willie. He married his cousin, Jane Secamore. You'll see her portrait in the Great Hall. She left him at the altar."

Isla listened, wondering what was coming next, and when Lady Lebanon spoke she was shocked to silence.

"She left him at the altar – but she had several children."

"A horrible idea! Dreadful!" gasped the girl.

'I don't agree." Lady Lebanon sat straight-backed and seemed to be giving judgment. Isla had the feeling that her words had in them a finality which could not be disturbed. "I don't agree. Jane was one of the greatest of the Lebanon women. You realise you are a Lebanon yourself, Isla – that your great-grandfather was the brother of the eighteenth viscount? Whatever happens your children will be in the family when you are married. They will bear the Lebanon name."

Isla heard her sigh. She seemed to relax, for her manner was easier and her voice had lost the strain.

"If you find your life with Willie impossible, I shall be very understanding," she said.

She got up from the bed.

"The car will be ready at eleven."

With an effort Isla roused herself.

"I can't do it," she said. "I can't possibly do it! I don't love Willie. I – I love another man."

Lady Lebanon looked at her quickly.

"Young Ferraby?" A long pause. "Well, suppose you do? I've told you I would be very understanding. Don't you realise what you'll be doing? A wonderful thing – you will be founding a new race. The family will find a new strength. The Lebanon women have always been greater than the men."

Something swished against the door. Lady Lebanon heard it and turned quickly.

"What was that?" asked the girl in a frightened whisper.

"It's Gilder. And that's another reason why you must marry quickly. These men are getting out of hand. I may not be able to control them after tonight."

She came back quickly to the girl, bent over her and whispered: "Gilder mustn't know you're going to be married. You understand that, Isla? At all costs he must not know."

There was a knock. She went swiftly to the door, and unlocked it. Gilder was standing outside, Isla heard the deep boom of his voice, and then the door closed on him.

She was dropping back into unconsciousness, and roused herself, noticing that Lady Lebanon had left the door ajar. She dragged herself across the floor and closed it, then, coming back to the bed, almost fell upon it, drawing the clothes over her.

She was asleep, yet awake. Her mind was working; insoluble problems came in procession, were examined and despaired of. Yet her breathing was regular.

She had been lying there a quarter of an hour when somebody tried the handle of the door. It yielded, and Gilder came quietly into the room.

"It wasn't locked after all."

The terrified man outside was shaking.

"Where's her ladyship?"

"Never mind about her ladyship. Give me that blanket." He tiptoed to the side of the bed, and, clutching the girl by the shoulder, shook her.

"Come along, miss. I want you to come with me, miss." She did not move; not by a flutter of eyelid did she show signs of wakefulness.

"She's right out," he said. "Listen in the passage."

"Why not leave her?" urged Brooks.

"I'm taking no chances," said the gaunt American. "Go and look when I tell you!"

When the man returned he was hushed to silence with a warning finger. Isla was sitting up in bed, her eyes wide open, and she was talking softly to herself.

"She's out!" said Gilder under his breath. "The blanket!"

He took the wrap from Brook's hand and wrapped it gently about her shoulders.

"I can't do it," Isla was saying. "I must have time. I don't want to marry."

Gilder opened his mouth and looked at Brooks.

"Hell! Did you hear that?"

"I can't marry today! I won't! I can't do it," she muttered.

Her feet were on the floor now. Gilder guided her to the door, but she must fumble for the handle herself, and find it, open it without help. He knew enough of somnambulism not to thwart her. He could turn her shoulders in the direction he wanted, and no more – but that was enough.

Beyond the second stairway the passage narrowed. A short distance down were the two rooms that he and Brooks occupied. He opened the door of his. His bed was made, and pulling back the covers, he gently pressed her down. She curled up on the bed with a sigh, and Gilder pulled an eiderdown over her.

"She'll sleep. Anyway, I'll lock the door on her. Go back to the room and bring her dressing-gown and slippers. Hurry!"

Brooks made a move and stopped.

Suddenly he uttered an exclamation and slapped his thigh.

"I've lost it!" he said. "You haven't seen it?"

"What's that?" asked Gilder.

"My gun."

Gilder scowled at him.

"Got a gun, have you? There's a fool thing to carry. Where did you leave it?"

"It was in my pocket an hour ago."

Gilder looked thoughtful.

"That's awkward. You were a damned fool to carry it, anyway. Go and look in your room, and see if it's there. Anyway, what do you want a gun for? Have you gone all weak and childish?"

Brooks went up to his room, and came back with a report of failure.

"Forget it," said the other impatiently. "You'll find it in the morning. Go bring that gown and slippers."

The door of the old lord's room stood open, though Brooks could almost have sworn he had closed it after him. Of one thing he was certain, that he had left the lights on. The room was now in darkness. It must have been Lady Lebanon. He had to close the door, for the switch was behind it, and he was reaching for the key when something slipped round his neck – a soft, elastic something. In a flash he put his hands between the cloth and his throat and lurched back. The grip tightened. He wrenched his hands from the scarf and grabbed behind him, but he touched nothing. The skilled strangler was prepared for that possibility, and Brooks went crashing to the ground, the world blotted out.

25

In the hall below Mr Tanner had finished his game, and stood watching the shameless efforts of Sergeant Totty to assist the accidents of chance. He made a little noise of protest when Totty deliberately took a card from the top of the pack and put it at the bottom.

"A man who would cheat himself at patience would commit almost any crime except robbing a bank to feed the poor," he said.

"A man who doesn't make his own luck is a fool," said Totty.

He shovelled the cards up and dropped them, yawned, looked at his watch and lolled back in his chair.

"Ferraby was saying he didn't like this shop. He said it gave him the horrors."

Totty smiled.

"I've known worse. Do you remember that night years ago, Tanner, when you and me waited for Harry the Fiddler, in the cats'-meat shop? Lord love a duck! cats used to follow me for weeks after that! That fat fellow's got a gun."

"Who – Brooks?" Tanner was interested.

"That's the chap. I saw the shape of it in his pocket when he had his coat off and was tidying up here half an hour ago. He's going to be troublesome."

"It'll be more troublesome for him than for us," said Tanner cryptically. "In fact, I think it's going to be very awkward indeed for him – what's that?" He heard a thud. "Go up and see."

Totty rose slowly.

"Up there?" he said.

"Yes. Are you scared?" snapped Tanner.

"Yes," said Totty shamelessly. "You didn't expect me to say that, did you? Still, to oblige you."

He went up the stairs quickly enough, and Tanner, listening at the foot, heard no sound until his name was called.

"What is it?"

It was Gilder speaking.

"Come here!" called Totty urgently. "Quick!"

Tanner flew up the stairs into the old lord's room. Brooks was lying on his back, and the detective was struggling to untie the knotted scarf that was about his throat. It was no easy task, and there was a very little margin of time.

"He's a goner, I think," grunted Totty.

"Let me get to him, mister."

Gilder went down on his knees, tore off the man's collar and the top of his shirt, and massaged his neck. Gilder's face was wet; tense with anxiety. For the first time Tanner saw in him evidence of real emotion.

"He's not dead," he said. "Can you get me some brandy?" Totty ran downstairs, found the decanter and brought it up. Under the influence of the liquor the man showed signs of life. The eyelids flickered, the hands twitched convulsively.

"He'll be all right, I guess." Gilder breathed the words jerkily. "Help me carry him to his room. It was a pretty close call, hey? Old Brooks! Gosh! His gun wouldn't have been any kind of help."

Yet apart from this exhibition of concern for the life of his friend, the big fellow was perfectly calm; he was neither horrified nor agitated by an event calculated to shake even his stout nerve: it was the possible consequence that seemed to distress him.

They carried the semi-conscious man into his little bedroom and laid him down. And then Tanner remembered that the old lord's chamber was Isla Crane's bedroom – and she had not been in the room.

"Where is the young lady?" he asked quickly.

Gilder looked up, then dropped his eyes.

"I don't know" – doggedly – "I guess she's about the house somewhere."

It was his last desperate and vain attempt to bring the appearance of order to an untidy situation.

"Go and find her." Bill's voice was harsh. "Where is Ferraby?"

Totty met him half-way up the stairs, and explained the situation to a young man who became instantly thrown off his balance.

"Don't ask questions, and don't go to pieces," snarled Tanner. "What the hell is this – a girls' school? Go round the house, wake everybody in it to find Miss Crane – that's your job. Totty, you needn't stay with this man; he is nearly recovered. Where's Gilder?"

The footman had disappeared. Unnoticed he had slipped from the room after Ferraby's arrival.

"Get him!"

Totty took one step to the door, and then without warning the lights in the room went out. The two men groped out into the passage; that was in darkness too.

There was a simple explanation.

"Somebody has cut us off at the main switch. You located it, didn't you, Totty?"

"Half an hour after I arrived," said Totty. "I can find it."

"Have you a lamp in your pocket? Good! And keep your truncheon in your hand. You may have to use it. I'll work back to the hall. This fellow isn't going to take any hurt in the dark."

They left the groaning man on the bed, and Totty went cautiously along the passage, felt his way down the stairs into the servants' quarters. He was sparing of his light, for if it showed him the way, it also located him and made it easier for the unseen enemy to attack.

The main switch was in a little cellar, approached from the kitchen, and he found the door to the cellar was wide open. Flashing his lamp down the stone steps, he took a tighter grip of his rubber truncheon and went down one stair at a time. He listened, thought he heard heavy breathing and cast his light around, but he could see nothing, though there were one or two recesses in which a man might hide.

"Come out of that!" he commanded.

There was no answer.

His first job was to turn on the lights. From where he stood he saw that the master switch was disengaged, and was hanging down. The apparatus was attached about six feet from the lowest step of the stair, and he felt gingerly along the distempered walls. He reached for the vulcanite handle when something struck him violently at the back of the head. He dropped his lamp with a crash, and turned to grapple with the unknown. Momentarily dazed, he struck out at random – and missed. Something flew past his head and crashed against the wall. He heard it break and the fragments scatter on the brick floor. It was coal, he guessed. Painful but not dangerous.

He struck out again, but hit the air. Feet moved swiftly up the steps, and the door slammed. Totty heard the bolt shot home and accepted the situation philosophically. First he pushed home the switch, and instantly the cellar was alight, for the lamp had been burning when the connection was cut. At the far end was a heap of coal, evidently used for the kitchen. It was from here that the missile had been taken. Totty picked up his lamp, tested it, then, taking a piece of string from his pocket, he tied the handle of the switch tight before he looked round for a means of opening the door.

There was no necessity to use force, as it happened. Ferraby's voice came down to him from the kitchen, and a minute later the bolt shot back and Sergeant Totty emerged, a little dizzy from his adventure, but very little the worse.

Totty's head was sore, but there was no wound.

"A bump as big as a plover's egg, but otherwise not so much as a scratch," reported Ferraby after a quick examination of his colleague's injury. "You ought to go down on your knees and thank the Lord that he only hit you on the head!"

"Have you found that young lady?"

Ferraby was less agitated now.

"No. She's in the house somewhere, and Tanner isn't really worried. That doesn't mean anything – are you all right?"

He didn't wait for Totty to reply, but dashed off. The sergeant took a long cold drink, made his way back to the hall to answer Tanner's rapid fire of questions.

"No, I didn't see him; I felt him," he said grimly. "That fellow's quicker than a rat."

"Threw coal at you, did he?" said Tanner. "You're a lucky man – he forgot that he had a gun in his pocket! I remembered it after you'd gone – to tell you the truth, I didn't expect to see you again alive."

Totty gulped.

"Thank you for your sympathy," he growled. "Where did he get it – the gun?"

"He took it from Brooks tonight. It was the first thing that Brooks spoke about when he came back to life. He spilt everything, though it wasn't necessary so far as I was concerned."

"Do you know who it is?"

Tanner nodded.

"Yes. When Lord Lebanon told me about his drugged whisky, it was the clearest possible case. I happen to know the drug that was used – I think I said that before."

He dropped his hand on Totty's shoulder.

"If we get through tonight without any further casualties I'll be down on my knees to the Chief Constable tomorrow asking him to enlarge your rank. I'd hate to see you an inspector, but I'm afraid it's got to be."

Totty smiled modestly.

"I don't know that I've done anything," he began.

"You haven't!" said his candid superior. "I've been trying to remember a piece of real help you've given me, and I can't think of a single darned thing that was the slightest assistance, but that's why men get promotion – for doing nothing."

He strode up and down the room, his old restless self. Mr Totty regarded him with the expression of a wounded fawn.

"Her ladyship's in her room and declines to come out. I think she's breaking. I knew she would sooner or later. Hallo, Ferraby!"

That dishevelled young man was almost at the end of his tether.

"I can't find her anywhere – "

"Don't look. She's in Gilder's room, and sleeping. I went in and saw her a few minutes ago. Here's the key of the room if you want it."

"In Gilder's room?" gasped Ferraby. "You've got the key?"

Tanner nodded. He showed it in the palm of his hand. "She's in no immediate danger and, I hope, no ultimate danger."

"Thank God for that!" Ferraby's voice was unsteady.

"These are the worst minutes I have ever lived." And then he remembered: "Lord Lebanon wanted to know what it's all about, but I haven't told him," he said. "I saw him outside his mother's room, talking to her. He told me she refused to see him."

"She wouldn't open the door to him, eh? Well, I didn't expect she would. Lady Lebanon has a very excellent reason for wanting to be alone at this particular moment. Where is the young fellow?"

He had hardly put the question when a tousle-headed and excited young man came running down the stairs. He had seemingly been aroused from his sleep, for he was in pyjamas and dressing-gown, and his feet were bare.

"You'll catch cold," smiled Tanner. "There is no reason why you should be the only casualty of the evening."

"I say, I can't get my mother to see me – " began Lebanon.

"She's not quite herself tonight," said Bill soothingly. "I shouldn't worry. Totty, go up and ask her ladyship if she'll come down. Tell her I particularly wish it. And, Ferraby, quieten all those servants and send them back to bed."

The two were left alone. It was as Bill Tanner designed.

"Where's Isla? I looked into her room, and she wasn't there My God, Tanner, this must be the climax!"

"I think it is," said Bill Tanner.

He had a feeling that the real climax would come when Lady Lebanon made her appearance. Would she come down? Would she find an easier way than facing the tragedy of her failure and the gaunt exposure of the secrets she had sacrificed so much to hide?

"What is it all about?" Lebanon's voice was unusually firm. "Please forget that I've been a soft, easy-going fool, and allowed everybody to run my life. I've decided it's about time I took charge. I'm going to leave this beastly place. Marks Priory is on the top of me, Tanner. You know who's in that room, don't you – the room that she wouldn't let you see? My father? I'm not Lord Lebanon."

Bill stared at him. This was the one revelation he did not expect. And yet instantly he corrected his surprise. Nothing Lebanon told him now could astonish him.

"He's the fellow who's been causing all the trouble," the young man continued. His words came with the impetuosity of a stream in spate. "He's gone – I'll bet he's miles away by now. He could get in and out of this house as he liked. That surprises you, doesn't it?"

"It does a little," said Tanner quietly.

The young man was sitting in his mother's chair, his hands lightly clasped before him, and with that attitude, in that light, he looked curiously like the woman whose son he was.

Bill drew a settle to the opposite side of the desk.

"Family, family – good God! I'm sick of hearing the word!" He leaned forward over the desk. "Don't you think it's time we put an end to all this? First Studd, then Amersham, and now poor Brooks."

Bill shook his head.

"You're a little premature. Brooks isn't dead."

"Isn't he? Somebody said he was… I'm glad. He's not a bad fellow. Don't you agree with what I say, Mr Tanner? The line should be wiped out – this line?"

"I don't understand what you mean."

The boy moved impatiently.

"This sort of thing has been going on for heaven knows how many years. You ask my mother. She's got all their dates, all their names, all their damned pedigrees, all their party per fess and their saltires! The Lebanons have always been like that – didn't you know?"

He dropped his voice confidentially.

"My father was like that. He was fifteen years in the old lord's room, as mad as a damned hatter!" He laughed softly. "Those two fellows used to look after him."

Tanner nodded. This was no news to him.

"Gilder and Brooks – yes, I guessed that."

The boy leaned his head on one hand and stared into vacancy. "But he never strangled anybody," he said slowly. He was speaking to himself; his voice was tremulous with the pride of achievement.

The old lord had never strangled anybody. He had done many mad things. Had been a menace to life and happiness, but he had lacked that inspiration – to come softly behind an unsuspecting victim and choke out his life.

Slowly Lebanon's face came round, and Bill looked into the fiery, laughing eyes.

"My father's dead – you know that. As mad as a hatter. Did I tell you he was in that room? Well, I was lying. I lie very easily. I've got a marvellous power of invention. I'm quick. Didn't I hear you say that – a quick worker?" He chuckled. "No he never strangled anybody. He didn't know how to do it."

He leaned across the table confidentially and spoke quickly. "The first time I saw it done was in Poona. A little fellow slipped up behind a big man and put a cloth round his neck and" – he leaned back – "by God, he was dead! Fascinating!"

Bill said nothing

"I tried it on a girl." He leaned forward again. "An Indian girl. She went out like that!" He snapped his fingers.

The boy's face was alive, eager, and, but for the queer light in his eyes, unchanged from the weak, drawling youth Tanner had known an hour before.

Here was the secret – no secret to Bill Tanner – of Marks Priory. This dapper little man had cheated the world, had cheated the police, cheated all but his own mother, who knew and suffered and gave her life to his protection – the Last of the Lebanons.

"Extraordinary, isn't it – how quickly people die?"

He put his hand in the pocket of his dressing-gown and drew out something: a long, red scarf, and chuckled with glee.

"Look at this! I've got lots of them: I brought them back from India. Amersham took some away from me, but he didn't know where

I kept my stock. I've surprised you, haven't I? I'm not a big fellow, but I'm strong. Feel!"

He thrust out his bent arm, and Tanner's hand felt the great biceps. It was indeed a surprise to him; he had never suspected such strength in the boy.

"It's rather a lark," Lebanon went on. "You'd never dream it about me. People say: 'Oh, look at that little whipper-snapper,' eh?"

And then he grew more serious.

"Of course, they made an awful fuss about this Indian girl. The fellows in the regiment didn't realise I had the strength to do it," he said. "It was a tremendous surprise to them, too."

"Is this the girl you told me about at Scotland Yard?"

Lebanon chuckled.

"Yes. Of course, Amersham wouldn't have had the nerve to do it, only I wanted to pull your leg. I get a lot of fun out of pulling people's legs."

"There was considerable trouble about it, wasn't there?" asked Tanner.

He kept his voice even; an observer might have imagined that they were gossiping on some uninteresting, commonplace happening. All that evening he had known what he might expect when the denouement came. He had sent his two assistants away, knowing that he would never hear from this young man's lips the true story if they were present.

"Yes, the babus made a fuss about it," said the boy resentfully. "The mater sent Amersham to bring me home. He was an awful cad of a fellow – a dreadful outsider. He was a man who would sign his name to other people's cheques…ghastly, isn't it?"

Again his tone grew confidential.

"Don't have anything to do with him," he said, with quiet vehemence.

To him, Amersham for the moment was alive, a living and hateful restriction upon the freedom of his movements. Amersham the forger, and Amersham the doctor. Amersham the doctor might appear at any moment and order those disagreeable courses of action which brought him discomfort.

"After he brought me to England the mater sent for those two fellows who had looked after father... Gilder and Brooks. Of course, they're not real footmen; they're a sort of – well they look after me, you understand?"

"Yes, I have understood that," said Tanner.

Then a thought amused the boy.

"You know that room my mother wouldn't show you? Well, it's all padded, you know – rubber cushions all round the walls. I have to go there when I realise things."

"When you're a little tiresome?" smiled Bill.

"When I realise things." He was angry. "I know what I'm saying. It's realising things that is so terrible. It's only when I'm excited that my brain gets clear."

Bill leaned over the table, and Lebanon drew back quickly.

"Don't touch me." His hand went to his breast.

"I want a light. Be the perfect host," said Bill.

Instantly Lebanon melted.

"I'm sorry – awfully sorry."

He lit the match and held it steady whilst Tanner pulled at his cigar. When he had blown it out and carefully deposited it in the ash-tray: "Are you friend or foe?" he asked.

"Why, what a question! I'm a friend."

Lebanon shook his head.

"You telephoned to Scotland Yard and asked them to send three doctors to certify me. I heard you on the phone. I was listening at the door."

"They're coming to see me," protested Tanner.

"That's a lie! They're not. They're coming to see me."

His face went hard. "But I can fool them, as I fooled you, and as I've fooled all the clever people – Amersham – all of them. She was under his thumb, my mother. I'll tell you why. She administered my father's estate when she ought to have put it under commission – Lunacy Commission, isn't it? You know the law better than I do. And then she's been looking after my estate too, and naturally she'd have got into trouble if it had been found out. Amersham threatened he'd go to the police once, and got a fearful sum of money from her."

There was one aspect of his disorder that had puzzled Tanner. "Why did you – why were you so unkind to Studd, your chauffeur?"

Lebanon's face fell.

"I'm terribly sorry about that," he said. "He was such a good fellow. But I'm afraid of Indians. Some of them tried to kill me...they were very angry over this girl I told you about. She was such a stupid girl – a Eurasian or something. I didn't know about this beastly ball in the village. I saw the Indian; I was horribly frightened of him, and..."

He was very penitent; there were tears in his eyes. He had been very fond of Studd. They had had this in common, that they both detested Amersham, and Studd used to do little jobs for his employer, unknown either to his mistress or to the doctor.

"I cried for a week after that happened. Mother will tell you – all the servants will tell you. I sent beautiful flowers to his funeral. I was really sorry. And I sent his sister two hundred pounds. She was his only relation. I stole the money out of mother's cash-box, but it's really mine, you know. Mother was very annoyed about it, but then she so easily gets annoyed."

He looked round towards the stairs, then to the door.

"Shall I show you something?" he asked, a half-smile on his face. "If I do, will you swear you won't tell anybody?"

"I'll swear," said Tanner.

Lebanon put his hand inside his dressing-gown and brought out a revolver. Bill Tanner had expected that, too.

"It's the first one I've been able to get," he said. "I took it out of Brooks' pocket." He chuckled. "That was rather clever, wasn't it? I've always wanted one."

Then he looked straight into Tanner's eyes.

"You can't strangle yourself, you know. It's rather difficult, and they look so ugly." He shuddered and closed his eyes. When he opened them again his face was drawn. "Sometimes I think the whole line ought to be wiped out – all their escutcheons and their shields. The line! God Almighty! To carry on the line! Isn't it ridiculous?"

Tanner did not answer immediately, then: "Poor old boy!" he said softly. Lebanon's eyes narrowed.

"What do you mean – me? Why do you say that?"

"I've got a young brother of your age."

Lebanon's suspicious eyes were fixed on him.

"You don't like me, do you?"

"Yes, I do. I've been a very good friend of yours – I was very nice to you at Scotland Yard at any rate."

The boy's face brightened.

"Of course you were! That was clever of me to go up there. wasn't it? I mean, that was the last thing you'd have expected. I killed Amersham that morning, and slipped away when all the fuss was on. I gave them a scare too. Mother must have sent Gilder off in her own car, and he knew where I was going, because I'd told him that morning I'd go to Scotland Yard and have a talk with you."

Tanner flicked the ash of his cigar into a tray, and again the young man drew back, covering the pistol with both his hands.

"Yes, that was a stroke," said Tanner.

They sat without speaking for fully a minute. There was a clock somewhere in the room. Tanner heard for the first time the monotony of its tick.

"I wonder where he's put her?" asked Lebanon suddenly. "Isla."

"Where who's put her – Gilder?"

Lebanon nodded.

"She was looking awfully like that Indian girl this evening. I went behind her and put my arms around her. Didn't you hear her scream? She ran down the stairs and Totty was there, or I'd have followed. And Gilder too, of course. He's never far away. Haven't you noticed that? He's generally around somewhere near her. I believe Gilder would kill me if I hurt her. You think Gilder's a brute, but he isn't really. He's very kind, especially to Isla. Nobody watches after her as he does, especially since she knew – and she does know. That's why she's frightened. She came downstairs the night I smashed up this place."

He looked round interested.

"I don't remember doing it, but I suppose I must have done. I nearly got Amersham that night. It took two of them to pull me off. By God, he was scared! Isla saw the struggle from the stairs. She's been frightened ever since. I don't blame her, do you?"

Bill shook his head.

"It's queer. When I did get Amersham last night, she saw me again, coming in through the door with the scarf in my hand. Mother took it away from me, and sent me up to bed. I'm terribly strong," he said again. "You wouldn't think so."

Bill nodded.

"Yes, I always thought you were pretty strong," he said.

He was beginning to feel the tension. His eyes never left that pistol under the boy's hand. This was not the climax he had planned. Yet he felt he could hold him in his present mood, quieten him, and after a while the paroxysm would pass and the boy would be normal again. That was a hope which was fast vanishing.

He had dealt with this type only once before, and the symptoms were not very encouraging. The peak of this mental disturbance had not yet been reached – and there was the pistol under his hand, fully loaded. He could see the grey noses of the bullets in their steel chambers, and the barrel was pointed in his direction.

"I worried them tonight" – Lebanon was laughing softly – "when I didn't take that drink. You know what was in it, don't you?"

Bill nodded.

"Bromide of potassium. They thought you were getting a little excited and they wanted to calm you. I suppose they've done that before?"

"Lots of times," said Lebanon, "but I fooled them tonight."

Tanner took the whisky and soda that he had put on the desk, drank it deliberately and rose.

"I'm going to bed," he said.

He pushed back the settle, yawned and stretched himself. When he looked round the boy was behind him, that same strange look in his face which he had seen before.

"You're not going to bed," Lebanon breathed. "You're afraid!"

Bill smiled and shook his head.

"Yes, you are. I frighten people."

"You're not frightening me," said Tanner good-humouredly. "Be sensible and give me that gun. Why do you want to fool about with a thing like that?"

"There are lots of things I could do with this."

Tanner heard a startled exclamation from the stairs. He did not turn his head, but he knew Lady Lebanon had appeared on the stairs.

"I could end the line with this."

"Willie!"

The whole demeanour of the boy underwent a startling change. He cringed back, tucked the pistol into the fold of his gown.

"What are you doing, you foolish boy? Give me that revolver."

"No, I won't!" he whined. "I've always wanted a pistol. I've asked you for one dozens of times."

"Put it away!"

For an instant of time he turned his back upon Tanner, and Bill leapt at him. He had not misstated his strength: it was staggering. Totty came flying in and joined in the struggle, but, with an effort which was beyond understanding, Lebanon wrenched himself free and ran to the stairs. As he did so, Gilder appeared. For a second the boy hesitated, and then...

The crash of the explosion was deafening. The pistol dropped from the boy's fingers and he sank down on the lower stair.

Instantly the three men were by him. One glance told Tanner all he wanted to know. Lady Lebanon stood stiffly by the desk, her face averted, her proud chin raised.

"Well?" she said harshly.

"He's dead. He has shot himself," said Tanner huskily. "My God, what a tragedy!"

She did not answer. Her hands were clenching and unclenching. The agony of her was pitiful to watch. Then she turned towards the stairway and came slowly towards them.

She passed the body without so much as a glance, stood for a second on the stairs, holding on to the wall for support.

"Ten centuries of Lebanons and no one left to carry on the line!" she moaned.

The men listened in awed silence.

"A thousand years of being great – gone out like a candle in the wind!"

They heard no more but the murmur of her voice receding into the distance.

Bill looked down at the dead man at his feet.

"A thousand years of being great," he said bitterly.

26

"To me," said Chief Inspector Tanner, reporting to his superior, "the case at first looked very much like a very ordinary crime of revenge. There were two or three suspects. The first of these, of course, was Amersham. He was present in the field when Studd was killed, and there was, moreover, a motive: they were both running after the same girl, and Amersham was intensely jealous. He had a bad record, and I confess I was fooled when Lebanon came to Scotland Yard and told me that story about Amersham having been involved in a strangling case in India. That for the moment clinched the suspicion to the doctor. As a matter of fact, it was not until after his death that I had a wire from India, giving me the fullest particulars about the crime.

"Lebanon was obviously the guilty party, but he'd been certified insane, and the Indian authorities were very glad to see him out of the country. He'd been acting very queerly, taking pot shots at his beaters when he was out shooting, and was under observation when the murder of this girl was committed.

"If I'd had the least suspicion of Lebanon I would have known that it's one of the commonest phenomena for a man mentally deranged to pass suspicion on to somebody else, and to credit other people with his own acts. But Amersham, with his bad record, and his peculiar relationships with Lady Lebanon, seemed a fairly reasonable point at which to start one's investigations. That is, of course, before I learnt of his death.

"I can dispose of Amersham very briefly. He was a thief and a blackmailer. He had the good luck to be employed by Lady Lebanon to attend her husband. The family doctor, who had kept her secret, had died, and she must have found considerable difficulty in procuring a successor, because any decent medical man would have immediately reported the facts to the authorities and the Lunacy Commission would have dealt with his estate.

"Amersham was in every way an ideal person. He was not unclever, he had some knowledge of mania, and when he saw the advertisement in *The Times* asking for the private services of a medical man with a knowledge of mental cases, he immediately applied, and had the good luck to get the job.

"The salary was a big one, and he was in clover from the start. But he must have realised his opportunities, and gradually increased his hold over the Lebanon family until he dominated the woman and eventually her son."

The Chief Constable interposed a question, and Bill Tanner shook his head.

"No, sir, there is no history of any early symptoms as far as the boy was concerned. He was not very brilliant, but he managed to pass through Sandhurst into the Army. The Indian medical authorities have a history of a slight sunstroke, which may have accelerated an hereditary weakness, but until he started shooting at his beaters there was not the least suspicion that anything was wrong with him. The Army authorities, of course, knew nothing about his father, though a great-grandfather had been confined in a lunatic asylum. In fact, there is insanity on both sides of the family.

"When the old lord died, her ladyship must have thought she'd got rid of a man who was becoming more and more of an encumbrance. We know that Amersham did not go to Marks Priory for three months, and then the trouble in India came, and she was glad to send for him.

"He agreed to take charge of the boy and hush up the Indian matter, and the price he demanded was a quiet little wedding at Peterfield. I was rather puzzled as to why they went to Peterfield, but Lady Lebanon has a lot of property in the village apparently, and in fact the Lebanons have the gift of the living.

"The marriage seems to have been one of convenience. There was no pretence of love or any associations of married life. But she did demand from Amersham a certain line of conduct. Amersham had his own establishment, his own life. They had brought back Gilder and Brooks to look after the boy, and nothing very remarkable happened until the killing of Studd, which in one sense was an accident.

"What the boy had discovered was that there was a secret way out of the padded room where he was put at times. He had found the panel and the stairs leading to a door which had been used in the old lord's time to bring him out into the grounds for fresh air. There are tiny grooved rails on each side of the steps into which the wheels of his bath-chair fitted. This must have been before Gilder's time, because he was ignorant of the passage and of the door.

"The vitality of young Lebanon was extraordinary. You can never have a better instance than what happened on the night of his death. Within a quarter of an hour he made an attempt upon a police cyclist, smashed his way into Mrs Tilling's cottage, got back to the house and changed into evening dress – all within fifteen or sixteen minutes.

"When the boy came to the Yard I had no idea that he was anything but normal. He seemed a weakling, one of the pampered mothers' darlings one meets with in every grade of society; a little insolent, perhaps, to his social inferiors in spite of his claim to democracy; but, generally speaking, quite a nice, wholesome young man.

"Why he came is pretty obvious. He had killed Amersham in the night and he wanted to make an early appearance before the police began their inquiries, and shoot the suspicion in any direction but himself. You and I have seen that happen scores of times in normal criminals, but it is extraordinary that this boy, with very little knowledge of the world, should have had the enterprise to do what he did.

"As soon as he was missing, Lady Lebanon sent one of the keepers in search of him. Gilder had heard him talk about going to Scotland Yard, and followed him, and did not leave him till he was safe at Marks

Priory. They returned in the same car – I didn't know this until Gilder told me.

"His appetite for destruction grew. He had only had one bad outbreak before the murder of Studd and that was when he smashed up the common-room at Marks Priory. The killing of Amersham was planned with remarkable ingenuity. It is probable that Lebanon had shown himself to the man he murdered a few minutes before he took his life. He waited outside passing down through the passage, and when Amersham was half-way down the drive, at a point where he had to go slow because of a sharp bend, he leapt on the back of the car and killed him.

"On this occasion he didn't go straight back to the house. Either he lost his way – at any rate, he found himself in a belt of trees that runs parallel with the road, and continued up there till he was suddenly halted by Tilling, the gamekeeper. In a frenzy of fear Lebanon sprang at him. There is no doubt whatever that the gamekeeper must have recognised who his opponent was, for he put up a pretty poor show. He was strong enough to deal with Lebanon, and one supposes – that is his story – that he only exercised enough force to restrain his master from doing him any harm. Tilling was shocked – probably more shocked than he was by the flirtations of his wife. It was he who took Lebanon back to the house.

"Lady Lebanon was in a dilemma. For the first time her secret had gone outside a select circle that could be depended upon to keep it. She was already distracted by the knowledge that something had happened to Amersham. In fact, they were searching for his body – she and Gilder and Brooks – when Tilling came on the scene with this rather subdued youth.

"For some reason they were not able to find the spot to which Amersham had been dragged, and their first care was to have Gilder take the car and leave it on the roadside a few miles from the village.

"There remained Tilling to be dealt with, and Lady Lebanon, knowing that the police would be on the spot in the morning, and that possibly this gamekeeper might be a source of danger, decided to send him to her cottage near Aberdeen. She provided him with money, and gave him his route, and Tilling went off, I should imagine, with his brain in a whirl.

"I think she could have taken the risk of his remaining on the estate, and she would have done but for the fact that she knew this man was under suspicion, and that probably he would be subjected to a stiff cross-examination at my hands, and that to save himself he would blurt out the truth. Tilling went off on his bicycle to Horsham, and eventually to Aberdeen.

"That was the last of Lebanon's definite crimes. All that followed were accidental and arising out of circumstances which he regarded as desperate.

"Towards Miss Isla Crane – I discovered this afterwards – he had the bitterest animosity, and, although she isn't aware of the fact, and so far as I am concerned will never know, he had made three attempts on her life, and had planned to kill her the night he was shot.

"With the cunning of a madman he did not tell Gilder his plan, knowing that Gilder, who had constituted himself a sort of guardian angel to the girl, would have done everything in his power to save her hurt. But Gilder knew. You can't look after a madman for very long before you develop another sense, and he removed the girl from her room to his own – just in time. It was his companion, Brooks, who was almost strangled.

"The old lord's room, by the way, has three entrances: one by the bed, which was the way the murderer came in, and two others that had been screwed up, probably by Lady Lebanon's orders.

"That is all there is to tell you, sir. The only thing I want to add is a recommendation that Sergeant Totty shall be promoted acting inspector."

The Chief Constable opened his eyes wide.

"Good God! Why?" he asked, shocked.

Bill scratched his head.

"I'm blest if I know, but he'd better have it," he said.

EDGAR WALLACE

BIG FOOT

Footprints and a dead woman bring together Superintendent Minton and the amateur sleuth Mr Cardew. Who is the man in the shrubbery? Who is the singer of the haunting Moorish tune? Why is Hannah Shaw so determined to go to Pawsy, 'a dog lonely place' she had previously detested? Death lurks in the dark and someone must solve the mystery before BIG FOOT strikes again, in a yet more fiendish manner.

BONES IN LONDON

The new Managing Director of Schemes Ltd has an elegant London office and a theatrically dressed assistant – however Bones, as he is better known, is bored. Luckily there is a slump in the shipping market and it is not long before Joe and Fred Pole pay Bones a visit. They are totally unprepared for Bones' unnerving style of doing business, unprepared for his unique style of innocent and endearing mischief.

EDGAR WALLACE

BONES OF THE RIVER

'Taking the little paper from the pigeon's leg, Hamilton saw it was from Sanders and marked URGENT. *Send Bones instantly to Lujamalababa… Arrest and bring to head-quarters the witch doctor.*'

It is a time when the world's most powerful nations are vying for colonial honour, a time of trading steamers and tribal chiefs. In the mysterious African territories administered by Commissioner Sanders, Bones persistently manages to create his own unique style of innocent and endearing mischief.

THE DAFFODIL MYSTERY

When Mr Thomas Lyne, poet, poseur and owner of Lyne's Emporium insults a cashier, Odette Rider, she resigns. Having summoned detective Jack Tarling to investigate another employee, Mr Milburgh, Lyne now changes his plans. Tarling and his Chinese companion refuse to become involved. They pay a visit to Odette's flat. In the hall Tarling meets Sam, convicted felon and protégé of Lyne. Next morning Tarling discovers a body. The hands are crossed on the breast, adorned with a handful of daffodils.

EDGAR WALLACE

THE JOKER

While the millionaire Stratford Harlow is in Princetown, not only does he meet with his lawyer Mr Ellenbury but he gets his first glimpse of the beautiful Aileen Rivers, niece of the actor and convicted felon Arthur Ingle. When Aileen is involved in a car accident on the Thames Embankment, the driver is James Carlton of Scotland Yard. Later that evening Carlton gets a call. It is Aileen. She needs help.

THE SQUARE EMERALD

'Suicide on the left,' says Chief Inspector Coldwell pleasantly, as he and Leslie Maughan stride along the Thames Embankment during a brutally cold night. A gaunt figure is sprawled across the parapet. But Coldwell soon discovers that Peter Dawlish, fresh out of prison for forgery, is not considering suicide but murder. Coldwell suspects Druze as the intended victim. Maughan disagrees. If Druze dies, she says, 'It will be because he does not love children!'

OTHER TITLES BY EDGAR WALLACE AVAILABLE DIRECT
FROM HOUSE OF STRATUS

Quantity		£	$(US)	$(CAN)	€
	THE ADMIRABLE CARFEW	6.99	11.50	15.99	11.50
	THE ANGEL OF TERROR	6.99	11.50	15.99	11.50
	THE AVENGER	6.99	11.50	15.99	11.50
	BARBARA ON HER OWN	6.99	11.50	15.99	11.50
	BIG FOOT	6.99	11.50	15.99	11.50
	THE BLACK ABBOT	6.99	11.50	15.99	11.50
	BONES	6.99	11.50	15.99	11.50
	BONES IN LONDON	6.99	11.50	15.99	11.50
	BONES OF THE RIVER	6.99	11.50	15.99	11.50
	THE CLUE OF THE NEW PIN	6.99	11.50	15.99	11.50
	THE CLUE OF THE SILVER KEY	6.99	11.50	15.99	11.50
	THE CLUE OF THE TWISTED CANDLE	6.99	11.50	15.99	11.50
	THE COAT OF ARMS	6.99	11.50	15.99	11.50
	THE COUNCIL OF JUSTICE	6.99	11.50	15.99	11.50
	THE CRIMSON CIRCLE	6.99	11.50	15.99	11.50
	THE DAFFODIL MYSTERY	6.99	11.50	15.99	11.50
	THE DARK EYES OF LONDON	6.99	11.50	15.99	11.50
	THE DAUGHTERS OF THE NIGHT	6.99	11.50	15.99	11.50
	A DEBT DISCHARGED	6.99	11.50	15.99	11.50
	THE DEVIL MAN	6.99	11.50	15.99	11.50
	THE DOOR WITH SEVEN LOCKS	6.99	11.50	15.99	11.50
	THE DUKE IN THE SUBURBS	6.99	11.50	15.99	11.50
	THE FACE IN THE NIGHT	6.99	11.50	15.99	11.50
	THE FEATHERED SERPENT	6.99	11.50	15.99	11.50
	THE FLYING SQUAD	6.99	11.50	15.99	11.50
	THE FORGER	6.99	11.50	15.99	11.50
	THE FOUR JUST MEN	6.99	11.50	15.99	11.50
	FOUR SQUARE JANE	6.99	11.50	15.99	11.50

ALL HOUSE OF STRATUS BOOKS ARE AVAILABLE FROM GOOD BOOKSHOPS
OR DIRECT FROM THE PUBLISHER:

Internet: **www.houseofstratus.com** including author interviews, reviews, features.

Email: **sales@houseofstratus.com** please quote author, title and credit card details.

OTHER TITLES BY EDGAR WALLACE AVAILABLE DIRECT
FROM HOUSE OF STRATUS

Quantity		£	$(US)	$(CAN)	€
	THE FOURTH PLAGUE	6.99	11.50	15.99	11.50
	GOOD EVANS	6.99	11.50	15.99	11.50
	THE HAND OF POWER	6.99	11.50	15.99	11.50
	THE IRON GRIP	6.99	11.50	15.99	11.50
	THE JOKER	6.99	11.50	15.99	11.50
	THE JUST MEN OF CORDOVA	6.99	11.50	15.99	11.50
	THE KEEPERS OF THE KING'S PEACE	6.99	11.50	15.99	11.50
	THE LAW OF THE FOUR JUST MEN	6.99	11.50	15.99	11.50
	THE LONE HOUSE MYSTERY	6.99	11.50	15.99	11.50
	THE MAN WHO BOUGHT LONDON	6.99	11.50	15.99	11.50
	THE MAN WHO KNEW	6.99	11.50	15.99	11.50
	THE MAN WHO WAS NOBODY	6.99	11.50	15.99	11.50
	THE MIND OF MR J G REEDER	6.99	11.50	15.99	11.50
	MORE EDUCATED EVANS	6.99	11.50	15.99	11.50
	MR J G REEDER RETURNS	6.99	11.50	15.99	11.50
	MR JUSTICE MAXWELL	6.99	11.50	15.99	11.50
	RED ACES	6.99	11.50	15.99	11.50
	ROOM 13	6.99	11.50	15.99	11.50
	SANDERS	6.99	11.50	15.99	11.50
	SANDERS OF THE RIVER	6.99	11.50	15.99	11.50
	THE SINISTER MAN	6.99	11.50	15.99	11.50
	THE SQUARE EMERALD	6.99	11.50	15.99	11.50
	THE THREE JUST MEN	6.99	11.50	15.99	11.50
	THE THREE OAK MYSTERY	6.99	11.50	15.99	11.50
	THE TRAITOR'S GATE	6.99	11.50	15.99	11.50
	WHEN THE GANGS CAME TO LONDON	6.99	11.50	15.99	11.50
	WHEN THE WORLD STOPPED	6.99	11.50	15.99	11.50

Hotline: UK ONLY: 0800 169 1780, please quote author, title and credit card details.
INTERNATIONAL: +44 (0) 20 7494 6400, please quote author, title and credit card details.

Send to: House of Stratus Sales Department
24c Old Burlington Street
London
W1X 1RL
UK

Please allow for postage costs charged per order plus an amount per book as set out in the tables below:

	£(Sterling)	$(US)	$(CAN)	€(Euros)
Cost per order				
UK	2.00	3.00	4.50	3.30
Europe	3.00	4.50	6.75	5.00
North America	3.00	4.50	6.75	5.00
Rest of World	3.00	4.50	6.75	5.00
Additional cost per book				
UK	0.50	0.75	1.15	0.85
Europe	1.00	1.50	2.30	1.70
North America	2.00	3.00	4.60	3.40
Rest of World	2.50	3.75	5.75	4.25

PLEASE SEND CHEQUE, POSTAL ORDER (STERLING ONLY), EUROCHEQUE, OR INTERNATIONAL MONEY ORDER (PLEASE CIRCLE METHOD OF PAYMENT YOU WISH TO USE)
MAKE PAYABLE TO: STRATUS HOLDINGS plc

Cost of book(s): —————— Example: 3 x books at £6.99 each: £20.97

Cost of order: —————— Example: £2.00 (Delivery to UK address)

Additional cost per book: —————— Example: 3 x £0.50: £1.50

Order total including postage: —————— Example: £24.47

Please tick currency you wish to use and add total amount of order:

☐ £ (Sterling) ☐ $ (US) ☐ $ (CAN) ☐ € (EUROS)

VISA, MASTERCARD, SWITCH, AMEX, SOLO, JCB:

☐☐☐☐☐☐☐☐☐☐☐☐☐☐☐☐☐☐☐

Issue number (Switch only):

☐☐☐

Start Date: **Expiry Date:**

☐☐ / ☐☐   ☐☐/ ☐☐

Signature: _____

NAME: _____

ADDRESS: _____

_____

POSTCODE: _____

Please allow 28 days for delivery.

Prices subject to change without notice.
Please tick box if you do not wish to receive any additional information. ☐

House of Stratus publishes many other titles in this genre; please check our website (**www.houseofstratus.com**) for more details.